*Laurel Springs'*

# LOVE'S ARRIVAL

AMANDA SPEIGHTS

HIGH PLAINS WOMAN
PRESS

This is a work of fiction. Unless otherwise indicated, all the names, characters, businesses, places, events and incidents in this book are either the product of the author's imagination or used in a fictitious manner. Any resemblance to actual persons, living or dead, or actual events is purely coincidental.

Copyright © 2023 Amanda Speights

All rights reserved. No part of this book may be reproduced or used in any manner without written permission of the copyright owner, except for the use of quotations in a book review.
To request permission please contact the author at hello@amandaspeights.com.

Library of Congress Control Number: 2023903819

Paperback: ISBN 979-8-9878676-0-0
Ebook: ISBN 979-8-9878676-1-7

Editor: Christine Wheary
Cover Design: Roseanna White
Author Photo: Melissa DeMers

Publisher: High Plains Woman Press

www.AmandaSpeights.com

*To the little girl who was told she'd never make anything of her life.*

# 1
# Livvie

*1872 (present day) Boone, Missouri*

Life can change as unexpectedly as the prairie winds. Yesterday I was Roy's wife, today I'm his widow. That's the difference between the two days. The July sun still shines, the leaves on the oak trees rustle, and the mockingbirds perform a melodious tune.

The preacher's voice is a rehearsed tone. "Dear Heavenly Father, we commit Royal McLain to you this day..."

It's hard to breathe. Surely, this isn't really happening. Everything is closing in on me. The preacher's prayer and the condolences of the few people departing are heavy as bricks on my chest. Roy's last words play repeatedly in my mind. "Livvie, it was Wes." His own brother shot and killed him. Sadly, it's not a surprise.

A touch on my arm and a sound brings me back to the grave.

Everyone else has gone.

Turning to the woman beside me, her skin fair and youthful beneath her feathered hat, I wonder if I appear as young as she, or has this life aged me beyond my twenty-five years. "Marybeth, I'm sorry. What were you saying?" I ask, shaking thoughts of Wes from my mind.

She wraps an arm around me. "It's all right; I don't expect you to be yourself right now." I lay my head against hers. She and her family are all I have left.

I nod. "Yes, I suppose you're right." I don't know how I'm supposed to be, honestly.

Marybeth runs her hand down the copper-blonde braid that drapes over my shoulder. "Why don't you come and have dinner with us?"

The beginning of hunger pangs gnaw at my stomach. No wonder, I haven't eaten since breakfast yesterday morning. "Yes...thank you. I think that'd be real nice." For the first time, I'm free to accept her offer without fear.

"I'll wait in the buggy. No rush." She walks away, leaving me to stand alone beside Roy's resting place.

"What am I going to do now, Roy?" Kneeling on the grass, the earth is cool under my legs, and I'm thankful for the solitude. For the first time, tears trickle down my cheeks. My chest is a hollowed-out place.

Smoothing my fingers over the spot where a wedding ring should sit, I think back to Mother's words from years ago regarding her own parents: *You have to be born lucky to have what they had, and you and me, we're not them.*

At twelve years old, I lounge at Mother's feet and pour over a box of love letters between my grandparents. Letters they had written to one another while courting. Letters full of hope and dreams, but above all, love.

"What were they like?" I ask.

"I don't remember, Livvie. I was younger than you when they died." Mother remains focused on her knitting.

"And that's why you had to live with Aunt Martha." I know the story. The parts Mother is willing to share, anyway.

"Yes. Now don't be getting any foolish notions in your head about love and thinking some Prince Charming will take you away because it's not going to happen. You weren't born with that kind of fortune." Mother preaches this often.

I hold a letter, as if it were fragile, studying the handwriting. This is how love looks. The tender words within these pages. I want this for myself someday. If my grandparents could have it, why can't I? As I place the missives back into the box, a glimmer catches my eye. Lifting the papers, I see it. A ring. Gold with intricate designs and a sapphire stone in the center. I gasp. "Mother, what is this?"

Mother glares down from her needlework and speaks to me in a tone as though I am stupid. "It's a ring, Livvie."

"Yes, I know, Mother, but whose is it?"

"It was your grandmother's wedding ring." Her focus returns to knitting.

"It's divine." I turn the band, taking in every detail before placing it on my small ring finger. I must hold it upright to keep the blue stone from falling to one side but that doesn't matter. All I want is to know how it feels to wear such a glorious piece of jewelry. Deciding

*Grandfather's proposal was as romantic as his letters, I place the ring back in the box. A flutter tickles my belly, a sensation I have never felt before, but rather enjoy.*

Here on the ground by Roy's fresh grave I come out of my reverie of the past, still brushing over my ring finger. I sift cold dirt through my hand, a welcome reprieve from the oppressive heat that envelops me. It's suffocating. Is it the air or is it death? My world has closed in on me. "Goodbye, Roy. I hope you find happiness wherever you've gone."

I stand and turn, hitting against the broad chest of a tall man wearing a black suit. "Livvie." His voice booms.

"Wes! You frightened me. Must you stand so close?" I wipe a tear from my cheek. He mustn't see my fear. Nor can he know that I realize he's the one who murdered Roy.

He takes my arm. "I didn't want to disturb you, but I do want a word."

Perhaps he wants a word with Roy, his spirit, or the box that holds his body. Who or whatever it is you speak to when someone passes from this life to the next. Perhaps he is sorry; surely not. His heart's cold enough to inflict frostbite.

"Of course, I'll leave you." I turn to move but he grips my arm — hard.

"I mean with you." His voice is gruff.

I must lift my chin high to look up into his face. My heart races. What does he want? My breath catches in my throat at the sight of his furrowed brows and wrinkled forehead. I turn my attention to a button on his suit coat. The evil in his eyes causes my body to shake. I can't look at him. His foul breath, a mixture of bourbon and tobacco, lingers.

"Now that Royal's gone, it's only reasonable you and me marry." His words send chills up my spine.

He's asking—no, telling—me to marry him, right here at his own brother's grave. Wes McLain is the devil himself. He never cared about his younger brother, so why would he care about his brother's wife?

"I know this ain't the best time or place for ya to be talkin' about it, but I have to leave tomorrow for Jefferson City on business, and I won't be back for a few weeks."

*Business.* How many times had I heard those words? I turn my face away, my already queasy stomach lurching. He should be long gone after killing his brother. Unfortunately, the law has no proof, and anyone who saw what happened fear him too much to tell.

"As I said, I know this ain't the best place, but it's only reasonable we get married today. I leave tomorrow at dawn." He releases my arm. "Now, you know I've never been the marryin' type, and I know you can't give me young 'uns. As I see it, you need someone to be carin' for ya, and I could use someone to be cookin', cleanin', and…providin' for me. If you know what I mean." He smirks.

My stomach tightens and twists. "Why do we have to get married so soon?"

Had he known Roy and I never actually married, perhaps he would see living together without a document was an option. Nevertheless, he's possessive, so conceivably not.

As much as I hate and fear the man, perhaps I'm fortunate

that he offers to take me as his wife. I have no place to go except back to the cabin. I don't know how I'll do the work around the homestead that only Roy could do. Perhaps I do need him. That's what Mother would advise. I wasn't born to be loved, so wanting it shouldn't get in the way of living. Wanting and needing are two different things.

He continues, "I figure you'll have time to move in while I'm away."

Of course, he won't be helping me with the move. That's just like him.

What will happen to my house and my belongings? He'll surely sell it all and keep the money.

"And it'd be right nice to have someone sweet smellin' to come home to." He grabs my chin and lifts my face, forcing me to look up at him. My body tenses at his touch. He looks nothing like Roy. Roy was handsome and his whole face lit up when he smiled. But Wes rarely smiles and his disproportionate ears in comparison to his small head do no favors for him. It's never been a surprise the two men don't share the same father.

Not wanting him to sense my unease, I lift my chin from his hand and take a step back. "My neighbor is expecting me for dinner. I don't want to keep her family waiting." I don't dare tell him the neighbor I refer to is the sheriff and his wife.

"Then I'll see you this evenin'." His eyes travel over my body. "That dress you got on will be fine enough to wear."

Dry grass and wrinkles cover my black skirt. He's already telling me what's acceptable to wear and we're not even married yet. "This evening." I lift my skirts, turn, and walk away.

If I refuse to marry him, he'll surely strangle me as he had done to Eliza the whore. If I agree, it will only be a matter of time before he beats me anyway, worse than Roy ever did. My heart races as I recall a memory of Wes's wrath on me back in Ohio.

*Upon entering our apartment, my stomach sinks when I see Wes and Roy sitting at the table. I hadn't figured on them coming home for a few more days, at least.* "Gentlemen. I wasn't expecting you home this early." *I hang my hat on the hook by the door, hoping they don't hear the disappointment in my voice.*

"Is that why you were over visiting with them whores?" *The question doesn't come from Roy but Wes.*

*I glare at him, puzzled, but he doesn't look at me. He runs his finger around the rim of his whiskey glass.*

"I visit them often when you two aren't here because I have nothing else to do. A woman can only do so much cooking, cleaning, and reading. She needs companionship."

"Oh, so now you're ungrateful for what we've given you?" *he snarls.*

*I gape at Roy, expecting him to stand up for me. He's supposed to be my husband, after all. Who is Wes to treat me so?* "I'm not ungrateful. I just can find little to do and those girls are my family."

"We're your family." *There's venom in Wes's voice.*

*There's no sense in arguing with a man so full of hate and violence. Not knowing what to do with myself with the two men in the place, I take to peeling potatoes but not without staring Roy down. He doesn't dare move his gaze from his glass. Coward.*

*Wes isn't finished.* "You're not to be associatin' with them whores."

"They're my family," I repeat, fighting the tears that threaten to come.

Wes stands. "They're a bunch of whores. They're not your family. We are and no sister-in-law of mine will be associatin' herself with a house of whores. You hear me?" His voice thunders through the room.

My blood bubbles like a pot of stew. I lean over and hiss in Roy's face, "Coward."

Wes moves from his chair, tipping it back. At the sound of the chair hitting the floor, his hand grabs the back of my hair. "He's your husband — you show him respect, you hear me, bitch?"

Still holding the knife in my hand, I contemplate stabbing him. What good would that do? It would be his word over mine, and as a woman — no one will listen to me.

"I said, did you hear me?" He pulls my hair tighter and yanks my head down harder.

I close my eyes and nod. Yes, I heard him.

That night in bed, I lay on my side and cry quietly to myself. This will become the norm over the years. Roy climbs in beside me, and as usual, pulls down his drawers, lifts my nightgown, and enters me from behind. I hate him. Where has the Roy gone who swept me off my feet just months ago?

As I climb into Marybeth's buggy, I know what I must do.

# 2
## Justus

*1866 (six years earlier) Longhorn, Texas*

My thoughts turn to the Rattlesnake Saloon. I'm wishing for whiskey and a woman after a long three-month cattle drive, but while away, I promised myself I was going to be a better man. One my ma would be proud of. I scratch at the scruff on my face. Instead, I'm going back to Mister Granger's ranch for a hot bath and a long sleep.

"I only see one piece of mail for you, Mister Bennett," says the older woman behind the counter. I thank her and step out of the general store to read the missive from Mary. Mary's like a second ma to me, and it's always a good feeling to get news from home.

Once outside, the wind is hot and arid, and dust parches my throat; the imagined taste of whiskey on my tongue temps me again. I force myself to swallow the thought and the dryness away. Sitting my Stetson back on my head to provide what little shade I can get in this barren town, I open the envelope.

*Dear Justus,*

*I'm afraid I write with rather unfortunate news. It's your father; he's had a stroke. Doc isn't sure he'll make it. Oh, I do hate writing such things to you. Please respond at once.*

*Sincerely,*

*Mary*

My mind goes back to the last time I saw Father, young and strong. This just can't be. I read the note again. *Doc isn't sure he'll make it.* The postmark reads four weeks ago. He may be gone by now. My heart is numb to this message. I glance about the dusty small town with tumbleweeds blowing and catching on the porches of the few businesses here. I had better go pack to be on the stagecoach tomorrow.

I step off the wagon in Laurel Springs, Colorado Territory onto the thirsty earth, dirt as dry as my tongue. At least the brim of my Stetson shades the sun from my eyes.

Women stroll the sidewalks with their long skirts swishing about. Children dart around people and horses stir up dust as they clomp up and down Main Street.

Pausing, I take it all in. I'm impressed with the growth of the town over the last five years that I've been gone. There are many new businesses, including a hotel with a restaurant, another eatery, a theater, and the stage station. Houses now dot the landscape where only Mother Earth once rested.

With my well-worn traveling bag in hand, I start in the direction I remember the livery to be. To both my relief and reluctance, it's still there.

"I'll be right with you." The caretaker keeps his focus on examining the hoof of a horse. His blonde hair is hidden by his wide-brimmed hat, but I know the man like I know my own face.

I do my best to paste on a smile. "I'm in no hurry," I say, not knowing how Clint will receive me.

He stops at my words and raises his head. "If it isn't Justus Bennett. How are you, my friend?" He limps toward me with his arms out wide.

*My friend.* I play the words over in my mind. With trembling hands, I grab him and pull, bringing him in for a strong hug. "How are you, Clint?" I stand a head taller than him.

Clint points to my legs with a half-hearted laugh. "It looks as though ole Johnny Reb treated you better than he treated me."

I swallow around a lump in my throat. Not a day or night has gone by that I haven't thought of that fateful day Clint was blown up. I nod. The floor's dusty and strewn with hay. I don't know what to say and shift on my feet. His injuries are my fault.

Clint breaks the awkward silence. "You headed for the ranch?"

"I am. Is he..." The words *dead* or *gone* won't come.

He sighs and his brows furrow. "He's not well but he's still with us."

Turning toward the door, I gaze into the expansive sky. Will

Father be able to find forgiveness in his heart for me? Will he see that I'm a man now? I was a grieving kid; I didn't mean to do what I did.

"The missus will be happy to hear you're home. She'd expect me to invite her long-lost cousin to Sunday dinner."

I turn back to Clint and smile. "Mary wrote that you married my cousin. That does my heart good." The scent of hay and leather mingle in the air. "I don't know if I'll even be here Sunday."

"If you need a place to stay, you're welcome to bunk with us."

"Thanks, brother." I may just have to take him up on that offer.

"Come on, let's get you a horse." Clint motions for me to follow as he limps toward a stall.

On the ride out to the ranch, I'm reminded of how much I love and miss this land. The stately mountains, rolling hills, and the pines that dot the landscape. The sky east of the range is wide open and as blue as a robin's egg. If Father turns me away, maybe I'll build myself a cabin in the rocks and become a hermit. I've been tired of Texas for a long time, with nothing but wide-open space as far as a man can see. Ironically, the vastness feels small.

It's been five years since I've been home. Now, here I am, approaching the place I once thought I'd destroyed. The place I swore I'd never return. Same as the town, it's all grown considerably. There isn't one, but two barns, several other outbuildings, the bunkhouse, and a couple of smaller homes besides the one Father had built for Frank and Mary.

The heat of the sun beats down on my back as I walk toward the main house. It's large, to be sure, but it doesn't appear as massive as it had when I was a boy. Between the great ponderosa pines of the house is a bright glistening white, as though it had just been re-chinked. The open porch covers the entire front of the log home—a beautiful place to sit in the early mornings when the mist is rising off the land and the deer are grazing on the grasses.

I tie the horse to the hitching post, then wipe my hands down the sides of my denim breeches, knowing the sweat on my palms is from more than the hot sun overhead. I've fought many a battle against the Rebels, but never have I felt my stomach turn quite this way. Standing at the door, I raise my hand to grab the door knocker but then hesitate. I can't turn back. No. I'm not a weakling. A surge of courage runs through me. I take hold of the iron ring and strike the wooden door several times.

The moment the door opens, an orange tomcat darts out onto the porch and Mary chastises the feline. "Why, you little scoundrel. You scared me half outta my wits." A smile forms on her face before she looks up at me. I hadn't written to tell her, or anyone, I was coming. Hell, I almost didn't come at all.

When the realization of who I am dawns, both hands fly to her mouth and tears flood her eyes. "Justus! Oh, Justus, you're home." She holds out her arms to me.

A lump lodges in my throat as I move into her embrace.

"You've matured." With her hands on my arms, she pulls

back and takes a long look at me. "But it's you, all right."

I can't help but grin. "Pardon, ma'am, do I know you? You must be Mary's younger sister."

"Oh, you." She swats my arm. "You may have grown, but you haven't changed. Ever the charmer."

"It's good to see you, too, Mary."

My eyes dart to a young man, about seventeen, entering the room.

"Oh, Caleb." Mary turns to her youngest son. "It's Justus. Can you believe it?" She beams.

I reach my hand out to the boy. "Caleb, you're nearly a man now. I wouldn't have recognized you if your mother hadn't said your name."

He blushes. "You've changed, too."

Mary lays her hands across her breast. "Yes, it does something to a mother's heart to see her baby is about to flee the nest."

Remembering why I'm here, I remove my hat and hold it to my chest. "My father. Where is he?"

Mary's eyes are tender. "He's in the garden getting some sun." She hesitates before speaking again. "You need to prepare yourself, Justus; he's not the same man he was five years ago."

My eyes fall to my boots before meeting Mary's gaze. "Yes, I'm not expecting him to be."

"He can speak some, but you'll find it difficult to understand him."

Sweat and dirt from my travels cling to me. I pull at the collar of my shirt that's sticking to my back. "It's been a long trip. Is there somewhere I can freshen up before I see him?"

She lays a hand on my arm. "Of course. Let's see you to your room." She lifts her skirts and leads the way up the grand set of stairs, calling to her son, "Caleb, please fetch some fresh water for Justus."

She peeks over her shoulder at me. "Have you eaten?"

"Even if I had, I'd have to say no just so I can have some of your good home cooking."

She stops and turns slightly to look down at me. Smiling, she shakes her head. "Dear me, he *is* back." Laughing, she continues up the stairs.

As we walk down the long hall to my room, she speaks again. "It hasn't been touched since you left, except for cleaning, that is." The floorboards creak under foot. "He hasn't said much, but your father's been holding out hope you'd return." She opens the door and steps aside, folding her hands in her apron. "Caleb will be up right away with the water. Come to the kitchen when you're ready." She places her hand on my arm and gives it a pat, then proceeds back down the hall toward the stairs.

"Thank you, Mary." I say as I stare into the room, almost afraid to cross the entrance, as if doing so will pull me into another time I'm not sure I want to enter. A time when Ma would tell me bedtime stories and softly kiss my head goodnight before putting out the lamp for the evening.

Nothing has changed here. Mary was right about that. I exhale, step over the threshold, and close the door.

# 3
## Livvie

*1872 (present day) Boone, Missouri*

Sheriff Andrew Peterson sits at the dinner table, his youngest child beside him. I'm guessing she must be about three or four years old. He pretends to pull a coin from her ear.

"I don't have money in my ears," she states, feeling around the sides of her head, as if she isn't entirely sure.

This exchange makes me giggle. While it doesn't seem quite right to be laughing on this day, it helps to imagine Roy is away on business, rather than lying dead in the nearby cemetery.

There's a heaviness in my stomach from thinking about the decision I've made — I'm marrying Wes this evening. Regardless, I allow my shoulder muscles to gradually relax while I visit with the family. They are so playful with one another. I'm amazed to find their three children, although quite young, to be well-mannered. I must admit, I haven't had much experience with little ones, never having siblings or cousins or children of my own.

"Marybeth and I are happy you agreed to join us for dinner." The sheriff places his calloused fingers over his wife's hand resting on the table.

"We certainly are." Marybeth gives me a warm smile and her hazel eyes twinkle.

There's a sense of guilt for the many times over the years she invited me to church services or to join them for dinner, and I politely declined with an excuse. I wasn't raised with Bible teaching and I knew Roy wasn't keen on the idea. His lifestyle didn't marry well with the Bible folk in town, or with spending time with the sheriff and his family. I always took note, however, that Marybeth never seemed to pass judgment on me.

"Thank you so much, Sheriff and Marybeth, for having me."

Marybeth's smile is sincere. "It's our pleasure, Livvie."

Grinning back, I shift my eyes to my plate.

"How about dessert?" Marybeth stands.

"My wife makes the best pie this side of the Mississippi." The sheriff smirks proudly.

"Oh, he's just biased, Livvie. Andrew, I'm sure Livvie is a wonderful baker, as well." She comes back to the table with not one, but two different pies—blackberry and pear.

"Oh, I'm *sure* I don't bake as well as you," I say, admiring the flaky golden crust.

Marybeth has brought baked goods to me in the past when she's come to my home to visit while Roy was away. But this dinner of pot roast with all the fixings proves the woman to be an excellent cook, as well. How sorrowful I am that I've never shared a table with this beautiful family before. What joy I've missed the past several years. Now, with Roy gone, I can take such liberties without concern of what he might say or do. Then I remember—I'm to marry Wes. I shudder and push the thought away.

The sheriff leans back in his chair after finishing off a slice each of the blackberry and pear pie. He rubs his slightly protruding stomach and licks his lips. "I don't know how you ladies manage to keep your womanly figures."

"Perhaps because we don't eat two slices of pie." His wife snaps her napkin at him.

"Mother's baking doesn't last long when Father's home." The oldest child, a boy, speaks up with a roll of the eyes toward the man.

The sheriff pats his belly again, then turns to the children. "What do you say we go pick your ma some pretty flowers to thank her for this delicious meal?" Cheers erupt from around the table. "Livvie, please excuse us," he says, pushing himself from the table. With great excitement, the children trail him out the door.

I also stand when Marybeth begins clearing the table.

"Oh please, sit down." She gestures to my seat.

"I insist on helping after all the work you put into making this lovely meal. I can't remember the last time I ate so well. I'm afraid I'm not much of a cook." The dishes clink as I sit them beside the washtub. "Besides, your family dinner came late on account of waiting on me."

"Nonsense." Marybeth gives a shake of her head. She surveys the dinner mess and claps her hands together. "You know what? This can wait. Let's sit out front with a glass of lemonade and chat, shall we?"

Being this is my first time visiting at her home, I must remind myself it's all right to relax. Usually, we visit at my little cabin and I'm on guard the entire time, worried about Roy coming home, upset that I'm associating with the sheriff's wife. She's become such a good friend to me. My only friend.

A warm earthy breeze sweeps over the front porch of the Peterson home. Prairie grass waves, as though in a choreographed dance. The sheriff and his children pick white foxglove and purple prairie clover in the distance and chase after one another. Watching them brings a smile to my face.

Without prologue, Marybeth states, "I was once in your shoes."

"Excuse me?" I'm not exactly sure what she's referring to. Was she once married to another man?

"It's not something I talk about, but Andrew isn't my first husband." The woman stares ahead. "My first husband, Bryce, had a strong liking for whiskey and gambling. I was days away from giving birth to our first child when two men came to the house demanding to know where he was. He owed them money over a gambling debt he failed to pay. Although I didn't know his whereabouts, they thought I was lying for him, so they beat me within an inch of my life."

"Oh, Marybeth!" I gasp. I can't imagine such a thing.

"The next day, I gave birth to a stillborn baby girl." Sadness clouds her eyes as she watches her family play in the field. "I named her Josephine. Josephine Louise, after my mama. Those men caught up with Bryce weeks later and killed him. Andrew was the deputy who came to my rescue."

Marybeth gives a faint smile and takes a sip of lemonade. "I was so consumed in my grief over losing Josie, I didn't want anything to do with anyone, especially a man. Nope. Andrew would invite me to church picnics or just for a walk, and I'd give reasons why I couldn't go. No matter how many times I said no, he still always seemed to be around." She rocks her head back and forth and smiles. "I couldn't understand why he would want anything to do with me. I tried my hardest to avoid the man. One day, I gave in and went to a dance with him, thinking then he'd leave me alone."

She glances at me and gives a hearty laugh. "Mercy, was I wrong! That man stole my heart. Not only that, but he showed me true love was possible. I learned to trust again. Most important, I learned to forgive. Now here I am. Life isn't perfect. It never will be. We live in a fallen world."

"But my life is good. I have everything I need and more." The children's laughter travels up from the field. "Please don't think I'm boasting. I'm not. I want you to know you can have this, too. Now, I'm not trying to preach to you." She reaches over and places a hand on my arm. We've never discussed my relationship with Roy beyond general talk. "I know this is none of my—our—business, but Andrew overheard Wes McLain asking Brother Hanson to marry the two of you this evening. I don't know if you agree with that or not. Andrew knows all too well who Wes is, and—" She hesitates before proceeding. "You remind me so much of myself not that long ago. I would hate to see you end up in the situation I was in or worse. Here, you just buried your husband today, and I can't imagine Wes's intentions are good. I just can't."

They aren't, of course, and the image of providing for his "needs" makes my stomach turn. Truth is, my stomach's been tied in knots all afternoon at the thought of marrying that man tonight.

"I saw you talking with Wes at the cemetery. Did he tell you his wishes of marriage?"

Pulp floats on the top of my juice. "Yes, he told me. We're to be married this evening." Her eyes are searching my face. "Oh, Marybeth, I don't wish to marry that man, but I have no choice."

Marybeth gives me a hopeful smile. "We want to help you."

What is she saying? How can they help me?

"I know this is sudden, but we don't have much time, considering." She turns fully toward me and takes my arm gently, her eyes pleading. "Andrew has an aunt and uncle in Colorado, good folks. He can have Charlie—Deputy Carson—see you to the train station and you can take the train west. You'll be safe there. You can start over."

My mind spins and my chest tightens. So much has happened in less than twenty-four hours. Roy's been killed, Wes intends to marry me, and now the Petersons want to help me get away. This is truly happening. It's all too much. I don't know if leaving is the right thing to do. Being with Wes will offer some familiarity and he'd be gone most of the time, anyway. Perhaps it's better to have him care for me, rather than venture off to a place I don't know, to live with people I've never met. What about my little cabin Roy and I built together, and the animals? On the other hand, I know Marybeth's right; leaving would mean a fresh new start. I'd be free of Wes. How I long for a life like the one I witnessed today in the Peterson home. Nevertheless, life has taught me it isn't possible—not for me.

The smile I've been hiding behind for most of the day disappears. "I'm afraid, Marybeth." There, I've said it. I sob. "I'm afraid of Wes. I'm afraid of being alone. Now, the thought of leaving also frightens me. What if I make the wrong decision?"

She takes me into her arms as I weep. "I know it's all very overwhelming. Please trust us, Livvie. I promise we would only send you into the best of care. We feel strongly that this is the right choice for us to offer you." She looks me in the eye, wiping away the tears from my face. "Do you have any money?"

"Yes. Who knows where it came from, but yes, I have money." Using the still-fresh handkerchief tucked into my sleeve, I wipe my nose.

"That's all right—God can use bad things for good." Marybeth brushes back a fallen strand of tear-soaked hair from my face.

I take a deep, bracing breath, as though I'm about to jump into the cold Missouri River. "All right, I'll go." I can exhale now.

"This is best." Marybeth gives me a sympathetic smile, then raises her arm and waves to her husband. He's been doing a great job keeping the children occupied in the field. When he reaches the porch with his brood in tow, she nods to him, a signal.

"All right, my little children, I must go to work. You mind your mother now, you hear?" He kisses his wife on the temple, tips his hat to me, and leaves.

Once back inside, Marybeth hands me a piece of paper. "This is the name of Andrew's aunt and uncle, and where you'll be going. And give this letter to Doc when you arrive. Andrew's gone to get Charlie, who will be here soon to see you safely over to your place to get your belongings. Then, Charlie will escort you to St. Joseph, where you can board the train tomorrow morning."

"What about my cabin? Bess needs to be milked and the chickens fed." Maybe this isn't such a good idea after all.

"We'll take care of everything, I promise." She hugs me. It's a long, tight, comforting hug. A hug as I've never felt. "It's going to be all right. We'll be praying for you."

Normally, those words would mean nothing to me. But at this moment, they mean everything.

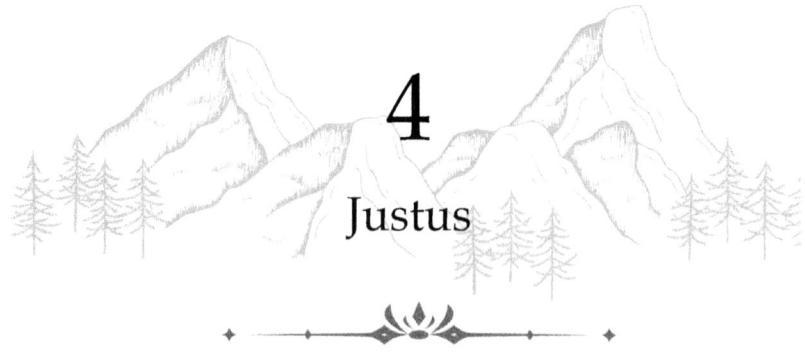

# 4
## Justus

1861 (eleven years earlier) Laurel Springs, Colorado Territory

I listen intently to make sure no one is coming. Voices of those offering their condolences flow from the sitting room. The clanging of dishes as the mourners eat and drink echo through the house. Still wearing my Sunday best, I sneak into the cabinet where Ma keeps the whiskey.

"It's only used for medicinal purposes," she always says when I tease her for having it. Being a good honest woman, I know she speaks the truth that it's the only reason she keeps it. I enjoy joshing with her. She's an easygoing woman that never minds my jesting. Her laughter rings in my ears, as if I had heard it that very day. But I haven't. Today we buried her on the hill beyond the house. She now lies beside my baby brother who hadn't lived more than a month. Her laughter's been silenced for good. Doc said it was her appendix; said there was nothing he could do. Surgery was too risky.

Tucking the bottle inside my coat, I start out the kitchen door, intending to head to our growing family cemetery.

"We have guests, son." The stern voice stops me. I pull my suitcoat tighter to conceal the bottle.

"I can't breathe in there with all those people, Father. I just need to be alone." He tips his head and walks away. Perhaps he understands, or perhaps he just doesn't want to deal with me.

Ma would never approve of me drinking whiskey for reasons other than medicinal ones, but I need something to numb my pain.

I can hear her voice as if she speaks to me now. *You need Jesus. That's what you need.* Ma sees any bad situation as a need for Jesus. Where is her Jesus now? Why has He taken her so young? She was barely thirty-four years old. She was my age, seventeen, when she married Father and gave birth to me. She was always so wise, but I feel as if I'm a lost and lonely little boy.

The relationship between Father and me hasn't been so easygoing. Although I stand head-to-head with the man, I must admit, I fear him. He's labored hard to build a successful ranch and he's put work above all else.

"When you take over…" Father always says. But I don't want anything to do with the ranch. I resent it. Now with Ma gone, what's even the use in living?

Sitting beside her fresh grave, her voice calls to me. *He's a good man, Justus. He just has a lot of responsibilities.*

Angrily, I tip the bottle and take a sip. The liquid is vile.

Shivers run through me as I forcibly swallow.

Where is God now? Why did He have to go and take Ma? She's the good one. She's been faithful to Him, and He just goes and takes her, as if she doesn't even matter. Thoughts whirl like an angry storm as I tip the bottle again and again. It doesn't take long before I grow acclimated to the pungent drink. In a rhythmic pattern, I wipe my tears with my sleeve, then take a swig from the glass. I thought the liquor would numb the pain, but it's only made it cut deeper, searing my heart, much like a branding iron on the backside of a steer.

"Why'd you have to go, Ma? Why'd you go and leave me here? I need you," I cry, longing for her to take me into her tender arms. I'd give anything to smell her sweet perfume one more time.

As the evening rolls on, the sun fades and darkness falls. Finding the night's coolness uncomfortable and the sounds of a storm looming in the distance, I head for a stall in the barn. Father will never stand for a drunken son, not even due to the sorrow of losing one's ma.

My stomach turns and my chest tightens. Ma will have to stay out in the cold dark night, all alone inside a pine box buried deep in the ground. It's not fair. She should be readying herself for the warmth and safety of her bed. I imagine her sitting at her vanity, wearing her soft pink nightgown and brushing her long pale hair, a lovely smile on her face. It's more than I can bear.

Sometime in the night, I wake from my drunken stupor, choking. I find myself in a stall of the barn, and the consequences of drinking whiskey hit me like a two-by-four upside the head.

My brain whirls, as if I were on a spinning wheel. What little is in my stomach begs to come up. I rub my burning eyes, but they continue to sting. The choking grows stronger. *Fire!* My pulse races and my jaw clenches. Smoke consumes the barn. Hiding away the whiskey bottle beside me, I fight to find a way out of the stall. Each inhale burns my lungs. I close my eyes against the sting of the billowing ash. Using my coat, I bury my face to filter the air that assaults my senses. Thick plumes of smoke roar around me, climbing up the walls and over my head.

Sickening chills run through my body as I think of the horses. Crouched down where the air is clearer, I crawl along the aisle between the stalls. I must save them. I feel my way along the stable doors and find the first latch. Opening the door, a lone horse rushes out. The fire draws closer. Another latch, but the horse rears up and refuses to escape.

"Come on! Come on!" I shout at her, but again, she raises her front legs in protest. *Her foal.* As any good mother, she is willing to risk her life to stay with her baby. I try to get to the newborn, but the mother won't allow it. "I'm trying to help you here," I shout at the mare. Frustrated, I maneuver my way to her side and give her hindquarters a good slap. She rears again and again spurning my attempts to move her from the stall.

The smoke continues to swell. I can't take it any longer and run for the exit of the barn. Frantic ranch hands with buckets of water pass me without notice. They race against time to rescue what they can before the fire consumes the barn and everything in it.

With my hands on my knees, I cough, working to clear my

lungs. The barn is now ablaze on one side. I must have knocked over a lamp. Oh, what have I done? Father! He worked so hard for all this. I can never face the man. I run for the woods, not knowing where to go, but knowing one thing's for certain. I can't go back.

# 5

## Livvie

*1872 (present day) Boone, Missouri*

Sitting atop Deputy Charlie Carson's wagon, a nervousness floats around my middle as I think of what is to come. The feeling is one of both excitement and fear. Will the sheriff's aunt and uncle be as kind as him and Marybeth? Will they welcome me, as the Petersons seem to believe they will?

Of course, they will. I've lived in this little town long enough to know I can trust the couple. I experienced their kindness many times over.

Roy's drunken saloon brawls come to mind. The sheriff had every right to jail him when they happened, but instead, he'd bring him home to "sleep it off" or to "sober up." Marybeth came over from time to time with a chocolate cake, a loaf of bread, or fresh vegetables from her garden. I've heard of them helping those in need around town many times. No one has an unkind word to say about the sheriff or his lovely wife.

I inhale deeply to calm my nerves and steady my breathing as my mind turns to my situation at hand. How angry Wes will be when he discovers I've gone away.

"Oh, do write often!" Marybeth insists. Her hand waves over her head as I ride away with the deputy. It's late afternoon now and the sky has clouded over, but the air is still and heavy.

A lump grows in my throat at the sadness of leaving my only friend behind. Life feels so unfair now, yet somehow promising. Can I make sense of it? No, but I'll trust it.

When we reach the door of my and Roy's humble cabin among the oaks and cottonwoods, the deputy helps me down from the wagon seat.

"Unless you need help with anything, I'll be out here waiting." He tips his hat and places a hand on his pistol.

He's doing more than just being kindly by waiting for me. He's keeping watch for Wes McLain.

I scan the horizon before entering the small room. Closing the door, I stop and stare at the bed. My breath catches in my throat. The vibrant block coverlet, meant to be our wedding quilt that I made when I first moved in with Roy, is gone. The two men who brought him home, bleeding to death, wrapped his body in it before taking it away to the undertaker.

This morning I'd washed myself, braided my hair, and put on the black dress. It was as though I was transfixed in my movements, even when I left the house. The missing blanket had been far from my mind.

This must be a bad dream. I close my eyes, pinching the bridge of my nose. My stomach turns as the walls close in. I open the door and hurry outside, fanning my face with my hand.

"Is everything all right?" The deputy steps forward.

"Yes, I just needed some air." My hand goes to my belly; again, my eyes scan the horizon.

"Why don't you leave the door open while you get your belongings?" He places his hand gently on my shoulder. "Do you need help?"

"No. Thank you. I'll be all right." I take a deep breath and go back inside, leaving the door open wide. Deputy Carson takes his place beside the wagon with his hand on his gun once more.

I pull my trunk from under the bed where I keep my grandparents' love letters and Grandmother's wedding ring. Treasures I'd never part with. Without care for neatness, I throw my clothing and other items of use into the case.

Not since the day Mother put me out have I needed to decide in such a hurry what's important and what isn't. My heart aches to think of what I'm leaving behind. What will become of everything here? What of the little log house in which I stand? Roy and I built this cabin with our own hands. It was long, hard, tiring work, but we'd done it.

The day Roy told me we'd be moving west comes to mind. Wes had him convinced of the possibilities moving to Missouri would bring. Ohio was home and the idea of moving so far away to a place where I knew no one terrified me. Would Roy leave me once we got to Missouri, the way Mother's second husband Jonathan had left Mother and me when we moved from New York to Ohio?

"We'll build our own house, Livvie. Just think of it. You won't have to live in this bachelor apartment with Wes anymore. We won't have neighbors for miles." His eyes are wide and his arms wave around the room as he speaks. "It'll just be you and me."

"But what about stores and a doctor?" I relish the idea of having our own house, but the thought of the unknown scares me.

"Wes says there's a general store, and a doc's plannin' on arrivin' soon."

'Wes says.' I hate those words, spoken by Roy almost daily. I know, in truth, that we have no choice. Wes is the boss of this family. One doesn't question or say no to him. I've witnessed his anger poured out on Roy and myself countless times.

The trip west proves hard, but Roy is true to his word. When we arrive in Missouri, we begin building our own home, without his brother.

On the day after completing the house, I'm able to take the pretty items from my trunk to decorate. A simple lace curtain for the window, blue cloth for the table, the good quilt for the bed, and a small rug for the kitchen area. The warmth from the sun invites me to open the door and let in more light. While stacking dishes on a shelf, Roy's shadow on the wall causes me to turn around.

"I think there's one thing that will make your decoratin' complete." He pulls his hand from behind his back and passes a fistful of wildflowers to me.

"Oh, Roy, they're beautiful." I take in the scent. "I have just the place for them!" Not yet owning a vase, I arrange them in a jar with water and set it in the center of the little table.

The truth is, it surprises me that we'd finished the house at all. From the moment we arrived in this new town, Roy spends his fair share of time at the saloon. Of course, the town has one of those. And

*Wes takes him away on "business matters" at every turn.*

My memories of the past fade. I've moved into the unknown before and made it. Surely, I can do it again. Still, a sense of sorrow comes over me as I stand thinking of the memories here, good and bad. The house has no idea I'm abandoning it. Perhaps leaving isn't such a good plan after all.

# 6
## Wes

My cabin's small and dark, but the image of Livvie adding feminine touches pleases me. The only time I've known a woman's touch around the house is when she lived with me and Roy in our Ohio apartment. And whenever I visit the occasional room of a young woman from a saloon or brothel.

I can't remember the last time, if ever, my bedding's seen a washing. Rubbing my hand over the growing hardness in my pants at the thought of having Livvie in my bed, I chuckle. "No one else has ever complained."

I consider relieving the bulge between my legs, but no, I'll save it for Livvie's sweet lips.

Taking one last look in the mirror, I smile to myself, then place my hat on my head. "It looks as if you're one lucky fella, Wes McLain." I give myself a wink, turn, and strut out the door.

Once outside, I consider hitching the wagon. Since Livvie will be moving in while I'm away, I reckon it won't be necessary.

No sense in going through all that trouble for one woman and her nightgown, anyway.

"She won't even be needin' a nightgown," I say, snickering as I mount my horse.

As I ride, I smile at the thought of taking her as my own. She's a decent cook, real good at sewin' and cleanin', and she's right pretty.

I pull my chewing tobacco from a pocket of my jacket and place a large dip on the inside of my lower lip. I've always wanted her for myself. I don't know how that little bastard Roy ever got her. Well, he ain't got her no more. I cackle at the thought. Staring into the horizon, I recall her sweet scent that I've taken in so many times. I can hardly wait to bend her over my bed after our little wedding ceremony.

As I approach the yard, movement catches my attention through the trees. I stop the horse, lean forward on the saddle, and squint. It's a wagon. Livvie's riding in the opposite direction with Deputy Charlie Carson.

"Now just where does she think she's goin'?" Speaking in a low gruff tone, I turn my head and spit tobacco juice into the tall dry grass.

# 7
## Justus

*1866 (six years earlier) Laurel Springs, Colorado Territory*

Mary and Caleb walk out to the garden where Father sits, leaving me standing in the kitchen doorway. Caleb carries a large tray that holds a pitcher of ginger water, two glasses, and a small basket of shortbread cookies.

Mary suggested it would be best that she go ahead to prepare Father. "He's going to be surprised you've come home, so I'll speak to him first. Also, you may need to help him with his drink, as he's a bit shaky."

I'm not sure what makes me more anxious, wondering if Father will accept me, or seeing him in this condition. Although I've helped many a wounded soldier on the battlefield, I'm not so sure I can handle any physical deficiencies he might have.

Mary approaches Father. I rub the back of my neck and peer

around. The garden has grown since I've been away. Ma would be pleased with the care Mary's put into it. The floral fragrance of rose, lilac, and lavender waft to my nose. They're pleasant scents. They're home. But they don't calm my stomach and I must push thoughts of Ma aside once more. Being back here, it's as if it were yesterday that I lost her.

The back of Father reveals a gray and balding head as he slumps in a rocker. He's aged more than the years I've been away.

Caleb sits the tray on a table beside Father and returns to the kitchen door to stand beside me. He gives me a sympathetic smile and my heart sinks.

Mary bends down to speak with Father. I can't hear what she says, but the man's head bows and Mary waves me over. I let out a deep breath before moving my feet in their direction.

"Justus, please have a seat." She motions to a chair. The table of refreshments sit between Father and me. "Are you sure you'll be all right?" She raises an eyebrow.

I nod, elbows on the arms of the chair and fingers intertwined. Glancing at the man beside me, I see there's a slate around his neck. I look to Mary. As if reading my mind, she smiles. "He uses it to communicate, just a little, but it's a helpful tool." She places a piece of chalk in his hand. "I'll leave you. If you need me, I'll be in the kitchen preparing the evening meal." She speaks to us as a teacher would speak to her young pupils.

I rub my hands together, as if it will conjure up the right words from my throat. Should I talk first or wait for Father to say something? I take a moment to observe the man beside me and the chalkboard around his neck. No, it's more than clear he has a difficult time communicating.

Studying my own hands, I take another moment before speaking. "Father, I—" Looking straight into the man's face for the first time stops my words from coming. His eyes stare at me. They're gray, as if the life has already left them. The right side of his face and body droop—lines and wrinkles tell of a hard life. His hair is much grayer than I could see from the doorway. How has he aged so much over the last five years? Perhaps it's the stroke.

I shift in my chair, clear my throat, and try again. "I'm sorry about the barn, Father." I gaze down at my hands again and wipe them on my knees.

At the sound of a grunt and the scratching of chalk, I watch him scrawl a question mark on the small board that hangs from his neck. I don't understand. "The barn. I burned the barn down. That's why I left. I ran away because I couldn't bear to face you. I joined the war and—" I survey my surroundings to avoid the face of the aged and ailing man.

The air is still warm, although the sun has crept west, closer to the mountains. I've missed those majestic forms that stand firm and proud. It's as though they guard against some unknown enemy from the other side.

Father's face contorts, then he spats, "No!" His voice is stern, the way I've always remembered it. "No. Lightning."

Still not sure what he's trying to communicate, I respond, "Lightning? No. I drank too much that night and knocked the lantern over in my sleep." As the words come out of my mouth, the truth smacks me. I'd put the lantern out before falling asleep, and if I hadn't, the hay around me would have caught fire. There was a storm brewing in the distance before I went to the barn. It made sense now. No other possibility for the fire, besides me starting it, ever occurred to me. I take a deep inhale of air. "It wasn't me." I'm not sure if it's a question or a statement. I collapse back in the chair and glance at the sky. The pieces are all falling into place.

Father shakes his head. "Not you. Lightning." Tears trickle down his face.

I reach over and place a hand on his knee. "I'm sorry, Father. I hope you understand I was just a boy. I feared you'd hate me for destroying what you worked so hard for."

He slowly beats his chest with his fist. "My fault…you left. No good…to you." He struggles to get the words out, but he continues, "Pray. I pray for you. God…forgive me."

Trembling, I bow my head before looking at him again through blurred eyes. "I forgive you, Father. God forgives you. I'm not the same boy I once was. I'm a man now and I'm home."

He takes his chalk and scrawls the word on his slate. *Home.* The letters are almost unrecognizable, as if a small child wrote them. He nods and produces a lopsided grin.

It's clear to me as we visit that he's a changed man—in a good way. I'm not accustomed to seeing the man smile, but he does a lot of it today. He even roars with laughter now and again.

The next morning, I awake for the first time in a long time in my own bed. A robin chirps from the tree outside my open window, and the sheer curtains wave like ghosts in the morning light. The thought of it all makes me smile. There's a warmth inside my chest.

After I splash water on my face, I dress and head to the kitchen in search of coffee and more of Mary's good home cooking.

Bursting into the kitchen with arms opened wide, I exclaim, "Good morning, family." The serious expressions on the faces of those who sit around the table halt my steps. "What's the problem?" My breath catches in my throat as I fear the news that's to come.

Mary's husband, Frank, stands. "I'm sorry, Justus. Your father, he's gone."

My stomach plummets. It can't be. Father was just fine yesterday evening.

Mary pulls me to a chair at the table. "He's been ready to go, but you know how stubborn he is. So stubborn that he had to wait for you."

Stunned into silence, I sink into the chair. My thoughts are in turmoil. I squeeze my eyes shut, then after a moment, square my shoulders. The only thing I know to do is trust in who or whatever brought me home. Ma would say it was God.

Mary pushes a stack of papers toward me. "He told me last night as I was tucking him in that he could go be with his Isabella now." She pauses and stares squarely into my eyes. "And Justus, he left everything to you. The ranch, everything. It's all yours."

# 8
## Livvie

1872 (present day) St. Joseph, Missouri

It's early evening when we—Deputy Carson, or Charlie, as he told me to call him, and I—pull into St. Joseph. The sun blazes as a raging fire, burning wild and out of control. Despite the inferno, the town is alive with activity. Ladies wave fans at their faces as they stroll the sidewalks. Men recline on chairs outside of the establishments. A group of children roar with laughter while splashing around in a watering trough. How wonderful to be them. No cares in the world except to play and cool off on a hot and muggy day.

My back aches from the wagon seat jostling over ruts in the dusty road during the long ride. Sweat trickles down between my shoulder blades—a reminder of how I'd love nothing more than to get out of this heavy black dress and wash up in a cool bath. At least I have the hat to shade my face. Food is my second wish, since I'd only eaten once today—the rather lovely meal with Marybeth and her family.

My thoughts then turn to the Petersons—their kindness is beyond my imagination. It's amazing that people such as them exist in this world.

And Charlie. He's been a pleasant riding companion, a complete gentleman on our two-hour journey from Boone. Filled with humorous stories from his boyhood to the criminals he's arrested, there seems to be no end to the tales he can tell.

"I want to be sure to get you settled in at the hotel before I take the team to the stables." He removes his hat to wipe the sweat from his brow. I'm so thankful for his kindness and tell him so. He chuckles. "Oh, just doing what my mama and pa taught me, is all."

During the trip, he confided to me that he plans to ask for Jenny McPhee's hand in marriage. Jenny is a lucky girl to have Charlie as a husband. He is more proof to me that good men are real and loving marriages are possible.

The next morning, after a good night's sleep and a hearty breakfast, Charlie sees to it that I board the train bound for Kansas City safely before he heads back to Boone. I've traded out my heavy black mourning attire and feathered hat for a sensible blue calico dress and bonnet. There's an ache in my chest as I wave to Charlie from my seat by the window, where I can watch the activity below. Another new friend I most certainly will never see again. Life is so full of bittersweet moments. There's that fluttering in my stomach again. I'm not sure if it's fear or excitement.

The whistle sings out as the engine begins to move, chugging and jerking. Before long, it settles into a smoother rhythm as it speeds down the track. A sway here and bump there. The red velvet seats remind me of the brothel. I smooth my hand over the plush material; it's soft and silky. I slide the hand in the opposite direction—hard and rough, much like my life.

Roy is dead now, and I've left behind the home we built together and everything I've known for the last seven years. Someone else will be milking Bess tonight, perhaps Sheriff Peterson. I play with the hair at the end of the long braid that drapes over my shoulder. Sheriff and Marybeth helped me escape Wes. That dirty, rotten man has been a plague in my life for far too long. Clutching my carpetbag, I gaze out the window, hopeful the sheriff's uncle, Doc Peterson, will receive Marybeth's letter in a positive way. Confident this man will be as kind as his nephew, I relax into my seat for the trip to Colorado.

Late in the night, I find myself on a second train in Kansas bound for Denver, dimly lit with oil lamps. Using my bag as a pillow, I attempt to sleep, but sleep doesn't come. Between the hard seat and the movement of the iron horse, rest is difficult. A crying baby does little to help matters. When it appears the child has finally reached the land of Nod, the wailing begins once again. Some passengers grumble and the poor mother apologizes for her teething infant.

As the train sways and bumps along the track, my mind wanders. I remember my eleven-year-old self and the day

Mother, Jonathan, and I ride away from the only home I'd ever known. Grandfather built the house with his own two hands.

*I cry as I sit in the back of the wagon and watch until the house is no longer in sight.*

*I want to jump out and run. Run as fast as I can back to that house with the white paint and carved porch columns. I want to sit where I so often think of my grandparents sitting together. Often, I will imagine Grandfather playing his fiddle while Grandmother sings. I frequently recall a quote from a letter Grandfather had written to Grandmother. "No opera singer could compare to the beautiful voice of my sweet Orinda."*

As I'm about to fall into slumber, an opening door to the car gets my attention. A tall shadowy figure in a hat and long coat stands in the entry, scanning the space. My stomach drops and my heart races. I hunker down in the seat, fighting the urge to get on the floor. That would likely draw attention to myself, for certain. I don't know how Wes has found me. He walks down the aisle, inching closer to me. I bury my face in my bag pillow with one eye peeking out, watching the man's every move.

# 9

## Livvie

*1872 (present day) Denver, Colorado Territory*

Thank goodness, the man who came into my car on the train last night wasn't Wes. My mind was obviously playing tricks on me; his hat wasn't even anything like Wes would wear.

A thunderstorm greets us this morning as we arrive in Denver. I wake to the sound of rain pounding loudly against the vehicle. It seems I'd fallen asleep after all.

Thunder crashes and lightning strikes across the angry sky. My heart sinks as I look out the window and see nothing but blurred figures. I've never much minded storms, so long as I wasn't out in them.

"Okay, let's get this over with," I whisper to myself and then descend the steps into the pouring rain. I need to get to the nearest hotel, but don't know where it's located. People are running around me. Some look as lost as I am.

By the time I have my trunk in hand, my dress is soaked through. "Excuse me. Can you tell me where the hotel is?" I shout over the rain at each person as they pass, but they, too, are in a hurry to get out of the storm and completely ignore me.

Cold, drenched, and alone, I begin to cry. I can't feel the tears that mingle with the rain streaming down my face, but I can taste them. They're salty on my lips. The sobs shake my body as I amble down from the platform.

The road is thick with mud and rushing water that pulls me in, as if it wants to swallow me up. Consumed by my emotions, I slip in the mire. From instinct, I reach out and grab a man's arm as I tumble to the ground.

"Are you all right?" he calls through the shower, helping me to my feet.

I stand, but a pain shoots through my right leg. "I think I hurt my ankle. I can't walk."

"Let me help you." Bending down, he places my arm around his neck, then takes my trunk in his other hand. He's a strapping man with broad shoulders, and I'm surprised by the butterflies that fill my stomach. He leads me to the porch cover of a nearby building. "What's your name?" he asks into my ear. I close my eyes at the warmth of his breath on my skin.

"Liv…Olivia," I yell back over a clash of thunder. It's best to go by my given name now. My real name. If Wes comes looking for me, he'd inquire about Livvie McLain, not Olivia Palmer.

"Where are you coming from?" He walks me up the steps and lowers me into a seat on the porch.

"Missouri." I'll never see this man again, so it doesn't matter if he knows where I'm coming from. But I remind myself I must get in the habit of calling myself Olivia Palmer.

The man is handsome and smells earthy, or maybe it's just the rain. Large chocolatey brown eyes with flecks of gold captivate me. His hair falls to his shoulders from under his hat and I have an urge to run my fingers through it. I'm surprised at myself for the attraction I feel for this stranger. His voice cuts through my thoughts of wanting to kiss his lips that show through the scruff of beard on his face. "I'm going to get you a doctor, Missus Palmer."

I realize I still have my arm draped around his neck. Embarrassed, I slowly slide it off, feeling his muscular shoulder in the process. "Oh, I hate troubling you like this." I wipe away the water from my face.

He smiles and my heart melts into a puddle. "No trouble at all, ma'am." And just like that, he is gone.

I remove my bonnet and drop it into my lap. Who was he and why does he have my insides as turbulent as the water running through the ruts in the road?

# 10

## Livvie

"You've got a bad sprain, all right," announces the doctor, who is old and gray with round spectacles on the end of his nose. I'm propped on my elbows, watching as he examines my ankle. He lowers my leg back down onto the bed. It's black and blue, and now too swollen to wear my muddy boot. "Not much we can do about it except keep off it."

"But I need to get to Laurel Springs," I protest. "I'm here for Doctor Edward Peterson. I came from Missouri to see him. Do you know him?"

"Just because I'm a physician doesn't mean I know every doctor in the state, ma'am," he says with a frown.

I lower my eyes. "Of course."

"I'll tell you what." The old man starts for the door, then turns. "I'll see if anyone is heading to Laurel Springs that can take you once this storm clears."

I rise from my elbows to my hands. "Yes, thank you so much.

I would be so grateful."

He dips his head and leaves the room.

*This is quite a predicament you've gotten yourself into, Livvie.* I roll my eyes and plop my head down on the pillow.

True to his word, the next day the doc has me on a wagon heading north to Laurel Springs with a man named Daniel. He's returning to Boulder, north of Laurel Springs, from purchasing supplies in Denver. He isn't at all talkative, but I'm all right with that. I much prefer my own thoughts over someone else's chattering today, anyway. Thankfully, the delay in travel provided me much-needed rest before surprising Doctor Peterson with my presence.

What will I do if he turns me away? If I go back to Missouri, Wes will kill me. If there is a God, as Marybeth spoke of, I hope He'd see to it that doesn't happen.

With no other options now, I settle in for a ride in the back of Daniel's wagon among his store supplies.

The sun is straight overhead when we arrive in the quaint little town of Laurel Springs. Taken in by the beauty of this country, I almost forget about my throbbing ankle and my body aches due to the jostling of the vehicle and crates pushing into me.

Laurel Springs lies at the foot of the majestic Rocky Mountains like a rug accenting an ornate piece of furniture. Rock outcroppings jut strong and bold from the range. I don't believe I've ever seen such an enchanted vision in my life. The greenery isn't like back east, but there are beautiful accents of it. Evergreens of pine and fir, mixed with maple and aspen.

It only takes one inquiry from Daniel of a passerby to get directions to Doctor Peterson's home. Within moments, he helps me limp to the door. To my surprise, it opens before we have a chance to knock. A frenzied pudgy gray-haired woman flings my other arm over her shoulder.

"Dear me! What happened? I saw you coming up the steps and I said to myself, I need to come help quick. Let's get you in here so the doc can get a good look at you. You must be new here, for I know everyone. Doc Peterson is Colorado's finest. Yes, he is. Now come right this way." The woman leads us to a small room off the foyer, decorated with only a bed, dresser, and chair.

After settling me on the cot, the woman grabs Daniel by the arm and leads him from the room. "Now you just wait out here and Doc will have your missus right as rain in no time at all." Before the woman can give Daniel or myself a chance to correct her, the two are gone and the door shut.

Soon after, a man enters, a complete opposite of the woman—tall, thin, and with slow movements. "You'll have to excuse my wife. She has a tendency to get excited." He sits in the chair and crosses his legs. "How can I help you, Missus…?" He raises an eyebrow, pausing to learn my name.

"It's Miss. I don't know that man, actually; he was kind enough to give me a ride. My name is Olivia. *Miss* Olivia Palmer. Yesterday I sprained my ankle slipping in the mud when I got off the train. Doctor Morris, there in Denver, said I needed to stay off this foot."

Doctor Peterson stands from the seat beside me and moves

to the end of the bed. With much care, he examines my injury. "So, if you've seen a doctor, Miss Palmer, what are you doing here? Has it gotten worse? It is fairly swollen and bruised."

I shift uneasily. "Truth is, I'm here because your nephew Andrew and his wife Marybeth sent me to you."

# 11

## Justus

1872 (present day) Laurel Springs, Colorado Territory

It's been six years since I returned home to Laurel Springs. Six years since we buried Father beside Ma. I took charge of the ranch the way I knew Father would have wanted; the way he would have done, had he still been alive. The herd has almost tripled over the years under my care—something I'm real proud of. I've realized how my time as a Union soldier prepared me for overseeing the ranch. I shake my head. It's funny how life prepares a man for what's to come and he doesn't even know it.

The sight of the main house in the morning light relieves some of the aches in my back and shoulders brought on by the long ride on ole Beau. I've been gone for weeks, although it feels like months. Driving a herd of cattle back from Denver is hard on a body. Do I have to be a part of the drive? No. But my heart can't sit behind a desk at the house. It's with the animals, the dirt, rain, snow, sleet, and sunshine. My heart longs for the nature of Mother Earth. The cattle drives give me long periods either to think or to keep my mind off what I'm missing in life.

More and more lately, I ponder over the future. Not the future of the ranch, but of my future. Mary has been pestering me about marrying. It would be nice to share my days and nights with a partner. Someone to greet me when I return from these long rides. Perhaps then, I wouldn't even feel a need to go. When I sit on the porch in the mornings with my coffee, I fancy having a wife beside me. I haven't felt a woman's touch in more than six years.

"You'll never have an heir to inherit this ranch if you never leave it," Mary often says. "And cattle drives don't count."

The problem is, every time I go to town, Bridget Murphy manages to sniff me out like a hunting hound, then ropes me into taking her to church or "for a stroll."

As much as I want to marry and have a family of my own, I don't consider myself worthy of a good woman. Any woman worth having deserves better than me. There are too many sins from my past that still haunt me. It wouldn't be fair to bring them into a marriage.

Handing Beau's reins to the ranch hand, I plod to the house. Ready for a good home-cooked meal and a bath, I take my Stetson from my head and smack it against my dusty chaps.

As I enter the house, I lay my hat on the small table beside the door. "Mary, I'm home," I call out. I know she's here because

I hear her clanking around the kitchen.

She greets me in the foyer. "Do you wish for a bath or to eat first?"

"I'll bathe, then eat." I start up the stairs.

"I saw your aunt in town yesterday. She insisted you come for supper when you've arrived home. I told her, 'That boy will never miss a meal.'"

My laughter booms from my belly. "You know me too well, Mary." I shake my head and trudge up the steps. "It'll have to be another time, I'm too tuckered today."

"Rest up, then, because I wasn't expecting you home and Frank's taking me to town to eat at that new restaurant," she says, walking away. "I won't be cooking for you tonight."

I holler down, "I know how to cook, Mary." Plodding up the remaining stairs, I mumble to myself, "You go on ahead and let that man treat you to a fancy supper. I'll go to my aunt's another day."

# 12

## Livvie

It's been well over a month since I came to live with the Petersons. They are as wonderful as I'd hoped they'd be. Everyone refers to Doc's wife as Miss Bea. She's welcomed me with open arms, just as she'd done with Rebecca, a young runaway slave, and her small son Thomas years ago. Everyone has been a light of joy in my new life here in Laurel Springs. Still, I can't help but feel I'm a burden on Doc and Miss Bea, considering they also have Rebecca and Thomas to support.

This evening, as I sit with the family in the parlor, the time seems right to voice my concern. "Since my ankle has healed, I can't continue to stay here. Also, I don't know how I will repay you for my doctoring when I don't even have a job." I have little money left. With a heavy sigh, I plop my needlework in my lap.

Miss Bea squeals, causing Doc to put his paper down. The older woman gives her husband a big grin with a shrug of her shoulders, the way an excited child would do. I glance to Doc.

He removes his spectacles and gives his wife a nod.

"What? What is it?" My eyes travel back to Miss Bea. Something's up here.

"Well, dear, Doc and I have talked it over, and…well—"

Doc, who is a man of few words, surprises me with what he says next. "We'd be obliged if you continue on here with us."

"Yes, dear, you've become a second daughter to us, and since you have no family, we wish to be yours. Ever since our Hannah got married and moved out, it hasn't felt the same around here. You can continue to stay in her old room and use it as your own." As if reading my thoughts, she continues, "I've already discussed it with her, and she's thrilled." Miss Bea gives a grin and another shrug of her shoulders.

Have my ears deceived me? I glance around the room, at a loss for words. Rebecca, who sits on the opposite end of the sofa helping seven-year-old Thomas with reading, gives me a warm smile.

I throw my hands up. "I…I don't know what to say."

Another surprising comment comes from Doc, who is placing his spectacles back on his nose and lifting his paper. "Say yes," he says slow and deep.

Warmth wraps itself around me like a soft blanket on a chilly day. How I cherish this family already. And Hannah and Rebecca are like sisters to me.

I smile. "Yes, I would love to stay." I right myself in the seat and hold my head high, confident in my answer.

Miss Bea squeals.

"Thank you so much." I place my hands to my heart. "I still

need a job, though. I can't just sit around here forever sewing and knitting." Miss Bea and Rebecca do most of the housework as it is. I would only continue to be in the way.

"Oh yes, of course, dear." Miss Bea tilts her head to one side and places a pudgy finger on her chin, as if retrieving a thought from the files in her mind. "You know, I recall seeing a 'help wanted' sign in the window of Lenny Johnson's tailor shop just yesterday. You do such fine work; I am right sure she'd be pleased to hire you."

I swear, I'm sitting on a cloud. "I'll walk down there tomorrow, then."

Jumping to her feet, Miss Bea claps her hands together. "This calls for a celebration. I'm going to make tea and popcorn." And quick as a wink, she is off.

What the future holds, I don't know. But Laurel Springs is now my home, and the Petersons are my family.

# 13
## Justus

I've spent the last few weeks catching up on the news around the ranch. I've reviewed and updated the business books and allowed for much-needed rest for myself and Beau.

As I sit on the hillside looking out over my land, with elbows perched on my knees, I think of Bridget Murphy. She wouldn't welcome horse rides beyond the hills. Nor can I imagine myself sitting on the porch in the dewy mornings discussing the beauty of Mother Earth or the troubles of wrangling cattle with her. I don't believe she'd even survive ranch life. The house isn't fancy. There isn't a library or a large, elegant drawing room. No maids or butlers. No way would Mary be a servant to the spoiled girl. No way would I put up with her high and mighty ways, either.

Mary's right, I won't widen my prospects to find a wife unless I take some time off. Frank and Caleb can handle ranch matters for a while. They did just fine after Father's stroke. I don't know if I'm ready for a wife, though. There's still so much

I hold on to from my past that I don't know how to let go. If I fall in love, I'm not sure how I'd tell her the things I've done.

"What should I do?" I speak into the air. A cool breeze sweeps over me. My eyes are shaded by my Stetson. All is quiet except for the rustling of the tall grass. "I suppose an answer will come in time."

My thoughts turn to the upcoming supper at my aunt's house. I'm thankful she and Mary are the closest to a mother I have on this side of heaven.

I asked Mary to bundle up some flowers from Ma's garden to take with me. She's included a jar of strawberry preserves since I'll be showing up partially unannounced. My aunt won't mind, though. She knows the life of a rancher, and besides, she always has a good meal with plenty of fixings on the table, no matter if there's company or not.

As I ride into town, I smile and lean back in the saddle. It's a beautiful early August evening. "Those mountains sure are pretty, aren't they, Beau?" The horse plods along without a response. "Great Spirit's got something special for us, ole buddy. I don't know what it is, but I can feel it."

I ride up to the house whistling "Oh! Susanna." I tie Beau to the hitching post, then take the preserves and flowers from my saddlebag and run up the porch steps. Still whistling, I knock on the door. When it begins to open, I grin and hold out my arms. A woman I wasn't expecting answers. My smile fades and my arms drop. This must be a dream. I try to speak but the words lodge in my throat.

"May I help you?" A smile plays on her lips.

The angel from the train station. Sun-kissed hair, eyes as deep blue as the sky when a storm rolls in—and her voice, sweet as taffy.

"May I help you?"

"Uh, yes." I square my shoulders. She doesn't recognize me. "Is my aunt here?" *Oh, you sound like a child.*

The angel's smile grows to show a set of beautiful white teeth. "That depends on who your aunt is." She surveys me with an amused grin.

"Bea." I grope for words. "Bea Peterson."

# 14

## Livvie

---

I could never forget those big brown eyes of the cowboy from the train station. My pulse quickens.

He fumbles over himself, which I find quite amusing. I pinch my lips together to keep a chuckle from escaping. Is that a bead of sweat forming on his brow? He tucks a jar under his arm, then removes his hat.

"Mister—?" I pause for his reply, so I may learn the man's name I didn't get when he carried me to safety that stormy day in Denver.

"Justus. Justus Bennett." He turns his head slightly. "We've met."

Was it a question or a statement?

I smile. "Yes, I believe we have. And thank you for your help."

He motions toward my foot. "All healed up?"

"Yes." I nod. I can feel my smile broaden as my heart races.

"Sorry I just left you there. I had to get to an important meeting." He appears as if he doesn't know what to do with his limbs. "That sounds foolish, now that I speak it out loud."

I chuckle. "Mister Justus Bennett, can I take something?" I hold out my hands and he passes the jar of preserves to me.

Thomas emerges from the house to stand beside me. "Hello, Justus. Can I pet Beau?"

"You sure can. Be sure to stay clear of his backside. And wash your hands before dinner. Your mother will have my hide if you don't."

"Thanks, Justus." The boy shoots out toward the horse.

"Please, come in." I motion to the entryway.

He steps forward and hangs his hat on the rack beside the entry. "Missus Palmer…am I correct?" Now it's his turn to pause for a response.

I give a closed-lip smile before speaking. "You remembered. Yes, *Miss* Olivia Palmer." I want to be sure to emphasize the *Miss*.

"Hmm, you look like an angel to me."

I glance down, then back to him. "I'm sure you say that to all the ladies."

I've heard his name spoken often in this house, and I know he's a single man.

"How is it I find you answering my aunt's door?"

"It's a long story." I turn and walk toward the kitchen, not wanting to appear too eager to be in his presence.

Miss Bea pulls biscuits from the oven. When she sees her nephew, she sits the pan down and darts to him. "Oh, Justus. I'm so happy to see your handsome face. I hope you're here for supper. You chose the best evening to come. Rebecca made duck and Olivia here made us a peach pie. I see you've met our Olivia." She hugs him and takes the flowers. "Oh, these are just lovely. Let me get a vase."

She leaves him with me to steal glances and flash smiles at one another.

I snap out of the moment and take a step forward. "I'll set an extra place at the table."

He traipses to Rebecca, who pours water from the steaming pot of boiled potatoes and places a kiss on her flawless ebony cheek.

"Justus, it's good to have you home." She speaks over her shoulder. "How was the drive?"

"Long, Rebecca. Long." He leans back against the counter and crosses his feet at the ankles, then crosses his arms. "I would have come sooner, but Beau and I needed rest."

"I'm sure you did," she says.

As I take an extra plate and glass from the cupboard, I feel his eyes on me. A tingle runs up my spine and I caution myself not to trip over my own feet, lest I fall and break Miss Bea's good dishes.

At the supper table, Doc is quiet as usual, focused on eating his meal as though no one else is in the room. The aroma from the meat, potatoes, and gravy waft through the air. Butter glides over the warm spongy bread and the corn is juicy and sweet. Does this evening's meal taste especially delicious? I peek up through my lashes and across the table at a certain cowboy whose dark brown eyes pierce my soul. He winks, sending tingles through my body. Justus rescuing me at the train station seems to be our little secret for reasons I'm not sure of yet.

Miss Bea continues to talk while soaking up the juice on her plate with a slice of bread. "Justus, our Olivia is working for Lenny Johnson. Olivia is a right fine seamstress, yes, she is. Tell him, Olivia."

I fidget in my seat. "Thank you for saying so, but Lenny is the talented one."

"Oh, don't be modest, dear. Lenny told me you're the best she's seen. You're certainly the best I've ever seen."

He gives a sideways grin as he lifts his water glass. "I do have some shirts and britches that could use mending. Sounds as if I should pay Lenny's shop a visit this week."

I peer into those eyes again, then glance back to my plate before I lose myself.

Miss Bea continues, "Yes, you should, Justus. I'm here to tell you, the gal's a right fine seamstress."

Not wanting those eyes to pin me once more, I stand and gather dishes. "Justus, could I interest you in a slice of peach pie?"

He wipes his mouth with his napkin. "I always have room for pie."

Rebecca stands. "I think everyone would love pie. I'll help."

I serve Justus first, since he's the guest. As Rebecca and I continue to serve the rest of the family, I notice him pouring sugar on his slice. Not a little but heaping spoonfuls of it. He must love sugar a lot.

Then Doc speaks up. "Justus, would you pass me the sugar, son?"

Then Thomas. "Me too. I want some."

"Hush now." Rebecca scolds the boy.

Why is this family pouring sugar all over my pie? I've never seen them do such a thing before. Is it because Justus did it?

I take a bite and know immediately. My heart drops. I shoot a look to Justus, who continues to eat his slice as if nothing is amiss. I examine each of the other members who sit around the table eating the pie as if it is a normal dessert. How could I have forgotten the most important ingredient aside from the peaches? What must he think of me?

"Oh, I'm so sorry. I'm afraid I forgot the sugar. It's ruined." I swallow past the embarrassment that's lodged in my throat.

Thomas pushes the bowl of sweetener toward me. "It's fine, Miss Olivia. Here, put some of this on it."

Justus stares at the heap of pie that lay on his fork. "It's not bad. But it's a good thing you're an excellent seamstress." A broad grin spreads across his face.

Something between a laugh and a sob escapes me.

Miss Bea tosses her napkin on the table. "Oh, mercy, Justus. Look what you've done. You've made the girl cry."

I hold my stomach as I double over in laughter, tears streaming down my face. "It's all right, Miss Bea. He's right."

Soon, everyone around the table joins in the merriment. Even Doc snickers.

# 15

## Justus

Sitting on the sofa, I hold the open magazine but stare at the flowered wallpaper on the other side of the room. My mind is focused on a certain copper-blonde-haired woman. If I had known she was here this whole time, I'd have come for dinner the day I got home from Denver. I have so many questions about her. Why is she here, for starters? Yes, I most definitely want to get to know her.

Every time I hear her voice or her giggles coming from the kitchen, my heart melts a little, like butter on a hot day. The way she laughed at herself for failing to add sugar to the pie makes me chuckle. She's as refreshing as a cool breeze on a summer afternoon.

My uncle plucks me out of my reverie. "She's just as smitten with you, son."

"Sir?" I realize I've been staring off with a smile on my face.

"Olivia. She's smitten with you, too. I can see it." Doc turns the page of the book he's reading.

"If she's working for Lenny Johnson, then she's not working for you or Miss Bea?" Am I being subtle in my way of asking why she's here?

"It wasn't safe for her in Missouri, so my nephew Andrew and his wife Marybeth sent her to us." It's as if Doc read my mind.

Why wasn't she safe? I'm not comfortable prying into her business.

"Do you think it'd be proper to ask her to a picnic after church tomorrow?" I'm willing to suffer through church if it means seeing Olivia.

"You don't need my permission, if that's what you're after. You'll have to ask the young lady." Doc peers down the end of his nose at his book.

That settles it, then. Before I leave this evening, I'll have my answer. There's a knock on the door and shortly thereafter, my chest tightens at the laughter I recognize all too well. Bridget Murphy.

# 16

## Livvie

Miss Bea hangs the dishrag up to dry, then turns to Rebecca and me. "Shall we see if the gentleman want to join us in the garden? It's such a lovely evening."

I've hardly noticed the near-perfect temperature or the sun soon to settle in the western sky. A smile plays on my lips as I remember the handsome cowboy with untrimmed hair and a scruff of beard who teased me at the supper table. I rather fancy his rugged look. He isn't like other men I've known. Clean-cut men that seem too proud to crack a smile, let alone make a joke. No. Justus Bennett is different.

A knock at the door interrupts my thoughts. "I'll answer it," I say, stepping forward.

A groan almost escapes me at the sight of the visitor, Bridget Murphy. I've crossed paths with the young woman at church and at Lenny's shop, but I don't know her personally. I only know Bridget's father owns the bank and the girl peers down her nose at most folks. She's quite demanding when she brings her garments to Lenny and me for hemming and such.

I motion for her to come in. "I'll go get Doc," I say, assuming she's come for his services.

Bridget gives me an exaggerated giggle and steps into the entry. "Oh no, darling. I'm here to see Mister Bennett."

"Mister Bennett?"

Bridget giggles. "Well, don't look so surprised," she says, stepping past me. Blonde curls flow from under her extravagant hat. A twinge of jealousy pricks my stomach at the lovely dress she's wearing. I play with the top button of my simple blouse. "By the way," she says. "I will be in the shop on Monday to pick up my gown. I do hope you've stitched it precisely as I asked."

I force a smile. "Of course."

Justus's voice comes from behind me. "Miss Murphy."

I turn to see him, hands by his side, then at his hips.

The young woman giggles again. "Oh, dear Justus. I saw your horse out front and knew you were here visiting your family. You should have come to see me at once when you arrived home from Denver. Anyway, I'm afraid I spent too much time visiting with a dear friend of mine. Would you be a gentleman and walk me home? It's getting late and you never know what kind of scoundrels are out this time of the evening."

Justus clears his throat. "Yes, of course." He glances at me, then back to Bridget. It's a nervous look. Is it shame or regret? I can't be sure. "Miss Palmer, it was a pleasure to meet you—again." He smiles at me. "I look forward to more peach pie in the future."

Despite my disappointment in Justus leaving with Bridget, I can't help but grin as I feel warmth creep into my cheeks. "It was a pleasure to meet you as well—again." I tip my head to him.

Miss Bea buzzes into the foyer. "Oh, Bridget, how are you, dear? Justus, you'll be in church tomorrow, won't you?"

He takes his hat from the rack and places it on his head, but before he can speak, Bridget interrupts. "Yes, ma'am, he will because he'll be picking me up. Isn't that right, darling?" She reaches up and touches the side of his face. "And be sure to shave. It wouldn't be proper to escort me to church with that horrid thing you call a beard."

So, Justus is courting Bridget Murphy. Clearly, he's not unlike other men after all.

# 17

## Livvie

This morning as I ready myself for church, my thoughts turn to Justus. There had been a glimmer of hope yesterday that he was different from other men, like Andrew or Hannah's husband Clint. I harrumph to myself while pulling my hair back into a tight chignon—a new way to wear my hair, since Wes would be looking for a long braid if he were to see me from behind.

Mother was right. I'll never have what women such as Marybeth and Hannah have, a man who is loving and gentle and whose face lights up when I walk into a room. I release an anguished sigh at my own misfortune.

Running my hands over my calico dress, I inspect myself in the mirror. "The sooner you accept that, Olivia Palmer, the better." I speak to the reflection that stares back at me.

Justus and Bridget will be together at church today. It feels as though someone has laid a stack of bricks upon my chest.

As a member of the family and a guest in their home, the Petersons expect me to attend services with them. Although I find everyone to be friendly, I don't understand the scriptures. Moreover, Reverend Moore shouts at the congregation until his chubby face is as red as a beet.

I frown at myself in the mirror, grab my Sunday bonnet, and head down to the kitchen.

---

The church service goes as I expect. Reverend Moore shouts scripture that I don't comprehend. And the congregation shouts back "amen" while they bob their heads. I'm thankful we've arrived before Justus and Bridget. This allows me the blessing of sitting in the front and not having to see them walk in together nor see them sit in front of me through the entire sermon.

Flirting with one woman while courting another. Just like a man.

I want so much for him to be unlike the men I've known my whole life. I watch Hannah and Clint sitting together with their two little ones, Chet and Mimi. Clint has his arm around his pregnant wife. Hannah is lucky to have him. Luck. Yes, the force of nature I was born without.

Thank goodness, the reverend finally stops hollering and closes the service in prayer. My sleepy eyes might not have made it a moment longer, as usual. Everyone files out of the pews, but I sit for a moment, bracing myself for the possibility of seeing Justus. Then I hear it; a laugh from the back of the room that makes my stomach roll. Bridget Murphy. Does the girl have no discretion?

I seek out the nearest family member, which happens to be Rebecca. "I'm afraid I'm not feeling so well. Some fresh air will do me good. Will you please let Miss Bea know I'll walk home?"

Thomas jumps up in excitement. "Can I walk with you, Miss Olivia?"

"Young man, she said she does not feel well. You will stay right here with me," scolds his mother.

"Yes, ma'am." The boy hangs his head.

I give him a smile and pat his shoulder before slipping out of the church.

The glossy green aspen leaves shimmer and flutter in the hot summer breeze. Which is worse? To see Justus and Bridget together or to walk in the scorching sun while wearing layers of clothing. At least my bonnet gives me some reprieve.

I've just begun my trek home when I hear the clomping of horse hooves slowing as they approach, and a deep voice calls out to me. "What's a respectable young lady such as yourself doing walking in the heat of the day all alone?"

Not recognizing the voice, I pivot toward the stranger. "I'm sorry, do I know you?" The man dismounts his horse.

"No, but you look as if you could use some company." His face is clean-shaven, and a thin black mustache rises and falls with the movement of his lips. He smiles, showing a lovely set of dimples.

What kind of a man is so bold? "What if I am married?"

"I don't believe a husband would allow such a specimen to

walk the streets alone." He glances around. His eyes are like the turquoise you find in the ditches after a good rain.

He makes me chuckle and I hold out my hand to him. "Miss Olivia Palmer." Curiosity about this man is getting the best of me. The cut of his clothing tells me he's a fashionable man.

He lifts my hand and brushes his lips over my fingers. "It is my pleasure, Miss Palmer."

"Do you live here in Laurel Springs?" I ask.

"No, ma'am, I'm here on business," he says.

My stomach sinks at that awful word, business. "And what is your *business*, if I may ask?"

"Banking." He motions to his horse. "Say, I'd offer you a ride, but I'm afraid you'd have to ride astride, and I don't take you as that sort of lady."

"You thought right. And I'm afraid you still haven't told me your name."

He removes his hat, showing a full head of black hair and gives a slight bow. "Asa McDaniels, ma'am."

I clasp my hands in front of me and give him a smile. "Oh, no need to call me ma'am, Mister McDaniels. Please, call me Olivia."

"And you may call me Asa." He sits his hat atop his head. "May I walk with you?"

"Certainly." I'm captivated by his stunning features. His blue-green eyes are a beautiful contrast to his dark hair.

He offers me his arm and we commence to stroll down the dusty road, his horse plodding behind us.

I find Asa McDaniels to be rather charming, despite his

well-groomed and smart appearance. His smile is warm and his moves graceful; the way he tilts his hat at me and the way he touches my hand. Why he's stopped to converse with me, I don't know. Clearly, he's a gentleman of high society, unlike most men I've known. And he's far from rugged. *Rugged. Like Justus.* I close my eyes and give a subtle shake of my head, as if to loosen the cowboy's grip on my thoughts.

As we walk, a wagon passes us. When I notice it's Justus and Bridget, my heart comes to a halt. Not wanting my pain known, I let out a laugh. One that is a bit too loud, even to my own ears. Have I lowered myself to the tactics of Bridget Murphy?

Once the wagon passes without a word from its passengers, I lift my chin and swallow. "Mister Mc…Asa, may I invite you for a lemonade?" I've never been so bold as to ask a man over. Truth is, Roy is the only man who's ever courted me. But Asa and I are now friends, aren't we?

"Why, Olivia, you surprise me, and I quite like it." His eyes twinkle.

I grin. I like the way he speaks to me. A refined man such as Asa McDaniels is not what I'm accustomed to. I am delighted and intrigued.

# 18

## Justus

(Earlier that morning)

"You're awfully quiet this morning, Justus," Mary observes aloud at breakfast.

I hover over my plate with a fork in one hand and a knife in the other. "I'm afraid I've gotten myself in over my head with Bridget Murphy."

"I've told you she's not the one for you."

"I know that, but I'm not so sure she does." My eggs lay limp on my plate. "I can't help but wonder why she was brought into my life, though."

Frank clears his throat. "For all one knows, she was brought into your life to show you what you don't want."

"Frank is right, Justus," says Mary. "Her father forced her on you. She is a spoiled little girl who would love nothing more than to marry the town's most wealthy rancher. I shudder to think of her running this house. Would it even be good enough for her? Your father built this house to your ma's specifications, and you know she wasn't a fancy woman. She was practical. She didn't see the sense in having a separate room as a library when she could have your father build shelves along one wall in his office and she believed she could entertain guests just as well in the same room where you all gathered as a family." Mary waves her arms about as if she's trying to convince me of what I already know. "And your father, he didn't need a room to smoke in. For goodness sakes, he just went outside."

I sigh. "I've had the same thoughts myself."

"Most important, Justus," Frank cuts in, "do you two share the same beliefs and values?"

I take hold of my coffee cup. "You're both right." I stare into the steamy black liquid. Oil has settled on the top. "She hasn't shown a genuine interest in anything about me or the ranch. She fusses about everything. And she'd make me cut my hair and attend every church service." I quiver. "She's not even as outwardly pretty as she was when I met her."

"Beauty is only skin deep, Justus," Mary interjects. "True beauty comes from within. That's why the good Lord looks at our hearts, not our outward appearances."

I sit back in the chair and cross my arms. "She made it clear I'm to pick her up for church this morning and to shave." I scratch at the whiskers on my face.

Mary rolls her eyes. "I see you've disobeyed one command. What about the other?"

"I said I'd be there and I'm a man of my word."

"Mercy, Justus." She wags her finger at me. "I suppose you're right, but you have to find a way to set that girl straight."

I nudge my chair back from the table, slide to Mary's side, and place a soft kiss on the top of her head. "Thank you for the breakfast, Mary. I best go help with chores before church."

Frank stands. "I'll come with you."

---

I can't take my eyes off Olivia throughout the entirety of the church meeting. She sits but a few rows ahead of me with her head remaining on Reverend Moore.

I don't particularly care for being here, and I especially don't care for the reverend's way of preaching the gospel. I'm only here because Bridget hoodwinked me into bringing her. Of course, if I'd gotten the chance to ask Olivia to a picnic, I would still be here. I just wish it were with Olivia.

In contrast to Olivia, Bridget fidgets and whispers, which I find quite childlike and rude. She keeps her arm wrapped around mine for the duration of the sermon.

Today is the day I must speak with her. She needs to know the relationship she believes we are in together must end. I realize I've led her on by not putting a stop to this sooner, but it can go no further.

Surely, Olivia thinks I'm courting the girl. The look on her face when Bridget came to Miss Bea's last night told me as much. I grimace. Asking her to a picnic today is out of the question now, but I must speak with her as soon as possible. She has to know the situation isn't as it appears.

When the sermon is over, I long to go to Olivia, but Bridget continues to cling to me. She chats with the other women and laughs too loud for my comfort. My chest tightens as I watch Olivia scurry from the church.

Once on the wagon seat, Bridget sits as close to me as she can get. Again, she wraps her arm around me in such a way as to make it difficult for me to drive the team.

"You will come to dinner, won't you?" she asks.

"Thank you for the offer, but I should get back to the ranch."

"Oh, that ranch. That's all you ever talk about. You have hired help that can see to ranch business for you. You don't always need to be there. You're the *boss*." She emphasizes the word boss and giggles as she squeezes my arm.

"'Boss' is not a title I place on myself. And the people who work for me are like family, not hired help." My pulse quickens, and I hear my voice come out a little too thunderous.

"Now, darling, I know how sensitive you are to others. But no need to worry, Father will show you how it's done."

I bite the inside of my cheek to keep from saying something I may need to apologize for later. I must end this so-called courtship with Bridget Murphy. But how, exactly?

Then something catches my eye. Olivia. She's walking with a man I've never seen before. Clean-cut and well-dressed. She holds his arm as they stroll leisurely, laughing together.

My stomach hardens. I shift away and swallow past the thickness in my throat. Perhaps they're already courting. I know nothing about her. But wouldn't Doc have told me she was taken? Of course, he would've.

Doc's words from yesterday ring in my ears. "She's smitten with you, too. I can see it."

# 19

## Justus

"Miss Murphy, shall we?" I remove my Stetson and point toward two rockers on the porch of the Murphy home. My mouth is as parched as the desert floor. I lick my lips, but my tongue is void of any moisture to wet them.

She puts her hand to her breast and a delighted smile springs to her face. "Why yes, Justus. I'd love that."

Diverting my eyes from her, I sit in the rocking chair to her right. It appears as though she believes I'm about to propose marriage right here and now.

She sits on the edge of the rocker with her left hand propped on the right arm of the chair.

Clouds inch across the sky, and a hint of thunder sounds in the distance. A warm breeze kisses a bead of sweat on my neck. I'm unsure if the sweat is from the heat or from the conversation I'm about to have with this girl. Sitting on the edge of the chair, I clear my throat.

She giggles. "Oh now, darling, don't be shy." She bats her eyes and glances down at her hand, then back to me. "Come out with it, will you?" She reaches out to swat my arm, her hand landing in the air.

I hang my hat on my knee before looking into her eyes. "Miss Murphy, I'm afraid I have allowed you to believe there is more between us than there is. I—"

She recoils, pulling her hand from the arm of the chair and places it over her bosom with an exaggerated inhale. "Why Justus Bennett, what are you saying? Are you claiming you never had feelings for me? It's that new girl, isn't it? That Olivia Palmer! I saw the way you two looked at one another last night."

"Now, don't be drawing conclusions, Miss Murphy."

"Miss Murphy?" She stands and stomps like a child who is not getting their way. "It is that Olivia Palmer. I knew it." Tears stream down the girl's face.

I stand, allowing my hat to topple to the porch floor. "First of all, I have always called you 'Miss Murphy.' Second, we aren't right for one another, and I know you know that. You need someone who…" I can't seem to find the words to express what exactly this spoiled child needs in a man. *God help him, whoever he is.* I place my hands on my hips and stare down at my boots before I peer back up at the hysteric girl. "Someone who's not me." That's all I can think to say. *Boy, I sure got myself into a predicament here, haven't I?*

She stomps her feet again and clenches her fists to her sides. With a tear-soaked face, she shouts, "I hate you, Justus Bennett. You are a lying, good-for-nothing brute. I never want to see you again." Then she runs into the house screaming, "Mama. Mama." The screen door slams behind her.

I glance around. That didn't go quite as planned. *But was there even a plan here, Justus?* What's a man to do? I pluck my Stetson from the floor and place it back on my head.

Sprinkles of rain dot the ground and the smell of earth tickles my nose. I deeply inhale the aroma. I'm free at least. A weight has lifted from my soul. Then I hear the screen door creak open and slam shut once more.

Connor Murphy stands to his full height, as though he is trying to make himself appear taller. Does Bridget's father, a short stout banker, think he can intimidate a tall rancher and trained soldier such as myself?

"What's going on here, Justus? My daughter tells me you've left her for that gal living with your aunt and uncle."

I shake my head and step toward the man. "With all due respect, sir, your daughter and I were never courting. I wanted to make sure she knew that and as you can see—" I hold out my arm toward the door as a demonstration of what had just happened.

Connor Murphy interjects, "But you've taken her to church and on walks. I don't understand. Were you leading my daughter on?" He places his hands on his hips and takes a step toward me.

Will the man try to hit me? I laugh inwardly at Mister Murphy's boldness, considering his stature.

I copy the older man's stance. "I never asked your daughter if I could pick her up for church, nor have I asked her on walks. She has a way of swindling me into things. I didn't know how to say no to her, if I'm honest, sir. But when it became clear to me that she thought we were courting, I knew I needed to set matters straight. Something I should have done from the start. Sir, I apologize if I ever gave the impression to her, or you, that we were courting."

"You're calling my daughter dishonest?"

"She's...crafty." I don't know how else to tell the man his daughter is a manipulator.

Connor Murphy relaxes his arms and lets his shoulders sink. "Have a seat, Justus." His tone is one of defeat.

Sitting back in the rocker, I listen as the man proceeds to speak.

"My daughter has always gotten her way." His elbow rests on the arm of the chair. He rubs a finger over his thick mustache while moving his head back and forth. "It's my fault, of course, and the missus, too. Now, I'm not trying to make excuses for Bridget. There is no excuse for her behavior."

I place my hands on my thighs and rock in a slow motion. My muscles ease at the turn of events with this man.

The sky continues to sprinkle water on the ground, making that relaxing earthy scent stronger. My horses swat flies from their backside with their tails, completely unbothered by the scene displayed on the porch.

"Bridget was a twin."

I shoot Mister Murphy a look. "You don't say? She never told me." But then again, we've never had conversations of any substance.

"It's not something we talk about. When the girls were three years old, they came down with a fever. Bridget pulled through. Dinah did not."

"I'm sorry for your loss."

The man's pain shows on his countenance. No parent should have to bury a child. I think of my own baby brother who lies beside my parents in our family cemetery on the ranch.

"We were just so thankful Bridget was alive and so afraid of losing her, too, that from then on, she got whatever she wanted. And honestly, Justus, I thought that applied to you. When I came out here, I considered buying your love for my daughter, but as you spoke, I knew I was wrong. I've always been in the wrong. She's seventeen now, and if she doesn't change her ways, no one will marry her. I know this."

I sit in silence, taking in what the man is telling me. Connor Murphy was going to try to buy his daughter a husband. I'm not sure how I would have handled that one. Thank goodness, I don't need to find out.

"I'm sorry, Justus. I know you and Bridget aren't right for one another."

"No, sir, we're not." I shake my head and rub my hands on my britches. I should get going before the clouds decide to let loose.

As though reading my mind, Connor Murphy stands. "Son, you should probably get those horses home before the flood gates open. You know these mountain storms can be quick but fierce." He reaches out his hand.

I shake the man's pudgy palm. "Thank you, sir. Thank you for sharing and for understanding."

"The best of luck to you, Justus." Mister Murphy tips his head.

Riding along in my wagon, I sag against the seat. That's all behind me now.

I had better put my focus back on the ranch and not worry about women. Either they're breaking your heart or you're breaking theirs. There doesn't seem to be any middle ground with me and women. Besides, no woman in her right mind would want a man broken by the war.

The rain is coming down steadier now. I pull the collar of my jacket up around my ears and tilt the front of my hat down. I don't mind the rain. I rather enjoy it. It washes away the old and gives life to the new. The sound of the drops hitting my hat is tranquil, even.

Passing my aunt and uncle's house, I can't help but think of the beautiful young woman who resides there. The angel with the dainty nose that turns up slightly. I smile at the image.

Then I see a familiar sight. The horse of the man she had been walking with is tied up outside the house. Even through the rain, laughter prickles my ears. There she is, sitting on the porch swing with that stranger. Her voice, sweet as honey. I have to look away. She isn't meant for me, either. She deserves better than a man who screams himself awake at night. I cringe at the thought. It's a plague I must bear.

# 20
## Livvie

"Olivia, Asa's here," Rebecca calls from the bottom of the stairs.

"I'll be right there." I stand before the mirror, smoothing out my dress. Courting Asa over the last few weeks has proven that possibly I have more luck than I've been led to believe. It's still hard to believe he sees anything in me when he could have someone as beautiful and fashionable as Bridget. Not wanting to keep him waiting a moment longer, I put out the lamp on the dresser and make my way down to greet him.

"Ahh, Olivia darling, don't you look lovely." He helps me with my coat.

I turn to face him and he gives me a wink. Strange, it doesn't affect me the way it had when Justus winked at me. But those dimples and blue eyes smiling back at me sends a tingling warmth through my chest.

The theater is dark except for the dimly lit stage.

I finger the extravagant necklace that hangs about my neck. "Thank you again for the pendant, it's beautiful." I think of his touch as he placed it on me during dinner. His fingers lingered longer than I felt comfortable with.

He leans over and breathes into my ear, "Only the best for my lady."

Goosebumps spread over my arms at his exhalation atop my skin.

"This is my first play," I whisper as we take our seats.

"You don't say? My darling, you stick with me, and you'll experience a lot of firsts." He nuzzles his face into my ear.

"Stop that." I move from him with a forced giggle. "The show's beginning."

It is a lovely and heart-wrenching tale of forbidden love. I don't believe I've ever heard such beautiful singing in my life. Perhaps Grandmother sounded as exquisite as this actress.

When the show is over, I fan my face with my hand in an attempt to dry my tears when a handkerchief appears. Asa smiles. "You're such a romantic," he says, kissing my cheek.

"Thank you. You're so sweet." I dab my eyes with the cloth.

"I have plenty, you keep it. You can think of me whenever you use it," he says when I hand it back to him.

I chuckle. "You mean when I blow my nose into it?"

"Whatever you use it for, darling—I'll be there with you in spirit." He holds out his hand to help me from my seat.

"Now who's the romantic?"

Pulling me close, he lets out a slight moan. "It's easy to do with a magnificent creature such as yourself."

My heart does a double take at his scent. "You're a dangerous man, Mister McDaniels," I joke, peeking through my eyelashes at him.

"Dangerous is my middle name, darling." He kisses my lips softly. "For now, we better get you home." He pauses. "Since you won't give me any loving."

At Doc and Miss Bea's, he helps me from the wagon.

"Can I invite you in for a cup of tea?" I ask.

"I had better call it a night. Work tomorrow."

"You're always working." I reach up and grab his tie playfully.

"A good man needs to be able to afford the finer things for his love." He swipes a curl from my eye.

"His love?" I cock my head.

"Oh, haven't I told you?" He gives a bewildered look.

I step back. I should have known he's married.

He catches me and pulls me close. "You're my love."

I let out a breath. "Me?"

"Could there be any other? I don't believe another woman exists." He glances about with a puzzled expression.

"Such a flatterer." I pat his chest.

He grabs my behind and pulls me close.

"Asa." I move his hand to my lower back.

"What do you say we go for a ride on Sunday? A picnic?"

"That would be wonderful. I'll have everything ready."

He bends down and brushes his lips to mine, then draws back.

"You're such a tease," I whisper.

"Ahh, I do believe the tease is you, my darling, walking around looking the way you do, like a delectable pastry I long to savor in my mouth." He pulls away and gets into the wagon. "I'll see you Sunday." He tips his hat and snaps the reigns.

Not sure how I feel about this man, I watch as he drives away.

Inside the house, I lean against the door. Is romance always this confusing?

"Olivia?" Hannah steps out of the sitting room with a smile on her face.

Rebecca peeks around her. "How was your evening?"

"Oh, the show was magical."

"Do tell us all about it." Hannah grabs my hand and the three of us practically skip to the kitchen like a bunch of giggling schoolgirls.

# 21

## Livvie

On Sunday after church, I put together a picnic basket of fried chicken, biscuits, potatoes, pie, and a jar of cider. I tuck a rolled blanket under my arm and head out to the porch to wait for Asa, who just happens to pull up at this very moment.

"I see I'm right on time," he calls out.

"I welcome a man who's prompt." I hand the basket and blanket up to him before he helps me to the seat.

"Kiss me, darling." He pulls me close and our lips briefly meet.

I pull away quickly as someone approaches on a horse. Embarrassed at Asa's openness about kissing me in the daylight in front of Doc and Miss Bea's, I tug at my bonnet. My heart leaps when the man and his horse become clear to me.

"Justus." Asa waves.

The cowboy tips his head, eyes on me, and moves past us without a word. My stomach tingles and my heart races.

"He's not very friendly, is he?" asks Asa.

"Please don't ruin our time fretting over him." I fold my hands in my lap. I don't know why Justus stared me down like that, as if I were doing something wrong.

---

We're finally alone, not at Miss Bea's, a show, or a restaurant. Alone.

"Did you make this chicken?" Asa licks at his fingers.

"Rebecca. She's real good at frying food. I did help with the potatoes and the biscuits."

"It all tastes delicious."

"Thank you."

When we're finished eating, I clean up while he walks off a little distance. If I could, I'd lie here under the warm golden sun and allow the rustling of the leaves on the nearby aspens to lull me to sleep. Instead, I sit with my face to the sky, taking in the gentle heat.

To my delight, Asa returns with a bouquet of wildflowers. He pulls one out and sticks it behind my ear. "For my beauty." Then he hands me the remainder of the spray.

"They're lovely." I lay them aside, then snuggle into his arm.

He kisses my head and runs his hand over my breasts.

"Please, don't." I move his hand. I'm not going to fall for this again.

My mind goes back to a time when Roy had taken me on a picnic at the lake. We had taken cover under a tree from a rainstorm.

*Once under shelter with our blanket, we sit close to one another to keep warm from the cold droplets. We're giggling and before I know it, Roy pulls me in for a kiss. At first, it's soft kisses on the lips, then he runs his hands over my breasts.*

*I pull away. "I don't know about this, Roy."*

*"It's all right," he says, peppering my neck with wet pecks. "Ain't no one gonna see us."*

*I'm not sure how to feel. My mind goes back to Mother's husband, Vernon. The shame of that day not so long ago. I enjoy Roy's company, though. He is handsome and kind. And he is gentle. This can't be bad, right? I kiss him back. I like the way he makes me feel. There is a burning sensation between my legs as he slowly slides his hand up my thigh. It's a good burning, though. I want more.*

*He lays me back on the blanket and lowers his pants. He's gentle and slow, breathing heavy in my ear. I tense at the expectation of it hurting, but it doesn't hurt at all. It's pleasurable, in fact. He moves faster until he groans and jerks just as Vernon had done. My stomach twists. Afterward, Roy lays with me and caresses my cheek and neck.*

*"Will you marry me, Livvie?"*

He never did marry me, and the way he made love to me that first time was the best it had ever been.

Asa's voice brings me back. "We're all alone, but still, you won't let me touch you."

"I want it to be the right time, is all." I peer into his face, searching for something to be there, but I'm not sure what I'm looking for. Something to tell me he's the one for me, perhaps.

He props himself on one elbow. "This is the right time." He runs a finger down the buttons of my blouse. "Come, darling."

He leans in to kiss me.

"No." I get to my feet. He's not hearing me. "I'm ready to go, Asa."

"Olivia, don't." He reaches for my hand, but I pull away.

He stands and grabs my arm, hard. I glance down, then back to his face. The grip he has on me is tightening. He's hurting me. He is no better than Roy or Wes.

His eyes soften and he lets go. "I'm sorry, darling. I didn't mean to take hold of your arm so hard." He lays his hand over his heart. "Please, Olivia—I'm in love with you."

I truly want to believe his words, but I'm not sure I can. I'm not sure I even care. In truth, his words don't move me. As much as I want to forget about Justus Bennett, he seems to be all I think about. My heart longs for the cowboy, but I don't want to admit this, not even to myself. "I appreciate you saying so." I stare at him.

He takes me in his arms. "I'd never hurt you, my dear flower." He lifts my chin and parts my lips with his tongue. His mouth feels foreign on mine, but I ease into his kiss. Perhaps he does love me. I'm not being fair to him. After all, this is what I want, to be loved.

He pulls away slightly. "I'll respect your wishes today. Grab your basket," he whispers. His lips hover over mine. I can feel his breath on my mouth.

Once home, he helps me from the wagon and lays a kiss on my cheek. "I can't wait to see you again."

"How was your picnic?" Justus's voice surprises me as I reach for the doorknob. I hadn't seen him sitting in the corner of the porch.

"It was very nice." I reach for the handle again, then stop. "I'm surprised to see you're still here."

"Wasn't ready to go home." His eyes bore into me. It makes me feel uneasy, but at the same time, sends flutters through my middle. He appears jealous. Yet, I'm unsure why, considering he's courting Bridget Murphy.

He nods toward the road. "What do you know about this Asa fellow?"

"Probably as much as I know about you, and yet, here I am, alone on a porch with you," I say, wondering if he catches my sarcasm.

He doesn't say another word, just continues to stare at me.

"Good day, Justus." I can't let him see that I want nothing more than to be in his arms, the way I was when he lifted me to safety at the train station.

I go to my room and change before taking a short Sunday nap. When I remove my blouse, I notice bruises on my arm. He didn't mean it, though. Asa said he was sorry. At least he did that much. Roy never apologized when he left bruises. Well, I suppose in the beginning he did. This is just an act that men do. They can be rough, that's all. I pull down my sleeve and dismiss any idea that Asa cannot be a good man.

After my rest, I make my way downstairs and find myself surprised by Justus's presence once again. Surprisingly, he's alone in the sitting room.

"Where's Doc?" I ask.

"He left to see to a patient." His gaze remains on the

newspaper in front of him.

"Let me guess, you weren't ready to go home?" He irritates me. I'm not sure *what* irritates me so much about him being here. Perhaps the fact that he's not mine, but Bridget's. The man ignores me. "Shouldn't you be with Miss Murphy?" Now I'm just being petty.

He slams the paper into his lap and looks as though he intends to reprimand me, but Thomas runs into the room with excitement. "Justus, will you play ball with me and the boys?"

Justus exaggerates a sigh of relief. "I thought you'd never ask."

I groan as I watch him go. I don't know whether I wish to declare my true feelings for this man or wring his neck.

# 22

## Livvie

My week went by quickly, as work kept me busy. Thank goodness, Justus hasn't shown his face again. I haven't seen him since Sunday when Thomas pulled him from the sitting room for a game of ball. That man confuses my thoughts and emotions. It's best I don't see him.

"Asa, won't you come in for a cup of tea before you two are off?" Miss Bea asks, moving her arms as if guiding him in the direction of the front room.

He puts his hand to his chest and bows. "Thank you, ma'am, for the offer, but I'm afraid we have reservations and I don't want to keep the restaurant waiting."

"Oh, all right. Yes, you better be going. Olivia dear, you look beautiful." She stands back to admire me before ushering us out the door. "Have a good time, you two."

I'm excited for dinner at the finest restaurant in Laurel Springs, and for time with Asa. Lenny has yet again loaned me a dress to wear for the occasion. My pocketbook can't compete with Asa's, so I save my money for the things I need.

"It's such a lovely evening, isn't it?" I wrap my arm around his.

"We'll see." His tone is one of contempt.

I pull away. "Whatever is wrong, Asa?" He was fine moments ago. I think through my recent actions, wondering if there was something I might have done or not done between the front door and the wagon.

He guides the horses away from the house. "When I dropped you off on Sunday, I saw you talking with Justus Bennett."

I laugh. "He only asked how our picnic was, and I told him we had a very nice time. That's all. Then I went in the house."

Asa continues to look straight ahead. No sign of emotion. "I don't want you talking to him. In fact, I don't want you around him at all."

I frown. "How can that be? I live with his aunt and uncle. I can't tell him he's not allowed to come over, and it would be rude for me to ignore him." My stomach feels as though it's filled with a bucket of rocks, an all too familiar feeling.

"Then it's time for you to move out. You're an adult; you can get an apartment."

"Move out?" My chest tightens. I don't want to move out.

He grabs my arm and squeezes. "Did I stutter?" he says through clenched teeth.

"No." I pull away. My throat is thick. Experience has taught me it is best not to argue with him.

As we approach the restaurant, a boy about Thomas's age stands outside the door. "A flower, mister? For your missus."

He holds out a single rose from the dozen or so he carries.

What a sweet child. No doubt he's trying to make money to help his family. So young and innocent. My heart warms and I wish I could wrap him in my arms.

"Go on now. Get out of here, boy." Asa pushes him away.

My mouth falls open. How can he be so cruel? Even Roy would not have done such a thing.

The boy lowers his head and steps away.

"Asa. He's but a child." My body tenses.

"He's a beggar."

"Maybe he has no choice." I strain to make eye contact with him, but he looks past me.

"Everyone has choices." He opens the door, motioning for me to enter.

The restaurant is grander than I had imagined. Although, I've just lost my appetite and the place has no appeal to me now. I'm sure Justus would never have done such a despicable deed. I think of how kind and playful he is with Thomas and Hannah's little ones.

A woman leads us to our table. A quaint space in a dark corner. I must admit, it is a romantic setting. It's too bad I'm not feeling a bit amorous. Asa pulls out my chair. Perhaps he's just tired. He has been doing a lot of traveling and his work is straining for him. I'm judging him too harshly. Roy would always remind me I need to stop jumping to conclusions. "Thank you," I say as calmly as I can muster.

Once seated, he holds out his hand for mine. I remove it from under the table and place it in his. "I'm sorry, darling, for my conduct. I just get so jealous at the thought of another man wanting you." His mustache lifts at the corners.

I accept his apology, but this is another infraction upon his character I can't ignore.

He moans. "Thank you for accepting my amends." He gently kisses the back of my hand, lingering a moment. "Your skin, it smells heavenly."

His breath is warm on my hand, sending unwanted goosebumps up my arm. "Thank you." I manage a closed-lip smile.

He lets out a raspy moan as his eyes rove over my chest while placing my hand back down on the table. Thankfully, the waitress approaches, saving me from having to acknowledge his carnal appraise of my body.

The remainder of our time at dinner and the ride back to Doc and Miss Bea's is pleasant enough. The food was better than I could have dreamed. Asa, on the other hand, talked about nothing but banking and his travels. Occasionally, he ran a smooth finger down my neck while prattling on about matters I have no interest in.

"Olivia," he calls after me as I approach the front gate.

I turn and smile. "Yes?"

"It's time to move out," he says in a sharp tone.

My stomach churns and my smile falters. "Yes," I say, gaping at the ground. As if the evening wasn't spoiled enough, he's just managed to make it even worse.

"I'll be back next week." He snaps the reigns.

How will I tell Miss Bea I'm moving out? I love it here and

want desperately to stay. I have to move because of Justus. It isn't fair and stirs anger in me. More anger with Justus than Asa. But why? It isn't Justus's fault. This is my home, my family. I will the tears not to come, not wanting anyone to see them when I go in the house.

I take a deep breath, slowly guiding the fresh air into my belly, then I release it even slower. This is no time to allow my emotions to control my decisions. I pinch my cheeks, as I'm certain they've lost all color. Squaring my shoulders, I march to the front door.

## 23

### Justus

---

"When are you going to stop playing around and tell her how you feel?" Clint asks as we watch the children play hopscotch from his and Hannah's front porch.

"What are you talking about?"

"Olivia. Everyone sees it."

Have I been that obvious? "She's courting Asa."

"He hasn't been around in weeks. Hannah says Olivia hasn't heard hide nor hair of him."

How could anyone just up and leave a woman as special as Olivia? I never would. "That doesn't mean anything. Besides, I'm sure she thinks I'm a damn jackass."

"You are a damn jackass." Clint gives me a push. "A damn jackass for not telling the woman how you feel."

"I don't know, Clint. I don't exactly have the best record with women. It's best I just keep my eye on the ranch."

"The ranch is the only thing your eye's been on for far too

long. Besides, you've never been in love before, either. And you've spent too much of your life with whiskey and ladies of the night."

I wag my head and chuckle. "Clint, I haven't known the scent of a woman in at least six years."

Clint claps a hand on my shoulder. "Do you want to go another six years, brother?"

Mimi runs over. Her face is hidden within her sunbonnet but her dark curls bob. "Cousin Jusdis, will you play hopscotch wid me? Da boys made dares dis big." She holds out her chubby little hands to show what a big amount is to her.

I grin at the little girl who warms my heart. "Come on, Mimi—let's show those boys how a real hopscotch looks."

I take hold of her small hand and she giggles. "Dank you, Cousin Jusdis."

After a time visiting at Clint and Hannah's, Thomas and I leave to walk back to Doc and Miss Bea's. Along the way, I stop to talk with some fellows looking over a mustang. I give Thomas a few pennies to get himself candy from the mercantile.

"Thanks, Justus," he says with big round eyes.

"Just don't eat it all at once or your ma will have my hide."

Thomas grins. "I promise I won't."

"You come right back here, you hear?" I call after him. Thomas waves while running in the direction of the store. I laugh, remembering what it was like to be a boy. "Who does this fine stallion belong to?" I ask, petting the silky black ribs of the horse.

Moments later, a commotion just down the street catches our

attention. Slowly, the men and I head that way to see what the ruckus is when I notice a well-dressed pudgy man has Thomas by the nape. "What's this about?" I shout, running to the scene.

The man's face is red with anger as he pulls on Thomas. "This here boy tried to steal my money."

"I swear I didn't. I was returning his wallet." Tears run down Thomas's face and his eyes plead with me to believe him. Of course, I do.

"I suggest you release the boy," I say, stepping chest to chest with the man.

"I will not," he spits out. "I am waiting for the sheriff."

I grab him by the neck and push him against the building. His eyes are wide with fright.

"The boy speaks the truth," says a woman. "I saw the wallet fall out of the man's pocket and the boy picked it up and handed it to him."

"Is that so?" Still having the pitiful man pinned against the wall with his eyes affright, I tell him to show me his wallet. His shaky fingers produce the leather pouch. "Count the money," I demand.

The man proceeds to finger each bill.

"I trust that it's all there," I say.

He nods.

"How much?"

"That's none of your—" I press harder on his neck.

"Sixty-two dollars."

"Give the boy two dollars."

"I will not," chokes the man as I press harder, squeezing for good measure.

"Make it five, you bastard," I say through clenched teeth.

He shakily counts out five dollars and slams it into my chest.

"Are you from around here?" I ask.

"I am not," he says indignantly.

"Good, because we don't want your kind around here. Make sure you leave and never come back, you hear?" The man purses his lips as I push away from him and hand the money to Thomas.

"What's going on here, Justus?" asks the sheriff, strolling up to us.

"Nothing I didn't already take care of. Come on, Thomas."

Now I will need to explain this incident and my behavior to Rebecca. I'm reminded of the beast inside me that I can't seem to let go.

# 24

## Livvie

It's a cool October day. The trees are adorned with lovely hues of yellow, orange, and some deep burgundy leaves. I pull my shawl tight around myself. The air is refreshing as I breathe it in and relax into the bench that sits in the middle of Miss Bea's garden.

It isn't like Asa to go so long without coming to visit me. Maybe he's hurt. No, business must have detained him. Perhaps he's found another, someone who will afford him the intimacy I've refused to give. I think of him calling another woman "darling" or gently kissing her lips the way he kisses mine. If I cared, I might worry myself to tears, but I don't. I'm only disappointed that not seeing him is causing me to prolong telling him I deserve better. I will no longer be joining him for any more picnics, shows, dinners, or the like. I pity the next woman who falls for those dimples or turquoise eyes.

I think of Justus rescuing poor Thomas from that awful man

who accused the boy of stealing. I wish I had been there to see Justus giving that vile man what he deserved. For shame.

*Oh, Justus.* My mind is lost in thoughts of the man when I hear the back door open and close, but I don't look back.

"A penny for your thoughts?" Justus sits on the opposite end of the bench.

Wouldn't Asa love knowing I'm sharing a seat with Justus Bennett. I laugh inwardly. "Enjoying the out of doors before the snow comes." My eyes remain on the mostly harvested landscape.

"I come to take Thomas fishing. Would you want to join us?"

Now that I know he's no longer giving his time and attention to Bridget Murphy, I can't be upset with him anymore when he speaks to me or teases me. He likes to josh, that's who he is; I've come to understand this.

I haven't fished a day in my life. "I think you boys would have more fun without me."

He sits in the crook of the bench, one arm on the rest, the other on the back. My breath catches at the sight of him. Quickly, I turn back to the garden.

"Oh, I don't know about that. Do you know how to fish?" He taps the back of the bench. His hand is almost touching me. The proximity causes my heart to skip a beat.

I shake my head. "I've never been fishing."

He sits up in astonishment. "You've never fished? That settles it, then, you gotta come with us." He grabs me by the hand and pulls me to my feet.

I laugh. "I don't think that's such a good idea. I'd be more of a problem. You most surely won't catch anything on account of me," I say, pulling back.

His grip remains on my hand; gentle, not harsh or mean. "Nonsense."

Thomas runs out the back door. "Justus, I'm ready."

"Olivia's coming with us," Justus says, eyes on me.

"All right," says Thomas, lifting his rod in the air. "You'll have so much fun, Miss Olivia. Justus is the best fisherman I know."

Justus smooths his hand over Thomas's head. "I'm certain I'm the only fisherman you know."

Thomas grins, showing a space where a couple of teeth should be.

I love this soft side of Justus, as well as his humorous side. My heart melts a little more each time I'm near him. But I must keep my fence up. I haven't told anyone, yet, that I plan to end my relationship with Asa. Just best to wait, I think. And I believe I need space to sort out the feelings I've been having for the man in front of me. It's high time I think about myself and what I want and need. Unfortunately, I hear Mother's voice sounding in my head that my wants and needs mean nothing.

# 25

## Justus

"Now you're going to put your bait on the hook, like so," I say as I show Olivia how it's done, not sure if she'll be able to handle the innards. I wipe my fingers on my britches. "It's your turn."

She produces a sly smile. "All right."

I watch her with amused anticipation.

She picks up the bait. "Sorry, friend," she says before threading the hook into its wiggling body.

"I'm impressed, Miss Palmer." I bob my head and grin. I'm impressed, indeed.

Then she reaches over and wipes her fingers on my pants.

I jump back. "These are my best slacks," I tease, excited that she touched me.

She tips her face to the sky and laughs. I swear, there's an angelic glow around her.

Thomas already has his line in the water. "I bet I catch a fish before you two," he taunts.

"We'll see about that," I call back.

Once I've given Olivia a lesson in fishing, we stand holding our poles in silence.

"This is relaxing," she says in almost a whisper.

"Yes, it is," I call back softly.

"Do you do this often?"

"Not as often as I wish." This is my favorite fishing memory so far. I have the loveliest woman in all the land standing but a few feet away from me. I'm treasuring this moment in my heart. If only she knew what she means to me.

Her shrieks pull me from my thoughts. I drop my rod and shoot to her side. It's then that I notice she's yanking on her pole. "I think I got a fish! I think I got one, Justus."

Hearing my name on her tongue makes my heart gallop. I pull the line in, and sure enough… "Why, you got yourself a fine trout, little lady." I hold it in the air. "Look here, Thomas—you've been licked by a girl."

"I had a nice time today," Olivia says once we're back at my aunt and uncle's.

"Why don't you come with us again tomorrow?" I wasn't planning on going fishing tomorrow, but I will if it means spending more time with her.

She gives me a sideways smile. "Justus, I shouldn't have gone today."

Asa. The thought of the man produces a bit of bile in my throat. I slide my hands into my pockets and shrug. "We're just friends."

Her eyes shift down, then back up at me. "Thank you for a fun day." She smiles and walks away.

So that's it, then. My throat tightens painfully. It's time to buck up. I take a deep breath and grab the pail from the wagon box.

"Don't forget your rod, Thomas." I call to the boy who's petting the horses. "And take this fish to your ma so she can fry you up a real nice dinner." I hand over the bucket.

"Thank you, Justus."

I wave. My shoulders slump as I make my way home.

# 26

## Justus

Once again, I turn my focus entirely on the ranch, no longer going to town. My heart just can't handle seeing Olivia. She's made her choice.

According to Mary, yesterday at church, Miss Bea invited us all for supper. When Mary shares the invitation with me, my response is swift. "No, thank you."

She gives me a knowing look. "You can't avoid that girl forever, Justus."

"Oh, yes, I can," I say, heading out the door.

Sunshine gives way to clouds, then flurries of snow, as I finish repairing the last fence post. Dinnertime can't come soon enough. My stomach rumbles and the cold bites at my ears. Ranching is hard work, long hours, and long days, but it relaxes my mind. There is nowhere in the world I'd rather be than right there.

It's ironic how life has come full circle this way. I was such a stubborn boy, not wanting anything to do with the ranch. The thought makes me grin. I imagine if Father could see me now, he most certainly would get a good chuckle out of it himself.

I gather my tools, then Beau and I make our way back to the semi-warmth of the barn. At least the building blocks the wind. I put the horse in his stall with fresh hay and water. Father always said a man shouldn't eat until he's fed his animals.

"Get yourself some chow and take a nap, ole boy." I give the horse a gentle pat on the head. "That's what I plan to do."

The house is warm and the scent of stew and baked bread waft in the air. My stomach does another rumble before I enter the kitchen. A clean-cut stranger with slick black hair sits with Frank, Mary, and Caleb at the table.

"You didn't tell me we were having company."

Mary moves to the stove to spoon a bowl of stew for me. "Justus, this is Reverend Flynn."

The man, who must be around my age, stands and holds out a calloused hand to me. "Please, call me Silas." He's not built like any preacher I've ever seen.

"Silas, it's nice to meet you, but I had better wash these hands before I go shaking yours." I hold up my dirty work-worn fingers before I go to the basin of hot water on the counter.

"I've been eager to meet you, Justus."

"Someone's been talking about me," I say over my shoulder.

"Frank and Mary tell me they've known you since you were a boy."

"Oh, so they've been giving you an earful about my shenanigans, have they?" I study the pair with a grin.

Silas chuckles. "Miss Bea as well."

"They're partial to me, Reverend. You can't believe a word they say." I sit down at the table with a steaming cup of hot coffee and butter a slice of bread.

"Please, it's Silas," the man reminds me.

I feel a cool breeze blow in from the window near my seat. I make a mental note to check the calking around it later.

Mary speaks up. "I was telling the good reverend that you stopped going to church because of your lady troubles."

With wide eyes, I swallow my food. "Now, why would you go and do a thing like that, Mary? That has nothing to do with it."

"Yes, it does. Now, don't tell lies, especially in front of a minister."

"Why don't you worry more about why Caleb still lives at home and less about me?"

Caleb protests, "Now don't bring me into it."

Frank speaks up. "You'll have to excuse these two, Reverend. They banter like a couple of old hens." He grins and takes a sip of his coffee.

Silas laughs. "It's quite all right. I enjoy good humor."

"Sorry, Caleb," I say. Eager to change the subject, I inquire, "So, you're taking Reverend Moore's place, then?" I hate the way that man shouts hellfire and brimstone sermons from the pulpit.

"Yes, this will be my first Sunday. I hope I can live up to the congregation's expectations. I know Reverend Moore has been here a long time, and people have great respect for him."

Mary places her napkin on the table. "I, for one, think you will be a breath of fresh air we all need." She scoots her chair from the table. "Pie, Reverend?"

"I'd love pie," he says with a chuckle.

Before Mary can get up from her chair, Stanley, a ranch hand, barrels through the kitchen door from the garden. "Justus, the old bull's gotten out and attacked Cook."

"Oh, dear!" Mary braces herself on the table.

Frank, Caleb, and I run for our coats and hats.

The young reverend goes to Mary's side. "Let's pray."

That's the last thing I hear before rushing out into the cold autumn air swirling with white flakes.

# 27

## Justus

"Caleb, hitch a team to a wagon," Frank shouts to his son.

Frank and I rush to follow Stanley to the scene near the barn. Men stand around, gripped by fear, ready to dodge the old bull at any second. Cook lay on the ground, writhing in pain, while the beast has a stance that dares any man to move.

Not wanting to frighten the animal, I whisper as I tiptoe closer, "Stanley, go get a bullwhip."

"Yes, sir."

My heart races. *Stay where you are, big guy.* The safety of my men is foremost in my mind.

Cook stops moving. I hold my breath. The only sound I hear is the beat of my own heart in my ears. Despite the cold and snow, sweat forms under my arms and over my back. If only I could remove my coat, but I don't want to frighten the animal.

The bull stomps his front hoof and lowers his horns. He isn't done with Cook yet. I take a step back and trip on a rock. The animal turns his attention to me and my stomach drops. This is it. I'm done. But before the beast can move, Stanley darts from the barn. "Yaw! Yaw!"

The bull raises his head and whirls toward the sound.

Stanley throws a rope to the ranch hand closest to the bull, then brings the whip down with a crack on the animal's nose. The beast stumbles back and gives a loud groan and snort. The man with the rope hooks the mighty horns, and Frank and I swoop Cook up and take him to the wagon that waits for us.

"Go, Caleb, go," Frank shouts as he and I tend to the bleeding man in the back. My mind flashes to the war and Clint, bloody and mangled. Much like then, we do our best to stop the bleeding by pressing rags here and tying rags there. Still, the life-sustaining liquid spills onto the wagon floor.

Moments later, Caleb brings the speeding horses to a halt in front of Doc and Miss Bea's.

Frank and I, covered in blood, heft Cook from the wagon and into the house. We find Doc in his examination room, tending to the knee of a small child. Doc hoists the boy from the bed and into the arms of his mother, giving way for his more serious patient. The mother shrieks as she covers the boy's eyes and rushes from the room.

"He was attacked by a bull. I don't know how bad he is." I run my fingers through my hair, not giving thought to the crimson liquid that covers them. I must have lost my hat when I tripped.

Doc nods to his nurse as she enters the room. "We'll take

care of him, Justus."

Frank and I exit, shutting the door behind us.

"Frank, you and Caleb go on back to the ranch. I'll stay here and wait for word about Cook."

He gives my shoulder a squeeze. "We'll be praying for him."

Miss Bea catches sight of me and throws her hands in the air. "Oh, Justus dear, we've got to get you cleaned up." She motions for me to follow her, and then hollers down the hall, "Rebecca, we need hot water in the basin right away."

Hours later, I stretch my long legs out and rest my head on the wall behind me. Other than washing up when I arrived, I haven't moved from the bench here in the foyer. The sun is setting outside but still no word from the room across the way.

I haven't lost a man since the war. I swallow around the lump in my throat and close my eyes at the thought.

Without warning, the front door flies open and a burst of cold air strikes me.

# 28

## Livvie

*(Hours earlier)*

I gaze out the shop window at the snow that falls in a steady stream. "You're lucky your apartment is upstairs, Lenny." I've enjoyed working for the young woman. She's simple, nothing especially attractive about her, but not homely, either. Her light brown hair compliments her freckles quite well. To make up for her plain appearance, she's rather humorous, which makes the workday go by quickly.

I drag my feet to the coat rack and begin to bundle up the best I can with what I have. The morning had been frigid but the sun was out, and I couldn't have predicted such snow at the end of my workday.

"At least you don't have far to go, and it's still daylight." Lenny turns her "open" sign to "closed."

"I suppose you're right." A shiver runs through my body. I really don't want to step into this frosty air.

We both jump at a sudden knock at the door. Lenny pulls the curtain back and turns to give me a smile that reads *this is your lucky day*. Asa stands outside, waiting to be let in.

"I happened to be nearby and thought I should give my lady a ride home so she won't have to walk in this dreadful weather." He brushes snow from his sleeves, allowing it to fall to the floor of the shop.

"What a gentleman you are," says Lenny sarcastically as she eyes the white stuff at his feet.

I'm not sure if I should hug him, grateful he's still alive, or be disappointed he's here. Where has he been? And how can he show up as if he hasn't been away for so long without any word? Well, it doesn't rightly matter, now, does it? This is my opportunity to bid him farewell.

I give my friend a peck on the cheek as a peace offering for the mess Asa has made. "I'll see you in the morning, Len."

Once in the wagon, Asa pulls me close. "Olivia, my darling, when do you plan to give your man some pleasure? I've been waiting for weeks upon weeks, but it's beginning to feel as if it's been years." He gives my backside a gentle squeeze.

I shake my head. "First of all, where have you been? You've been gone for *weeks* without a single word."

He gives an amused laugh and turns his team down a road that does not lead to the Peterson's. "Darling, you know I'm a busy man."

"You couldn't write a letter or send a telegram? And where

are we going?" I'm eager to get home. It's cold out and I'm tired.

"It's a surprise, darling." He kisses my cheek, knocking my hat askew.

I reach up and straighten it. "Asa, we really need to talk." I don't feel up to a surprise at this moment.

The team moves on straight out of town. He doesn't answer.

"Where are you taking me, Asa McDaniels?"

"I told you. It's a surprise."

"I don't want a surprise. I want to talk. Are we going somewhere we can do that?"

About a mile out of town, we come to a small cabin nestled among a cluster of fir trees. No light shows through the windows, but smoke billows from the chimney. It's as beautiful as something out of a painting, with the snow falling steadily but gently.

"Where are we?"

"Come, my darling." He lifts me from the wagon and carries me to the door.

"What are you doing, Asa? I can walk," I protest. What kind of surprise could this possibly be?

"Let me carry my lady, will you?" His smile is broad and the dimples I once found attractive now do nothing for me.

*I'm not your lady.* "Is this where you live now?" I ask, still not knowing where I am or what is happening. Although I've never been there, I know he stays at the Grand Hotel when he's in town. My stomach quivers as he opens the door and sets my feet gently on the floor. *Please don't be a proposal.*

"Make yourself at home." He lights a lamp that sits in the

center of the lone table.

"Asa, what's going on?" I clutch the collar of my coat.

"I bought it. This cabin, it's mine. Ours."

"Ours?" I say hesitantly.

Warmth from the little room wraps itself around me. The decor is sparse, much as the cabin I shared with Roy. I welcome the heat from the fireplace but know I can't stay.

"That's right, ours." He places his hat on the table and lays his coat over a chair. His movements are slow and deliberate. He gives me a sly smile as he makes his way toward me. Tenderly he kisses my forehead, then my cheek.

"But we're not married," I remind him.

I should protest more to being here. No good can come of this. I am a woman who longs for a man's touch, but not this way. Not with him. I must be honest with myself. I must be honest with him.

Goosebumps ripple down my arms. He cradles my chin in his hand and places soft kisses on my lips. "Asa, no. We can't. I can't." I move my face from his and turn. "Please, take me home where we can talk."

He reaches up over my head and rests his hand on the door. "It's cold out there."

"It's all right. Please, take me home." Big flakes of snow fall outside the window. A mixture of wood smoke from the fire and the fresh scent of his cologne lingers in the air. I must stand my ground. "I'm ready to go to the Peterson's, Asa," I say firmly.

"I'm not ready for you to go."

My feet are unmoving. I can't walk back to town in this weather.

He pours himself a glass of whiskey and drinks it in one gulp. He pours another and hands it to me.

"No, thank you. I should be going." I point behind me toward the door.

He throws the glass across the room. The crash causes me to jump. He begins to unbutton my coat.

"What are you doing? Stop it." I pull back.

"I'm doing what I've wanted to do since the day I first saw you walking all alone in the hot August sun."

"Asa, please. Let's talk about this." How am I going to stop him from forcing himself on me? As if she's here with us, I hear Mother's awful words. "You little whore."

"I'm done talking, darling." He tears my coat from my body and takes a step back. His eyes rove over my chest as he slips from his suspenders and unbuttons his pants. "You'll do the same if you know what's good for you."

My mind spins. Should I give him what he wants? I did that once before and it left me barren. I should run, but I'm not sure I can make it in this weather. My coat now lays at my feet.

Asa loosens the buttons on his shirt and pulls it from his trousers. "You're testing my patience, darling." He removes the shirt and tosses it aside. "Come on, don't be shy."

I clear my throat, afraid to speak, not wanting Asa to detect my fear. "I need to freshen up first."

He steps forward and takes my hand, then guides me to the cot near the fireplace. "I think you'll do just fine." He moves so that his bare chest touches me and sniffs my hair as if admiring the scent of a rose. "I told you to stay away from Justus Bennett, did I not?"

Fearful, I begin to make an excuse. "I…"

He cuts me off. "I know all about your little fishing trip," he hisses. He must see the surprise in my eyes. "That's right," he says. "I went to see you, and your Miss Bea so graciously told me you were gone fishing with him." He laughs. "I told her not to tell you I stopped by because I wanted to surprise you."

"Please, Asa, I'm not the least bit interested in him. I only want you," I lie, believing now that telling him I want nothing to do with him will send him into a rage. I just need to find a way to escape.

"Then prove it."

Warmth radiates from the fire. The burning logs crackle. Asa unbuttons my dress, causing the hair on my neck to prickle. My hands form into fists as I let out a long breath through pursed lips. With a pivot that sends him stumbling back, I slump onto the bed. "I'm afraid it's a bit warm. I feel faint."

"All the more reason to get that dress off you, darling."

"I'm not feeling so well." I hang my head.

He steps forward and grabs my arm. Face to face with me, one eyebrow rises. "I'm not playing these games, Olivia. Get. Up." His voice is stern. Any charm he once had is gone.

I glance down, then away. The fire poker's propped up on the hearth of the fireplace. With the back of my free hand, I brush the sweat from my forehead while staring him in the eyes. "You'll have to finish removing my dress, then." My tone is seductive.

He snickers. "That's my girl." Straightening to his full height, he releases my arm.

I stand, and without another thought, push him with all my strength. Then, leaping forward, I grab the poker.

He regains his footing and cackles. "So, you don't want to play nice."

I hold the poker with both hands out toward him. "Stay away from me, Asa."

He grins and holds his arms up in surrender.

I back myself toward the door. When I bend to grab my coat, he snatches the poker away, yanking me to the ground.

He taps the piece of iron on the floor near my face. "I think I quite enjoy this little game of cat and mouse." He reaches down and grabs the back of my head, pulling my hair from the chignon. Putting his mouth to my ear, he purrs.

My neck aches at the angle he holds it. "Asa, please."

He moans. "I love a woman who begs." Still holding onto my hair, he lifts me from the floor and drags me back to the bed, flinging the poker to the other side of the room. Then he tears my dress open, sending the loosened beaded buttons tinkling along the boards beneath us.

I close my eyes tight as he brushes my dress off one shoulder. Will he believe me if I again act as if I'll give in? Or perhaps I can reason with him? No. He's shown me he's not a reasonable man.

Pushing past my disgust, I fling my arms around him and kiss his lips. I kiss him hard and passionately. It's warm, wet, and makes my stomach turn.

He pulls his head back and gives a hearty laugh. "I knew you were a wild little filly under that ladylike ruse."

I grab the back of his head and pull him in again for another breathless kiss. Then, I bite his lip, hard. A copper taste fills my mouth.

He tumbles back with a yelp. With wide eyes, he slaps his hand to his mouth. "You bit me, you little bitch." He lunges for me, but I run for the door. He catches the skirt of my dress and I fall, smacking my face on the floor. Pain shoots through my cheek and brow bone, making me wince.

He grabs my hair and jerks me back to my feet. I'm close enough to the table to reach out and take hold of the heavy water pitcher. I swing it around and hit him upside the head. He pauses, then falls to the floor.

Not waiting to see if he's dead, passed out, or in shock, I run out the door into the snow, leaving my coat behind. I can make out the lights of town in the distance. I run as fast as my legs will move; I must get there as quickly as possible.

I don't look back. I can't. If I'm going to die, at least I'll die running for my life. The cold air stings my lungs with every inhale. Again, I hear Mother calling, "You make me sick."

Finally, I reach home.

"Olivia?" I hear Justus say, jumping to his feet from his seat on the foyer bench.

"Justu—" It's the last thing I remember.

# 29
## Asa

*(Later that evening)*

I saunter into the saloon and up to the bar. My hat is low and the collar of my coat high. Cheers erupt from the corner of the room where a group of men play a game of cards. The music is loud as the piano player pounds out a jovial tune. I narrow my eyes on him, but he pays me no mind.

The bartender slides a shot glass in front of me and fills it with a dark bourbon. "You look terrible, Asa."

I sneer. "Your face isn't all that pretty, either, Smitty." I drink the liquor in one gulp, wincing at the pain of the whiskey as it stings my broken lip. I slam the glass back on the bar and grind my teeth. *That little bitch.*

Smitty refills the glass, then sets the bottle on the counter in front of me and walks away.

A hand slides over my back and shoulders. My muscles tense at the touch. Can't a man have a drink without conversation?

"How's my favorite customer?" the raspy female voice asks as she runs a finger down my arm.

"I've seen better days." I tip the glass back, swallowing the drink whole.

The woman is gaudy. Her hair falls in ebony ringlets down her shoulders. The thick rouge she wears accentuates the lines on her face, aging her beyond her years. Her dress leaves little to the imagination. I've traveled that well-worn road enough to know every line and curve. My mind requires no curiosity.

She takes a seat beside me and pulls at the collar of my coat. "Oh, honey, what happened to you?"

I fill my glass with the bottle the bartender left. "I got on the wrong side of a little heifer, that's all. It'll heal."

She strokes my face with the back of her hand.

The scent of rosewater and tobacco emanate from her skin. "Why don't you let Darla make it all better?"

I guess this is as good as it gets. I swallow down another drink. I throw money on the bar, grab the bottle, and follow the whore up the stairs.

# 30

## Livvie

*(The next morning)*

My head pounds in my ears. What an awful nightmare. I peek my eyes open but only one unfolds. Light seeps into the room through the lace curtains. Swaths of red and orange hues blanket the sky outside the window as the sun wakes for the day.

I grimace at the pain when I touch my swollen face. It wasn't a dream. It's real. I bring my hand back down onto something—warm? I peer down. *Justus.* He's sleeping in a chair with his arms crossed on the bed, and his head rests on them.

Despite my aching head and body, I manage to maneuver myself onto one elbow. I pull the blanket over my shoulder, not wanting him to see me in my nightgown.

He stirs, and then his head shoots up. "Olivia, are you okay?

Can I get you something? Hot tea? Coffee?"

"Justus, what are you doing here?" His hair is messy and his eyes are red. And is that dried blood on his shirt?

His fingers comb through his hair. "Doc thought you might have a concussion. I-I offered to watch over you."

My stomach flutters at his words. He stayed beside me all night. I can't imagine he cares that much. *Push the thought from your mind, Livvie.* I won't put myself in that situation again. Look where it's gotten me.

I lay back on my pillow. "Was I run over by a team of horses?"

He moves from the chair and sits on the edge of the bed. "Who did this to you? Was it Asa? My aunt said he was here looking for you the other day when we were gone fishing."

I can't bring myself to answer. It shouldn't matter to him who did this to me. It shouldn't matter to him how this happened. The back of my throat burns where a lump threatens to form. A tear trickles down from my good eye and into my hair. Love is too much to ask for. Mother's words of my misfortune play in my mind once more. Every man close to me has hurt me—Vernon, Roy, Wes, and now Asa. Life has proven it's not in the cards for me to be loved and cared for by a man. I'm so ashamed, I don't even know how I can love myself.

With a soft touch, he wipes the moisture away. "He'll never hurt you again."

My skin tingles at his touch. I don't understand how he can make such a claim. I exhale. "This is my lot in life."

"Don't say that. It's not true."

I close my eye and rest the back of my hand over my forehead.

"You don't know me or anything about me. You can't say that."

"I know enough to realize you don't deserve this." He takes my hand in both of his. "I want to know everything about you, Olivia."

Rebecca's voice flows from the doorway. "I brought you breakfast, Olivia." She places the tray on the small table beside the bed. "Do you want me to bring your food to you, Justus?"

I speak before he can answer. "He'll eat downstairs."

He rises from my bedside without a word. His boots sound on the wooden floor as he moves through the room and down the stairs. I roll over and sob uncontrollable tears into my pillow. I've pushed him away for good.

# 31

## Justus

*(The evening before)*

Miss Bea and Rebecca tend to Olivia, who is in and out of consciousness, until Doc comes up from caring for Cook. Doc says only time will tell if Cook makes it. The old bull gored him in several places, and he has multiple broken ribs and a busted collarbone. The amount of blood he lost is the real concern.

After examining Olivia, Doc determines it doesn't appear as though she has any broken bones. He administers a tonic that will numb the pain and help her sleep. "She needs rest. But we'll have to watch over her through the night."

I'm quick to speak up. "I'll do it." Three heads all turn to me. I slide my hands in my pockets and shrug my shoulders. "If that's all right," I say hesitantly.

Miss Bea and Rebecca glance at one another and grin.

Doc nods. "That will be fine. Let the women get her into a nightgown and you can come back up. We'll send Thomas for the sheriff to get to the bottom of this."

When I return to Olivia's room, I sit and study every inch of her face. Every curve of her lips. Every lash of her eye. The lamp casts an amber glow about her. Despite the bruising and swelling, she still resembles an angelic being. My jaw clenches. *What happened to you, Olivia?*

How I long to reach out and smooth her hair. Instead, I lean back in the chair and watch as the blanket rises and falls with every breath she takes. At least I'm close to her. I'll be here when she wakes.

---

The next morning, I sit at my aunt's table and run my hand over my sleep-deprived eyes as I watch the steam rise and curl from the black liquid in my cup. *It's obvious my presence isn't welcome.* Olivia made that perfectly clear when she told Rebecca I'd be eating my breakfast downstairs.

I don't know what it is about her that makes my insides twist and turn in ways I've never known. How could Asa McDaniels do that to her? *If she were mine...* But she isn't mine.

There's a knock at the front door and seconds later, Miss Bea and the sheriff enter the kitchen.

"Have a seat, Sheriff, and I'll get you a cup of coffee," buzzes Miss Bea.

The older man sits across from me and leans back in the chair. "Justus."

"Sheriff. I hope you came to tell us you have Asa McDaniels locked up."

"I'm afraid Asa McDaniels is gone."

I straighten. "What do you mean 'gone'?"

"My deputy and I found out he was renting a cabin about a mile out of town. We went out there to talk to him. It's cleaned out. He's gone. That speaks of his guilt in my book."

I shove my fingers through my hair. A boiling heat rages through my body. "He did it, all right."

Miss Bea sets the cup of coffee in front of the sheriff. "Earlier this morning, Rebecca was able to talk with her about what happened. Apparently, Asa told Olivia he purchased the cabin." She shook her head sorrowfully. "He told her it was…for them."

The man nods and lifts his cup. "Well, that's a lie."

Miss Bea wrings her hands. "I'm afraid this is my fault. Asa came by on Saturday when Olivia was out fishing with Justus and Thomas. Asa said he wanted to surprise her and asked that I not tell her he was back in town. Oh, Sheriff, how can we be sure this man won't come back for her?"

"He's a coward. He's not coming back. But we've put out wanted posters on him." The sheriff takes a drink from his cup.

I just can't see how they'll be able to arrest Asa for what he did to Olivia. It's his word against hers, and women don't amount to much in the eyes of the law. "What judge is going to convict him for attempted rape? How can you even arrest him?"

The sheriff's eyes grow wide. He doesn't know the extent of

the circumstances. Leaning forward, he pokes his finger on the table as he speaks. "First of all, I'm the law in this town. Second, your family are prominent folks here. We wouldn't have a Laurel Springs if it wasn't for your kin. Last, the judge owes me a favor. Believe me, we've got our ways." He takes another sip of his coffee.

Miss Bea strokes my arm. "We appreciate that, Sheriff."

"How is she doing?" he asks, relaxing back into the chair.

I stare at my cup. "How do you think she's doing?" If only I could take this from her. The pain. The memory.

The sheriff shifts his mug. "I'll have to question her. The sooner, the better."

Miss Bea pats the table. "She gave some details to Rebecca, but I'll take you up to her room. She's expecting your visit."

The man follows Miss Bea out of the kitchen, once again leaving me to my tormented thoughts. Thoughts of infatuation for this woman and wanting to punish the man who hurt her.

# 32

## Livvie

*(Twelve days later)*

Not wanting stares or sympathy, I choose to stay home from church again today. Once the family leaves, I slip on my robe and pad down to the kitchen in bare feet. The smell of bacon and pancakes linger in the air and warmth radiates from the cookstove. I clutch my robe when I see Rebecca. "I thought you had gone to church."

Rebecca sits at the table with her bible lying open in front of her. "I offered to stay back in case you needed anything."

I pour myself a cup of coffee. The scent of the hot brew brings a sense of comfort. "Oh, you didn't have to do that." The cold floor under my feet makes me wish I'd put stockings on before coming downstairs. "I don't mind your company, though. May I sit with you?"

"Of course, you may." Rebecca closes the book in front of her. I nod toward the bible that rests on the table. "Have you always believed in God?" God is somewhat of a mystery to me, and I'm not sure I believe the way the Petersons do.

Rebecca smiles. "Oh, child, my mama had me reciting scripture since the day I could speak."

"Has He ever helped you? God?"

Rebecca sits back in her chair. "He was my mama and papa when I didn't have one. He's been my healer when I was ill, and my protector when I was in danger. My provider when I had nothing, my comforter when I was in despair, and my guide when I was seeking direction. Yes, He's helped me."

I gaze into my cup. "I don't know Him. My mother wasn't religious. And I hadn't heard much about Him until I met Marybeth Peterson. From the sounds of Reverend Moore's preaching, He doesn't seem like a loving father to me. I think He's waiting to send us all to hell."

Rebecca moves to the stove to refill her mug. "Sadly, some folks think the way to save souls is through fear, Olivia."

"How long have you been with the Petersons, Rebecca?" I ask, preferring to change the subject. I've never felt it was my business to ask such a question. Usually, Rebecca and I discuss what's happening around town, never anything personal. But we've grown closer over the last couple of weeks, and I'm curious to learn more about her life.

"Since the end of the war." Rebecca takes her seat at the table. "They saved my life. Thomas's, too." She stares off into a distant place or time. Her face is youthful but her eyes tell of an old soul.

"Really? May I ask how?"

Rebecca gives me a reassuring smile. "I'll just start from the beginning," she says. "The master sold my father and one of my brothers before I came into this world. I never knew them. I had my mama, my brother Moses, and my sister Rachel for a time. The master would come to our cabin at night after we were all to bed. I knew what he was doing to my mama. There was only a blanket used as a curtain that separated her bed from ours. I heard the sounds and saw the movements in the shadows. I could hear her sobs after he'd leave. She died during childbirth, and they took the baby away. We didn't even know if it was a boy or a girl."

"Oh, Rebecca." My heart is pained at her memory.

She sways her head. "I've only told Miss Bea my whole story. There's no use dredging up the past, but I guess I feel a calling to tell you, too." Her brown eyes twinkle at me. "We all have a story, Olivia," she says, as though reassuring me I'm not alone in suffering. My stomach tightens as shame fills me, but I push it down the way I always do. But my heart warms at the thought of Rebecca feeling comfortable sharing hers with me.

She takes a deep breath, bringing me back to her words. "Moses, Rachel, and I were sold after that. That's when I met Samuel." A smile lights her face. "We were friends as children. He was my protector, always. One time, he laid himself across me to take the whipping that was coming to me. Once grown, we married. It wasn't a legal marriage, of course, but I knew it was a marriage in God's eyes, and that's all that mattered to me." She peers down at her hands clasped on the table.

"Our first baby, Samuel's namesake, caught a fever at three months and died." She wipes away a tear that runs down her cheek. "Then came our girls, less than two years apart." Rebecca smiles wide again. "Ellen and Lydia." She beams. "They were so full of life, running, jumping, playing. I can still hear their laughter." Her eyes glisten. She gazes down at her hands again, swallowing back tears. "When the girls were five and six years old, the master died, and the family had to sell us. I remember the day they took us to the auction block in town. I hadn't been there since I was a child. The sun was out, bright and warm. Any other day, it would have been considered a beautiful morning. But on this day, the sunshine taunted me. It suffocated me. People stood around gawking, as if they were watching a show for their entertainment, peering at naked men shackled and in cages, as if they were animals." Her lips tighten.

"Samuel, my husband, was the first of us to be sold. Then the girls were next. Ellen clung to me, screaming, begging." Silent tears stream down Rebecca's face.

"I had no choice but to push her away. Tears soaked Lydia's cheeks, but she remained stoic, not even so much as a glance at me. But Ellen, she held out her arms and wailed. I feared she'd get a lashing and the inside of me begged her to stop. Oh, Olivia. That child vomited all over herself. And all I could do was stand there and watch. It was as if someone tore my heart from my body. My stomach tied in knots. I wanted to sweep her up and run. Run as fast and as far as I could. But all I could do was stand there, staring. I died inside that day."

I weep silently, listening to Rebecca's heartbreaking tale.

She continues, "I just give thanks to God that the girls were bought together. That's the only thing that kept me sane. Weeks later, I knew I was pregnant with Thomas and it gave me a purpose to live. At least I had a part of Samuel still with me."

"The war was going on and there was talk of slaves being freed soon. But I couldn't bring my child into that world. I heard there was no slavery in the West and I made up my mind I had to go. I cooked for the new master. And since my belly was growing, I'd sneak rice, peanuts, beans, and anything else I could that wouldn't go bad up under my dress to hide later for my escape. The master had dogs to guard the property, but I befriended them. I'd feed and pet them when no one was looking." Rebecca has a sly smile on her face and her chest puffs proudly.

"One night, everyone had gone to bed. There was a bad thunderstorm. That's when I knew I had to run. I snuck out with only a blanket and headed for the woods to dig up my sack of food. Where those dogs were, I don't know because I didn't see hide nor hair of them. I dug up my sack and ran west in that pouring rain."

"I camped out in the woods and made my way the best I knew how. Days later, I met up with a group of runaways. They were gathered around a fire, singing 'Amazing Grace.'"

She props an elbow on the table with her chin in her hand. "What a sight and sound to behold. Doc had been sneaking into the camp to care for the sick. When Miss Bea learned about me being with child, she insisted I come to Colorado with them."

Her teeth shine like pearls. "Not long after we arrived, the war ended. And my Thomas was born into freedom."

I had no idea this was Rebecca's life story. I'm in awe of the woman who sits before me. "And what about your husband and daughters? Do you know where they are?"

"No. I reckon I won't see them again until we meet in heaven, Olivia."

"Rebecca, how can you believe God loves after all you lived through? How can a loving father allow his children to face such trials?" Anger fills me and I need to understand. If there was a God, why has he allowed any of us to endure such pain?

"We're going to have trials and tribulations in this life. We live in a fallen world."

A fallen world. I've heard that before, from Marybeth Peterson. What does it mean?

A barrage of voices comes from the front door. One voice in particular has me seized with panic and horrified that I'm still in my robe and bare feet.

# 33

## Justus

*(Earlier that morning)*

The church pew's hard under my behind. I'm not sure what to expect from this new preacher, and I can't believe Mary talked me into coming. It's the last place I want to be. At least the room's warm on this cold October morning. I'm not surprised Olivia didn't show, with her face battered and all. Since I came in after the singing had started, I was able to avoid Bridget Murphy. If I can only be so lucky after the sermon. I made up my mind I'd come listen to the reverend today, to give him a chance, even if I don't believe in the bible. And I won't let that girl keep me from hearing the message.

No shouting comes from the pulpit as Silas Flynn speaks. "Good morning, church family." His voice rises so that all can hear him, but his tone is steady. A smile plays on his face with each word he enunciates. Mary was right—he's nothing like Reverend Moore.

"I want to talk to you about belief." Silas folds his hands and rests them on his bible.

"I assume you all at least believe Christ is real or you wouldn't be here."

"Amen." Heads nod around the room.

"Let me ask you. Do you *believe* that with God, all things are possible?" He scans the room. His demeanor is calm while he studies faces as they call back "Amen" and bob their heads.

"Do you *believe* He healed the sick and raised the dead? Do you *believe* He parted the red sea, brought His only son into this world through a virgin, and gave a donkey the ability to speak?"

Everyone appears to be believers.

Silas lifts the bible for all to see. "Then let me ask you this. Why do you limit Him? Why do you limit His abilities to the confines of this book or to the time in which it takes place?"

"You *believe* that He *did* perform miracle after miracle that's recounted in these pages. But do you *believe* that He *can* and *does*, to this day, perform miracle after miracle?"

"Do you have *faith* that He *can* and *will* perform these miracles in *your* life?"

Silas turns and walks around to the front of the pulpit. "One day, two blind men approach Jesus and beg for healing. Jesus asks them if they believe He can heal them, to which they respond, 'Yes.' They believe. Then Jesus touches their eyes and says, 'According to *your faith*, be it unto you.' And they were healed."

Again, Silas studies the silent group. As though he's about to reveal a secret, he leans forward. "According to your faith." He speaks the words at a deliberate speed.

Then, his voice rises. "What does that mean to you?"

"It means if you want to see miracles in your own life, you better step out in faith."

"Yes, step out in faith. Because faith without works is what, church family?"

"Dead," shout a few voices in unison.

"Exactly."

"Are you single? Step out in faith by making room in your life for your future spouse. Step out in faith by facing your fear and tell that lovely woman you wish to court her. Are you without a child? Step out in faith by making room in your home for that boy or girl. Quilt them a blanket."

Whispers sound around the room.

"You do believe Sarah gave birth in her old age, don't you? You do believe Mary was a virgin when she gave birth to Jesus, don't you? Then why is it so hard to believe that God would answer your prayers today?"

"Are you ill? Step out in faith and speak health over your body."

"I can't tell you how or when God will choose to answer, but I can tell you this. He will answer according to *your faith*. Let us pray."

I've never heard such words spoken before. I'm a believer. Not in the god of these people. Not in the god of my mother. But I do believe in a great spirit, and I believe it wishes for me to have a wife. But Silas is right, I haven't shown that I'm ready. The ranch has 100 percent of my time and attention. There's been no room for companionship. And as much as I wish for companionship, I'm afraid. I'm afraid because I know I'm a broken man. Looks like I have some changes to make.

Silas stands near the door at the back of the church, thanking parishioners for coming.

"I just don't know what to think about what you said today, Reverend. If my Sally makes a quilt for a baby she's not even pregnant for, isn't that odd?" Missus Whitley presses the reverend.

"Perchance He doesn't wish for her to conceive a child of her own, ma'am. Perhaps there is an orphan in need of a mother. Then he or she will have a nice blanket made just for them." He reaches for her hand.

"But Reverend, isn't that playing God? What if it's not part of His plan for Sally to have a child?"

Silas places his opposite hand on her back and guides her out the door. "I would love to discuss this with you more. Over a cup of tea?"

I chuckle to myself, watching the exchange before he ushers the old lady on her way.

"It appears Missus Whitley is going to give you a run for your money, Reverend." I extend my hand.

Silas shakes his head and gives me a big grin. "It appears so, my friend."

"Say, if you're not too busy this week having tea with the ladies and all, I'd love for you to come out to the ranch. I'll show you around and you can stay for supper. Mary's a fine cook."

"Yes, she is. I'd enjoy that. How about Tuesday?"

"Tuesday works just fine for me. See you then." I tip my head and exit into the chilly autumn sunshine.

"Oh, Justus, dear." Miss Bea hustles to me as fast as her short legs will allow. "Justus, why don't you come to have dinner with us today?" Her fancy feathered hat shades her eyes.

I'm not sure that's such a grand idea. Olivia made it clear she doesn't want to see me. But what about what Silas had spoken moments ago regarding stepping out in faith? Sometimes that means stepping into fear.

"Justus?" Miss Bea waits for my answer.

"I reckon I can do that. I want to check on Cook, anyhow."

"Oh, wonderful." She claps her hands.

Upon entering the house, the conversation centers on the reverend's sermon.

"Oh, I think he did a splendid job of delivering the message today. I don't know why Martha Whitley was pestering him. He was just speaking the truth." Miss Bea waves her hand, as if to dismiss the old woman's foolish notions.

"I'll have to agree with you, dear, he did well," states Doc while helping her out of her coat.

"I invited him out to the ranch on Tuesday so I can show him around," I offer as we stride down the hall.

Miss Bea clutches her hands to her chest. "Oh, Justus, that's wonderful. I think you two will make great friends. You should invite Clint." No doubt my aunt is hoping the good reverend will convert me. I chuckle to myself.

"I was thinking—" The sight of Olivia cuts my sentence short. She stands in the doorway of the kitchen, holding her robe tight around her. One eye is still battered with yellow and purple hues and one deep blue eye is as big as a scared doe. Her reddish-blonde hair flows down around her shoulders. I've only ever seen it pinned back. She looks more like an angel than ever before.

Her pale cheeks turn a bright shade of pink. "I'm so sorry. I came down this morning, thinking I was alone, and Rebecca was here, and we got to talking, and—" I look away, not wanting to embarrass her. Her toes curl.

Miss Bea shoos her down the hall toward the stairs. "Oh, dear, it's quite all right. Just get along with you now."

# 34

## Livvie

A warmth creeps up my neck and into my face. I glance away and pad down the hall as fast as my feet can take me. I can't believe this has happened. And in front of Justus, no less. I can't face him again. I'll skip dinner. My stomach rumbles. No, that won't do. The first order of business is to get dressed and do something with my hair.

Finding only Rebecca and Miss Bea in the kitchen now is a relief. The room is warm with the heat of the cookstove. And the smell of chicken stew simmering in the pot makes my stomach do another tumble. Rebecca slides biscuits in the oven and Miss Bea cuts apples.

"What can I do to help?" I ask.

Miss Bea waves her knife toward the cabinets. "You can set the table in the dining room, dear. I believe Rebecca and I have everything handled in here."

While laying bowls on the long lace-covered table, I think of the last time I saw Justus and how I'd treated him. In my anger and shame, I was so unkind. The clomping of his boots on the hardwood floor, leaving my room and making their way down the stairs, rings in my ears. I close my eyes at the recollection. Embarrassed at the way I treated him, I wonder how I'm to face him in a few moments when we'll be forced to sit across from one another at this very table.

"Olivia?"

I jump at the familiar voice, deep and alluring.

"I didn't mean to startle you," he says.

"It's quite all right." I set the last bowl on the table with a shaky hand and wipe my palms down the front of my dress. Looking this man in the eye is torture. Through my pride, I force a smile.

There's the haunting sound of his boots as he steps further into the room. He puts his head down, then shoves his hands in the pockets of his britches. He's the only man I know who wears denim pants. "Listen—"

"No, Justus, let me speak. I'm sorry. You were so kind to watch over me and I treated you badly." My chest aches at the sight of his big brown eyes staring back at me like a wounded pup. "Please, forgive me." Then my heart almost melts over the table at the warm smile that draws up one side of his face.

"I'll forgive you."

Relief washes over me. I let out a breath and nod in thanks.

"I will," he repeats, stepping closer to the table. "Under one condition."

A condition? "Certainly. What condition would that be?" I ask.

"You go on a walk with me after dinner."

I swallow. "Are you sure you want to be seen with me? What will people say?"

He draws a hand from his pocket and covers his chest. "It would be my honor, Olivia. Some busybodies may talk, but I don't care." He tilts his head. "Do you?"

*It would be his honor.* Instinctively, I lower my head and reach for my battered eye. How can he not care what people will think or say?

"Olivia." He leans in from across the table. "Will you oblige me?"

His eyes hold a sincerity I can't understand or resist.

"Yes. I'd be happy to."

---

Justus pushes his plate away and reclines in the chair. "Thank you for the meal, ladies, it was real good." He shoots a wink in my direction that sends a flurry of tingles through my belly. He looks at his aunt. "Olivia and I are going on a walk."

I lean into the table. "I must help clean up first, Justus."

Miss Bea wags her head. "Oh no, you just go right ahead. Go on, now." She shoos us away.

"I guess that settles it, then." He pushes his chair from the table. My eyes meet his smile. "I suppose so."

The warmth of the sun envelops Justus and me as we walk down the dirt path. The air is cool, but the temperature this afternoon is warmer than it has been. I'm grateful I brought my shawl rather than my coat. Loosening the wrap from my shoulders, I allow it to hang down my back. "It's such a beautiful day. I can't believe how quickly the snow is melting."

"Ahh, it's because we're so close to the sun." He grins. Sometimes I can't tell if he's teasing or being serious.

It's a quiet Sunday afternoon stroll since most folks don't dare do anything to break the Sabbath. The Petersons are more lenient about these things. Most religious folks around town act all high and mighty, but not the Petersons.

Justus softly nudges my shoulder with his. "Tell me about your life before you came to Laurel Springs."

"Oh, you're not up on town gossip?" I chuckle.

"I don't listen to gossip. And in case you haven't noticed, I keep to myself."

"Yes, it's always a surprise to me when I do see you. You're not around much anymore." I briefly touch his arm. "And I'm sorry about Cook."

"I'm glad he's improving, and his spirits are up. It's a shame that ole bull got ill-tempered and forced us to take him to the slaughterhouse. Once they show aggression in that way, though, we can't have 'em around."

"I suppose not."

"Cook was shown mercy, that's for sure."

That animal would have killed Cook if he'd not been stopped, from the story I heard. "By the bull?"

"By something or someone not of this world."

"You mean God?" I ask.

"You can call it God if you want. I call it Great Spirit."

Surprised to hear this from him, I ask, "You don't believe in God?"

"It's complicated. I believe we all have our own version of who God is and how we choose to worship Him." He puts his hands to his chest. "I'll admit I don't believe the same way my family does."

"No?"

"I believe the sun, the moon, and the stars are forms of God. I only go to church sometimes for my family. Mother Earth is my church. I don't read the bible. Great Spirit speaks to me here." He points to his heart. "And here." He points to his head.

"I love that," I say, and mean it.

He continues. "My ma taught me to believe. The way she'd been taught, of course. There was a time I turned away from God and any form of religion. I did some things I'm not proud of. Sometime after the war ended, when I was at my worst, I made a friend who taught me a new way to believe, and it spoke to me." The ground crunches under our feet. "Before that, I did things that would make my ma turn in her grave. The best way I can explain it is that I awakened. Great Spirit, in its loving way, picked me up by the nape of my neck and brought me home. Kinda how a mother cat does with her kittens."

Crows caw from the trees above. I wonder what kinds of things he'd done that he wasn't proud of. Perhaps he's referring to killing men as a soldier.

"I want to think my ma would be right proud of me now, though, even if I believe different than she did."

"Do you know what folks mean when they say we live in a

fallen world?" I ask.

"According to the bible, the world was perfect in the beginning. It was without sin. Then Adam and Eve, the first people, disobeyed God and that caused sin to enter the world. They believe that's why we have pain, death, sickness, drunkenness, lying." He shrugs. "You probably get the point."

"Do you believe that's why we have bad things happen?"

"I believe we have lessons to learn." He squints against the sun. "I'm still learning a whole lot of them."

It occurs to me that I've misjudged this man. I thought he was a scoundrel like many of the men I've known throughout my life, but as it turns out he's a real gentleman.

"How about your ma?" he asks.

"I don't know." I stare at the ground as we walk. "I haven't seen her since I was sixteen." There's no need going down that road with him. I hope he doesn't pry.

We come upon a giant boulder, and he motions for me to sit. "You would never know my father and Miss Bea were raised in the same home."

"Oh? What was he like?"

Justus stares off into the distance. "What mattered most to him, besides my ma, was the ranch. He only attended church to appease my ma and to rub elbows with wealthy churchgoers. Most of all for the wealthy churchgoers. He had to make a good impression as an upstanding, influential rancher. He started out as a simple farmer back east with a dream. One day he loaded me and my ma and our belongings into a wagon and we headed west." He picks up a stick and draws in the dirt. "He's part of the reason I ran off as a kid and joined the war. In time, he changed for the better. I'm glad I got to see it before he died." He regards me with those brown eyes that make me smile. He smiles back.

"You ran away to join the war?"

"No. I ran away because I was a scared child. I took my foolish self to Clint's and talked him into going with me. We didn't know where we were going. We were just out on an adventure like Lewis and Clark or Daniel Boone, exploring the West."

"We met a Union army recruiter who told us he wouldn't tell, if we didn't, that we weren't eighteen. He said President Lincoln needed strong men such as us. That was just the adventure we were looking for. Or so we thought."

With his elbows on his knees, he rubs the stick between his hands. "I saw things, Olivia, that I don't ever want to see again in this life. I blame myself for Clint's loss."

"But it's not your fault. These things happen in war." I place my hand on his bicep. Even through his coat, I can feel that it's solid.

"If I hadn't talked him into running away with me, he'd still be whole."

"He is whole, Justus. See, he has Hannah and the little ones, and another on the way. He has the stables. He's so blessed."

Justus straightens himself and pats my hand. "How is it that a lady such as yourself is unmarried at your age?"

A part of me wants to keep my past hidden away. Roy, Wes, Mother, Missouri, it's all behind me now and I'd prefer to keep it that way. "What do you mean to say 'at my age,' Justus Bennett?"

He throws his head back with a hoot. "It's just that you're beautiful and sweet as pie. You can't bake, but I understand you can sew."

I lean into him. "I'll have you know I *can* bake. I just made an embarrassing mistake one time. Thank you for reminding me."

"One time I'll never let you forget." He stands and holds his hand out to me. "We better head back. Don't want to cause a scandal by being gone too long out of sight." He offers his arm as we stroll back to the house.

I work up the courage to ask a question. "I know it's none of my business, but what happened between you and Bridget Murphy?"

He lays his hand over mine. "Ahh…your nosiness is quite all right."

I can't stop a chuckle from escaping.

"There was nothing between me and Miss Murphy. She wanted to believe there was, but I can assure you, there wasn't." He stops and looks me in the eye. "I never even so much as placed a peck on the back of her hand." He says this to reassure me, I can tell. "And she now knows there will never be anything between us," he says, continuing to lead the way back to the house.

I smile to myself as a weight lifts from my chest. Perhaps this is the beginning of a special friendship between the handsome cowboy and me. Only time will tell, but for now, I'll enjoy walking arm in arm with him.

"Did you two have a nice walk?" asks Miss Bea.

I smile at Justus. "It was lovely. There's more to this cowboy than just his boots and hat."

Miss Bea waves her hands. "I'm happy you two are getting along so splendidly because I need your help."

Justus shifts. "Help with what?"

"You know us ladies at the church do an annual pumpkin parade, and I need your help to prepare a float. Justus, you have the wagon, hay, and tools. Olivia, you have the sewing abilities and creativity. I think you two could work beautifully together to make the most magnificent creation." As usual, her arms move about in excitement as she speaks.

Justus and I glance at one another. Does Miss Bea need our help, or is she trying to play matchmaker? No matter, I'm sure Justus knows as well as I that we can't say no to his aunt.

Miss Bea stares at us, waiting for an answer.

I break the silence. "All right. What would you have us do?"

"Make me a float, of course. Use your imagination. But it must be done in two weeks. Make me proud." She reaches out, pats both our arms, and trots away.

Justus leans into me. "Sounds as though we got our work cut out for us."

I raise an eyebrow and nod. My heart skips a beat looking into his handsome face. It appears I'll be spending more time with this cowboy.

# 35

## Justus

*(Tuesday)*

"Silas, I'm glad you were able to tear yourself away from tea with the ladies to spend time with the men," I joke as I shake the reverend's hand.

Silas laughs, getting down from his horse. "The life of a preacher." He hitches the animal to the post.

"That's why I'm not a preacher. Among other reasons."

"It's a calling, all right." Silas scans our surroundings. "I can see you were called to be a rancher."

"I didn't always think so. I thought I was called to get as far away from here as possible," I tell him as we walk to the corral where a few horses are fenced. "After my ma died, I thought there was nothing left for me here."

"And your father?"

"We may as well have been worlds apart."

A horse saunters over and Silas pets her nose.

I go on. "I ran away, like a coward. Took Clint with me." The horse whinnies. "Worst thing I ever did, talking Clint into going."

Clint had tried to dissuade me from setting off, but I was hell-bent on leaving Laurel Springs. So, he reluctantly gave in and went with me.

I think back to that day when I convinced Clint into going with me, not knowing the destination, how we'd eat, or where we'd take shelter. But Clint was up for the adventure. When we heard the Army was recruiting, I thought it would be a great deed. Clint wasn't so sure.

"I don't know about this, Justus." Clint is hesitant.

"Come on. We'll go home heroes after fighting those Rebs and putting them in their place. My father won't be able to treat me like a boy any longer."

Clint keeps shoving the toe of his boot into the dirt.

I go on. "You know those Rebs are dirty scoundrels. They don't have no right keeping them colored folk as slaves. We gotta stop 'em."

"Well, I guess you're right about that. They don't have no business doing that. Colored folk are people just like you and me."

"Yes!" I shout.

Clint agrees to go see the recruiter. When we stand before the man and say we're seventeen, he informs us we're too young. "You have to be eighteen." Clint and I look at each other in defeat. "But," the man continues, "I won't tell if you don't." He scratches something on the paper in front of him and welcomes us as Army soldiers.

*Clint and I smile at one another in victory.*

"If it weren't for me, he'd still have his leg," I say to Silas.

"You blame yourself."

"I do. I talked him into leaving. I talked him into joining the war."

"Don't you think he had a choice in the matter?"

I stare out into the corral. Of course, he could have said no, but we were as close as brothers. I'd have done the same had the tables been turned.

I can feel Silas studying me. "Do you think Clint blames you?"

"He says he doesn't."

"Is he one to tell falsehoods?"

This preacher might be right. It could be I'm the only one holding onto this, and just like holding onto a hot coal, it's only burning me. "No, he isn't." I stretch away from the fence and study my boots. "I have nightmares about it."

Silas stares me down, one arm on the fence. "Have you asked God to take them away?"

"No, I suppose I haven't come right out and asked." I'm surprised at my ease in talking with this man. He's a preacher, for Pete's sake. He doesn't seem like a preacher, though. Something about Silas draws me in. I feel like I'm talking with a friend, not an elder of the church. All the preachers I've known have been old enough to be my grandfather.

I show him around the ranch and introduce him to the men. A few of them he knows from church but most don't attend. I explain what everyone does and how the whole operation works. "You ready to put some spurs on and get out there with us, Preacher?" I tease.

Silas pats my arm. "I think I'll leave that to you, my friend. Doing the Lord's work and helping Henry Tillman construct houses in town is more than enough toil for me."

I laugh. "Whaddya say we go on in and get a cup of hot coffee?"

"Sounds good to me." The sky is foggy and a burst of wind kicks up. "Looks as though we're going to have an early winter, what do you think?"

"Winter's pretty much already here." I clap the preacher on the back.

Warmth flows from the sitting room fireplace as we drink from our cups. I take a sip of my coffee, then clear my throat. "So, do you think you'll ever get married? Or have preachers stopped doing that?" I smile. It may be a personal question, but I feel comfortable enough to ask it.

"I believe you're thinking of Catholic priests. An evangelical preacher still gets married to a woman." Silas chuckles. "What about you?"

"What about me?"

"Will you ever get married?"

I rock back in my chair. "I don't know if I would make a good husband. Besides, I've done a lot of things in my past I'm not sure can be forgiven."

"We've all done things in our past, Justus, and it all can be forgiven."

"I don't right think I deserve a good woman, if I'm honest."

"You recently stopped courting Bridget Murphy. Do you think she deserves better?"

My eyebrows furrow. "So, you've heard about that. I wasn't courting Miss Murphy. She'd made up that fantasy in her head. I had to make it clear to her there was nothing between us when she started hinting at marriage."

Silas laughs. "I see." A log in the fireplace falls with a gentle thud and crackle. "How's Olivia?" he asks.

I lower my head at the mention of her name. It pains me to think of her. How I've longed to take her into my arms.

"I see I've hit a sore spot," says Silas. "Does she know how you feel?"

I shake my head. "Now, she deserves better than me."

"No matter what you did in your past, you're not that same man. She deserves to know how you feel. Show her the Justus of today."

"I've been trying, but she has this wall up. Besides, I'm not sure I'm worthy of her love if she were willing to give it."

"Why do you think you're not worthy?"

I run my hand over my face. I'm exasperated. Not at Silas, but at myself for all the wrong choices I've made in the past. "I've killed men and I've been with a lot of women." I narrow my eyes on the man. "I didn't care about a one of them. They were all whores." Little sparks, like fairies, fly up into the chimney. "I'm so ashamed."

"Are these sins you still commit?"

"I haven't killed a man since the war, and I haven't been with a woman in over six years."

"Well then, you have to find it in your heart to forgive yourself. That's the way to freedom."

"How do you reckon I do that?"

"You've taken the first step by admitting your wrongdoing out loud. Confessing it. Now you must show yourself some grace. It's time you close that chapter and write a new one. One you can be proud of."

"How come you haven't preached hellfire and damnation to me?" I study him skeptically.

"I don't believe condemnation is the way to bring folks to the gospel."

I nod in understanding. He's not going to lead me to the gospel, but I do have a fondness and appreciation for him. "What made you decide to become a preacher?"

Silas peers down at his cup. "Like you, Justus, I have a past I'm not proud of. A past I'm downright ashamed of. One day, someone pulled me out of the mire and set me on a solid rock. I thought leading others like myself to something greater was my calling."

"I sure am glad you left whatever tea party you were attending in town to come out here and visit with me today." I'm serious.

"Me too, my friend. Anytime."

"Say, is that how you stay up on all the gossip?" I ask, curious how he knew to ask me about Olivia and Bridget.

Silas laughs but doesn't have a chance to respond.

"Are you gentleman ready for supper?" Mary asks from the doorway.

I throw up a hand. "What kind of question is that, Mary?"

She wags her head and lifts her eyes to the ceiling. "Whatever was I thinking?"

Silas chuckles.

He's given me something to think about — making my feelings known to Olivia. But how will she receive my confession?

# 36

## Livvie

(Wednesday)

"I'm so sorry, Lenny, to have left you with all this work." There's a heaping pile of garments in need of repair.

It's been a little over two weeks since my incident with Asa. A part of me needed time to heal, as much from the emotional bruises as the physical ones. Yet, a part of me needed to get my life back to normal.

My thoughts have been turning more and more to Justus after our walk on Sunday. There's still so much about the cowboy I don't know but long to. It gives me peace to learn he, too, has skeletons in his closet of which he isn't proud. There's comfort in his brokenness.

"Oh, hush now." Lenny waves the apology away. "It's not your fault Asa turned out to be a good-for-nothing. Besides, I certainly wasn't expecting you back so soon." Lenny tears at a seam. "I knew something wasn't right about him." Her lips curl.

"If you knew something wasn't right about him, why in heaven's sake didn't you say something?"

She stops ripping through the seam and peers at me. "Would you have run if I had told you I sensed he was up to no good?"

Sitting back in my seat, I harrumph. "You're right. I would have said you were jealous." I give a giggle to show my friend I'm only teasing.

Lenny rolls her eyes. "Jealous."

I choose a garment from the pile and lay it in my lap. "Lenny, why don't we ever talk about our lives before Laurel Springs?"

"Because we're trying to forget."

"I suppose."

"You don't want to forget your life before?" she asks.

"Yes, I do." I study the flowers of the dress draped over my knees. "It haunts me. Sometimes I wake in the night, feeling as though I'm being suffocated by it."

She keeps her eyes focused on the task at hand. "I know what you mean. But I think relief will come when you stop focusing on the past and instead, focus on the here and now."

"You're probably right."

I still have so many questions about Lenny's past, but I suppose, if she's trying to forget it, then I won't be the one to dig it up.

It doesn't take us long to get back into our normal rhythm. We're soon mending, gossiping, and dreaming of our futures when we'll marry rich men and won't have to sew for the likes of Bridget Murphy any longer.

"Perhaps I'll marry her daddy," says Lenny with a twinkle in her eye.

"Oh, Lenny!" I gasp. "He's married."

"So, wives don't live forever. And that undisciplined little girl of his can learn to mend *my* finest dresses." She points to the ceiling. "From the attic. Where she'll sleep, of course, with the rodents."

"You'd make a horrid stepmother." I shake my head. "Her fairy godmother may just turn *you* into a pumpkin for being so wicked."

"No good fairy would be that awful girl's magical godmother." Lenny's eyes roll.

"You know you'd have to share her daddy's bed," I say.

"Oh honey, I've done worse for less."

I double over with laughter. "Lenny Johnson, you're terrible."

We're so caught up in Lenny's Cinderella story, we don't notice Justus at the door.

"Hello, ladies." His voice is deep and oozes with magnetism.

Both of our heads shoot up. I wonder how much of our shenanigans he heard. I calm myself to a more well-mannered state. "Oh, Justus, I'm afraid you caught us off guard."

"I see." He removes his hat. "I'm glad to hear your laughter. It's good for the soul, you know."

My cheeks warm at his presence and his words. Had the room grown hotter? I glance at the woodstove, as though it will tell me it has raised the temperature.

Lenny stands. "How can we help you, Mister Bennett?"

"Please, call me Justus."

"Very well." Lenny puts her hands behind her back, every bit proper and businesslike. The opposite of when we ladies are alone.

He glances from Lenny to me. "I hear Olivia is a better seamstress than she is a baker, so I thought I'd bring a couple of shirts that could use mending." His eyes remain on me.

"She's a real fine seamstress. I'm sure she's a real fine baker, as well." Lenny isn't going to let any man say anything disparaging about a friend.

My eyes lock on his.

"You haven't had any of her baking then, have you?" Justus smirks.

I step forward. "I know. You'll never let me forget." I grab the garments from his hands. "When do you need these shirts finished?"

"No, I won't. And I'm in no hurry."

"I'll have them done by the end of the week."

"I'll see you Friday, then, under one condition."

I squint my eyes at him. "Why do there have to be conditions with you, Justus Bennett?"

"Assurance."

"Assurance?" I raise an eyebrow.

"That's right. My condition is that you come to the ranch Friday evening for supper. I'll pick you up from my aunt and uncle's at five."

I stand there staring the cowboy down for a good solid minute before replying. "But you're already picking me up on Saturday morning to help you with the float."

"And Friday evening for supper." Our eyes have not left their intense showdown. It's as if we're the only two people in the room.

His smile liquefies my insides, the way a blazing candle melts over itself. Looks like I'm going to be spending lots of time with this man. Butterflies swarm in my stomach.

He places his hat back on his head. "Ladies." Then he turns and leaves.

Lenny gasps. "What was that about?"

I shrug and plop down in the seat. "What?"

"What? You two couldn't take your eyes off each other. He sure does fancy *you*."

"I think I fancy him, too," I say as I hold his shirts to my bosom. How I want to take in the scent of his clothing, but I resist the urge.

# 37

## Asa

I hand the butler my hat and coat. "Dietrich."

"Mister McDaniels, it's good to see you, sir. Adelyn is in her bedroom. Shall I bring you a drink, sir?"

"I'll get it, Dietrich."

"Very well, sir." The man bows before leaving the foyer.

I walk to my office and pour myself a glass of brandy, then sit behind the overly large mahogany desk, not yet ready to face Adelyn. I'm exhausted and my lip isn't yet thoroughly healed. I sit back in the seat and sip the whiskey. I'm happy to be back at my desk, but I hate being in this house. It's big and cold and doesn't belong to me. Nothing belongs to me.

"How long have you been home?" Adelyn stands in the doorway.

I set the glass down and move to my feet, straightening my suit coat. "Only about five minutes." She approaches me and I run my hand over her swollen belly. "How are you feeling, darling?" The sight of her looking like a sow about to give birth makes my stomach turn, but I must keep up the ruse if I want to see any of her daddy's money.

"I'm feeling better now that you're home. This baby is about to come any day, Asa. I was worried you'd miss the birth."

"Yes, I got home as quickly as I could, darling." I force a kiss to her hand.

She reaches up and touches my injured lip. "Oh Asa, what happened?"

"I'm afraid I tripped and fell. Embarrassing, but it's quite all right." I remove her hand from my face. "Why don't you go on back to bed? I've got paperwork to do before I retire."

"Will you sleep in my room tonight?" she asks hesitantly.

"I'm afraid I'll be up quite late, and I'm rather tired from being on the road."

There is sadness in her eyes, which does not move me. She's a means to an end, her daddy's funds. That's all she'd been when I married her almost a year ago. I've managed to keep myself away for most of that time. Of course, I had to force myself to produce an heir. It's not that she's an unattractive woman. She's engaging enough, but her neediness and her increased weight since being with child disgusts me.

"All right." She drops her gaze. "I'll see you at breakfast, then."

I turn her back toward the door. "Perhaps tomorrow night."

She nods and slowly waddles out of the room.

I move back to the desk, but her voice stops me. I turn and see her head poking around the door. "I'm missing a rather expensive necklace. I think one of the staff has taken it. I feel as if I can't trust anyone. Will you inquire about it?"

"I'll get to the bottom of it, darling. Now go on to bed."

I sit back in the large leather chair once more, entertaining visions of that necklace resting on the milky-white skin of Olivia Palmer.

## 38
## Livvie

The last two days have dragged out the way winter does once Christmas is over. Finally, Friday is here, and I'm as light as a feather as I parade down the staircase. Rebecca, Miss Bea, and Thomas "ooh" and "aah" from the bottom of the steps.

Thomas's eyes are wide. "Miss Olivia, you're a princess."

Miss Bea chimes in, "Yes, she is, Thomas."

Lenny insisted I borrow her sapphire dress with the white lace trim. I chose to layer my skirts rather than wear the hoops because I'm still a practical woman. Rebecca helped iron my hair into ringlets that she pinned at the top of my head, so they fall delicately, almost touching my shoulders. I'm not sure I've ever felt so pretty.

I take as much of a breath in as I can, considering the corset that squeezes my already trim waist.

A knock at the door brings everyone to a halt.

Miss Bea's hands go to her mouth. "Oh, that's Justus." She

scrambles to let her nephew in from out of the cold.

His eyes fixate on me, causing warmth to creep into my cheeks.

"Oh, Olivia. You're—" His eyes travel over my dress and hair. "Enchanting."

Miss Bea breaks the spell between us. "It's time to get you bundled up, dear; it's an icy one out there this evening."

Once in the sleigh, I hardly notice the crispness of the air. I can't be any warmer than I already am, cuddled beside Justus under a heavy bearskin blanket.

The skis slice through the snow as the horses trot along. And the bells that adorn the team echo through the dark of night. It's all so magical.

When we reach the ranch, Justus helps me from the sleigh and into the house. There are animals on the walls with their canines exposed. Ferocious. I hope I never meet a live one. I grip my coat tighter, although the room is plenty warm. Justus must notice my hesitation because he laughs. "Don't worry, they won't bite," he says.

"Let me take that." Mary springs forward.

I've met her at church but haven't had a chance to converse with her. "Thank you." I begin to unwrap myself from the many layers Miss Bea put on me.

"Oh, you look just lovely," she says.

"Olivia, Mary will take care of you while I put the sleigh and team away." Justus places his hand on my back. Reassurance, perhaps.

"Thank you." I glance from Justus to Mary. Oh, how I hope to make a good impression this evening. It's important that Mary approve of me, as I know Justus thinks of her as a second mother.

"Justus prefers to eat in the kitchen. I hope you aren't offended by that. The formal dining room hasn't seen a meal since he's been home." Mary's voice is as warm as the room.

Of course I don't mind, but I do feel overdressed. I run my fingers over my collar. "Oh, not at all. I much prefer informal."

Mary's wearing a white blouse and brown skirt, resembling what I wear daily. I now regret donning the dress that Lenny insisted upon. Better to overdress than underdress, I suppose.

"Is there anything I can help you with, Mary?" I must find some way to make myself feel useful in this awkward situation.

Although we're eating in the kitchen, Mary has the table set with silver and fine china. I am unworthy of silver and fine china. Or perhaps they always eat this fancy.

"Actually, everything is ready." Mary pulls out a chair before pointing to another. "Justus sits there, so you have yourself a seat beside him. My husband Frank and my son Caleb will join us any moment."

The room smells of pot roast, potatoes, and freshly baked bread. "It sure is a perfect evening for warm food." I fidget in my seat. *Warm food?* Had I really said that? *Oh, Livvie, pull yourself together.* I clear my throat. "You all live here, then?" I glance about the room, wishing to quickly change the subject.

"No, we have a house out yonder that Justus's father built for us years ago, but we're a family and always eat together when we can."

"Yes, I suppose it would be hard eating in the big ole house all alone."

Relief washes over me when the three men come in through the kitchen door. A cold gust of wind blows in with them.

"Sorry about that," says Justus as they hang their coats and hats on the pegs that line the wall. "It's starting to snow pretty hard out there."

Once everyone is seated around the table, Mary asks her husband to say grace. The meal is warm and wonderful. The company, too, is delightful as I get to know another aspect of Justus's family. They are all so welcoming, and the laughter puts me at ease.

"So, Olivia," Caleb asks, "where are you from?"

I want to forget where I'm from, but of course, people will be curious. He only wishes to get to know me, is all. That's understandable. Most folks aren't trying to run and hide from something. I move my food around on my plate. "Missouri."

"What part of Missouri?"

"Boone. It's a small town in western Missouri. I'm originally from New York but lived a good part of my life in Ohio."

Justus speaks up. "You don't say. My family's from Pennsylvania, although, I don't remember it." He laughs. "But we're practically from the same neck of the woods."

I smile at him, and he gives me a wink.

He winked at me. This is becoming a common thing with him. I feel my insides melt to my toes. Wondering if anyone noticed, I glance about the table.

"Mary and I come from Illinois," says Frank. "We got gold fever—"

Mary interjects, "You mean, *you* got gold fever."

He dips his head. "I stand corrected, Olivia. *I* got gold fever and decided to move my family to California. We had three young'uns at the time. Caleb here came later. Anyway, all we found was heartache. More people got rich off the miners than the miners themselves did."

He takes Mary's hand. "Smallpox took our son Adam."

I clutch my chest. "I'm so sorry to hear that."

"I decided for the sake of my family, we better head back east. By the time we reached Laurel Springs, we needed to restock our supplies, but that required a temporary job because we were plum outta money or anything of value to trade. Justus's father, William, brought me on as a ranch hand and Mary to help Isabella, Justus's mother, with domestic needs. I guess you could say we just became a part of the family and have called this place home ever since. William even had a house built for us beyond this here main house." He points behind himself with his thumb.

"Yes, Mary told me. That's some story, I must say." Before I have a chance to reel in my words, I ask, "Where are your other two children?" *They could be dead, Livvie.*

"Oh, they went and got themselves married and moved away," says Frank.

"And now I know how my mother felt when we left Illinois." Mary blinks her eyes, as if to keep tears from springing up. "Anyway, I have apple pie with fresh cream. Who has room for dessert?"

At that moment, our attention is caught by wind and ice beginning to beat against the side of the house and windows.

It's a wonder the large kitchen window is still in place.

"I forgot to check the chinking around that damn window," says Justus. "I sure hope it holds for the night."

Mary shudders, then moves to the counter. "Justus, I think it would be best for Olivia to stay the night. I don't think it's safe for you and her to be out in this storm, and I can't bear the thought of it."

The wind is howling like a pack of angry coyotes. I'm not sure how I feel about staying, although I agree, it wouldn't be safe for us to be out in the storm. The blowing snow and ice pummels the window. Weather such as this has caused men to lose their way and freeze to death.

Justus studies the window. "I think you're right, Mary. Olivia can stay in my parents' room."

After enjoying dessert, I help Mary clean up. She insists I shouldn't help since I'm the guest of honor. But I insist that it's only right after all the work she's put into such a lovely meal. In the end, she concedes.

We all enjoy more laughter over a game of cards and hot tea.

I've never played cards before, but everyone does a good job explaining the rules to me and I think I understand.

"Stop looking at the girl's cards, Justus," says Caleb.

"I'm just trying to help her out."

"Looks to me like you're cheatin'."

I hold up my free hand. "I can do this, you two, so stop your fussing." I pull my cards into my chest and tilt my head to Justus. "And Caleb's right, stop your peeking, will you."

"It's all right," says Justus. "I know when you think you

have a good hand, anyway."

"How?" I gasp.

"I'm not saying, but you got a telltale sign." He smirks and fans out his cards.

I don't know if he let me win, but in the end, I beat him with a flush. I grin from ear to ear as he lets out a slow whistle. "Well, I'll be," he says.

Frank laughs. "With that, I believe we can call it a night. Good job, Miss Palmer."

Once in bed, wearing a nightgown lent to me by Mary, my thoughts turn to Justus, whose bedroom is across the hall. I roll over, staring at the window where the curtain dances to the rhythm of the wind that rages outside. I try to allow the storm to lull me to sleep along with visions of the handsome cowboy playing in my mind. He is so close, yet so far away.

A knock on the bedroom door startles me from my musings. "Come in," I call.

The door opens and I see Justus's silhouette. "Olivia?"

What's he doing at my door?

# 39

## Justus

(An hour earlier)

I linger by the fire a little longer as Mary sees Olivia to my parents' room. The wind pounds outside while the crackling logs warm me. Knowing she'll be sleeping across the hall further heats me.

That blue dress of hers brings out the color in her eyes—and those eyes get me every time. She's the most beautiful woman I've ever seen. And her laughter, it fills my soul.

She proved to be competitive while playing cards earlier in the evening. I smile to myself at the thought of it. She didn't know how to play but caught on as fast as a baby coon. You only need to show them once. She's a woman who can handle herself, all right.

I could sit here by the fire all night watching the flames dance as I think about her. She did this funny little thing with her nose every time she believed she had a good card hand. I loved it.

Her features are soft and dainty, reminding me of a flower — colorful, glorious to look upon, and heavenly to smell. You'd think the slightest touch would cause it to wilt or the petals to fall. But no, it weathers any storm and any temperature. It's resilient.

"She's a special girl, Justus." Mary's voice interrupts my thoughts.

I glance up in surprise at her words. "You think so?"

"Yes, you can't fool an old hen. She's lovely and true."

"And you're the old hen," I state, matter-of-fact.

"Of course."

Mary knows I'm teasing her. I nod and glance back to the fire. "Just wanted to make sure we agreed on that."

"Yes, and if I could bend you over my knee and take a switch to you, I would."

I peer up at her, serious now. "Mary, what do suppose Ma would think of her?"

"I wouldn't doubt if your ma sent her, Justus." She kisses the top of my head. "I'm going home now. And don't worry — Frank and Caleb are waiting in the kitchen to walk with me."

"Thank you, Mary." I'd heard the two men talking, so I figured as much.

Ma bringing Olivia into my life is a beautiful notion. The thought sends a warmth over me. If only Ma was here now. I could use her words of wisdom. How wonderful it would be for me to introduce Olivia to her. I can almost sense Ma sitting in her rocker. I watch, willing her to appear. My chest squeezes as I stare intently at the chair. But she never shows herself, as the seat remains still and empty. I peer back at the fire and exhale, relaxing my tense muscles. Sometimes I wish the veil between this life and the next could be lifted, even if just for a moment.

After tending to the coals in the fire, I make my way up to my room. From the edge of the bed, I pull off my boots and sit there contemplating. Olivia's presence haunts me through the walls.

The icy wind threatens to break through the wood and thin glass panes. Despite the fires burning in the stoves downstairs, the air is cold upstairs. I would keep her warmer than any layer of quilts ever could. I know this and ache to wrap her in my arms.

In stockinged feet, I plod to the door across from mine and knock.

"Come in." The soft voice beckons me.

I can't see into the darkened room. The only light is the glow of the lantern behind me, shining from the table beside my bed.

"Olivia?"

"Justus?" There is surprise in the way she says my name.

"I just wanted to make sure you were all right. Do you have enough covers?"

"Yes, I'm fine. Thank you."

"All right, then." I start to shut the door, then open it again. "Olivia?"

"Yes."

"I'm thankful you're here."

"Me too," she says.

I can hear the smile in her tone, and it squeezes my heart a little.

The next morning, a fire roars within the cookstove in the kitchen. Olivia stands at the counter with her back to me. She's wearing that blue dress with her hair pulled into her usual chignon. How wonderful it would be to wrap my arms around her waist and lay soft kisses on her neck. I take a deep breath to shake the image, then clear my throat. "That's a pretty fancy dress for breakfast, don't you think?"

She turns slightly while pouring coffee into a cup. A grin. I enjoy seeing that sight first thing in the morning.

I move closer and take a mug from the cupboard. "How'd you sleep?"

"Surprisingly well."

"Why do you say surprisingly?"

Leaning against the counter, she shrugs. "Different house, a different bed, different noises. A storm howling outside."

"I understand that." The war's been long over, but I still sleep as if the enemy were around the corner. I pour the steaming black liquid into my cup.

She lifts a lid from one of the crocks on the counter and peeks inside.

"What are you looking for?"

"Sugar." She lifts another lid.

"I could put my finger in your coffee if you like."

She finds the one she's looking for and pulls it toward her. "Because you're so sweet?" She gives me a sideways glance and smirks.

"Yes ma'am." I give her a wink and move to the table. My heart is hitting against my chest the way the ice pelted the house all night. I'm thankful to see the big window still in place.

The sun is making its appearance in the eastern sky. Snowdrifts are high, leaving the men and me a lot of shoveling to do before Olivia and I get to work on Miss Bea's float in the barn.

"That dress looks beautiful, but I don't think you want to be working in it," I say.

"Mary said she'd bring me clothing this morning that's more appropriate." The dress rustles as she takes a seat. "I had a wonderful time last night."

I want to bring her into my arms. She's a ray of light in this dimly lit kitchen. She's staring at me, and I realize I haven't responded. Words have failed me. I stare back, yearning to kiss her.

# 40

## Livvie

The day has turned out to be beautiful in many ways. Although the air is crisp, the sun is glowing and every branch of every tree holds a layer of snow, sparkling like jewels.

Justus and I make great progress on the float. He pounds away in the barn while I stuff old clothing with straw and sew heads and faces on the bodies from the warmth and comfort of the house.

"Do you know how to ice skate?" he asks me at lunch.

"I've never been ice skating."

"We'll fix that today, then. I'm thinking you're about the same size as my ma. You can wear her skates."

"But where will we go?"

"There's a pond out back."

I'm not sure what to think of this idea, but he is right about one thing, his ma's skates fit perfectly. But can I stand in them?

"Don't you let me fall, Justus Bennett." I wobble with bent

knees, holding on to both of his arms with a grip no man can pry open.

He laughs. "If you fall, you won't die. I promise."

"But I don't want to break something."

"Listen to me carefully," he says. "I want you to march."

"March?"

"That's right, march. Lift your knees and march, soldier."

"I'm not one of your men, you know."

"Oh, I know," he says smoothly.

Legs shaking, I lift my right knee and set my foot down. Then I lift my left knee and set that foot down. All right, that's not so bad. I continue to march around the pond. My hands that are gripping his arms relax.

"That's it," he coaxes. "Now the next time you bring your foot down, I want you to glide with both feet."

I do it. A bit wobbly, but I do it.

"And again," he says.

"Am I skating?" I raise an eyebrow.

He chuckles. "You're skating."

I continue this for a few more feet, then he instructs me to glide with one foot. Slowly, he pushes me from him, so I no longer have an anchor to hold. His eyes light up. "You're doing it. Look at you."

I whoop. "I'm doing it. I'm skating."

He spins around me, so we're now holding hands. Slowly and cautiously, we skate in circles.

This must be what it feels like to be free as a child with no cares. If the wind were to blow, it may take me away.

After some time, Justus points to the bench where we sat to put our skates on. "Let's have a rest, shall we?"

"Tired already?" I taunt.

He lets out an exaggerated sigh as he sits on the seat with his arm over the back. It's a small bench and I'll have to sit in the crook of his arm.

He pats the space beside him. "Come sit."

My breath catches at our closeness. The wind begins to blow the top layer of snow, which chills me. If only I could lay my head on his shoulder.

"You're a skater now," he says.

"It seems as though I am. I think I could use more practice." I stare ahead, eyes on the marks we'd made in the ice.

He brushes back a fallen curl and places it behind my ear. My body tingles. "We can make that happen," he says.

My cheeks burn. Frozen in place, I don't know what to do or what to say. I can feel his eyes on me.

"You're the most beautiful creature I've ever seen." He continues to smooth my hair behind my ear.

Nervously, I look upon his face and study his features. His big brown eyes regard me and my breath grows rapid from gazing at his alluring lips. His finger is warm against my cheek. "Can I kiss you, Olivia?"

I nod. *Yes, please.* I close my eyes and part my lips, willing his mouth on mine. Holding my chin, he caresses my lips with his. Our tongues entwine. His mouth is warm and sweet. He rests his forehead on mine, causing his hat to tip upward. "I've wanted to do that for so long."

"So have I." I take hold of the back of his neck and pull him in. His hat tumbles off his head and onto the snowy ground. The moment is passionate, sensual. I'm kissing Justus Bennett and it's wonderful. Everything about it is right. Kissing someone has never felt so right.

# 41

## Livvie

Dark clouds have long covered the sun and the sky gives way to white flakes once more.

"I could sit here all day and kiss you, but we'd better head in," says Justus.

"All right." It's as if I'm floating outside of my body. I can't feel anything but a fire that grows inside me for this man.

By the time we reach the house, the wind has picked up. I try to bury my head down into my coat, but it isn't working.

"Looks as though we're in for another storm," yells Justus over the wind. "You go on in and I'll be there later."

As I hang up my coat, Mary comes blowing through the door with her face and head bundled in scarves and a hat.

"Oh Mary, you didn't have to come over in this weather. I can cook for Justus and myself this evening," I offer.

"It's quite all right. I'm here now. Besides, I wanted to make sure you were set up for a bath tonight and that you had a clean nightgown, seeing how you won't be going home yet." Snow falls around her as she removes her layers.

"Thank you so much. A bath would be lovely. What can I do to help with supper?"

"I'll fetch potatoes and carrots from the cellar, and you can slice them up. I think this will be a good evening for some fried vegetables and beef."

"That sounds good to me."

While my hands are busy with the cutting, my mind is on a certain cowboy. No one's ever kissed me the way he did. I replay it over and over in my mind.

"You must enjoy cutting carrots," says Mary.

I chuckle to myself. It hadn't occurred to me that I'd been grinning like a possum. "I was thinking about how much fun I had learning to ice skate." The statement is partly true.

When the men come in, their faces are red from the wind and cold. Caleb washes his hands at the basin. "Another night on the ranch. How do you feel about that, Olivia?"

"I don't mind. I love it out here." I glimpse at Justus, who waits for his turn with the hot water. He winks, making my knees go weak.

After another fun-filled evening of food and dominos, Frank calls it a night. "Come on, family, we had better try warming up our house before bed."

"Oh, Olivia, I forgot to heat the water for your bath." Mary jumps up and grabs the pail.

"I'll take care of it, Mary. You all get going while you can still see out there," says Justus.

"This lantern does all right," says Frank, igniting the light.

"I'll see you two in the morning for breakfast," says Mary, bundling up.

Justus ushers her out the door. "I know how to cook. You just stay home where you'll be safe and warm. Don't worry about us."

Once they're gone, Justus takes me by the hand and leads me to the sofa in the sitting room. "I thought they'd never leave."

I gasp. "Justus."

"All I've been able to think about is kissing your beautiful mouth again." He cups my face in his hands and claims my lips passionately. He gently takes in each one then slides his tongue deep in my mouth. I wrap my arms around his neck, savoring every stroke of our tongues. They glide over one another, as if we've always done this.

I need more of him. Tilting my head back, he brushes his mouth over my chin and down my neck. Goosebumps form on my skin.

He stops and stares into my eyes. "I have to tell you something."

I quickly search my mind as to what he could have to tell me. "What is it?" Panic rises in my chest. Perhaps this isn't really what he wants.

"That night I sat by your bedside watching you sleep with your face all bruised up, I knew you were the one. When you made it clear you didn't want me near you, it about tore my heart right outta my chest."

I exhale my relief. "I'm so sorry. I regretted it the moment I said it, but I couldn't take it back. I was too stubborn. It was then that I knew I was pushing away someone very special."

"Oh, Liv." He pulls me in. I'm drowning in his kisses. If I never come up for air, I'll be just fine.

He maneuvers me to lay on the couch while lying on top of me, lightly sucking on my neck. He's hard against my leg. I reach down and run my hand over the bulge in his pants. This is right. All of it is right. My body needs every inch of him. He pecks my lips softly and smooths my hair back. "Have you ever…?" He tilts his head.

I nod.

"Let's get you a bath." He places a kiss on my nose, gentle and tender.

I am bathed and wearing the nightgown and robe lent by Mary. Although I'm not a virgin, I don't know what to expect with Justus. My heart races at the realization this is truly happening. I step into his room where the lamp on the nightstand still burns. He sits on the edge of the bed, naked. His muscles are chiseled, the way the Greek gods look in the pictures I'd seen in the books at the library back in Ohio. I lean to put out the light, but he catches my arm. "I want to see you."

My chest tightens. I was rarely ever fully naked in front of Roy.

He stands and removes my robe, letting it fall to the floor. Then he pulls me in, taking my chin in his hand and brushes my lips softly with his. He grows hard against me again. Unbuttoning the front of my nightgown, he pulls it over my head and lets it, too, fall to the floor. Lifting me into his arms, he turns and lays me on the bed. I see his hardness throbbing between his legs as he hovers above me. He's certainly much larger than the pictures of the Greek gods.

He runs his mouth down my neck to my breasts. The sensations I feel are foreign. The way he kisses and touches me, I've never experienced such loving before. He takes my breast into his mouth. I moan at his wonderful touch. I had no idea lovemaking could be so incredible. Roy only ever pulled up my nightgown, entered me until he was finished, then rolled over and went to sleep. All in the dark. I push those thoughts from my mind.

"Your body is so beautiful." He takes in my right breast while still pinching and teasing my left nipple. I run my fingers through his unruly hair.

His kisses move down my body to my belly. I watch him in the golden glow of the light. Whatever he's doing, it's heavenly. He kisses the insides of my thighs, sending tingles to the bud that throbs within the soft curls. Can it get any better than this? Oh yes, it can. He makes his way to the folds between my legs, caressing that tender bud with his tongue. Moving his fingers inside me, he sucks as though he can't get enough of my juices that flow freely for him. I moan at his caresses.

"Does that feel good, Angel?" His voice is raw and sexy.

"Yes," I gasp as he continues hungrily feeding on me, moving his fingers in and out. Steadily fingering my honeypot, he licks at it, laps, and sucks, as if attempting to extract every bit of nectar.

"Yes. God, yes." I grab the sheets into the balls of my hands, squeezing with the pleasure that emanates from between my legs until my body convulses and I pulsate in his mouth. He lingers before moving up my body, kissing my stomach. Every nerve in my being stands at attention. I shudder as he sends prickles throughout every part of me with the slightest touch.

He finds my mouth once more before sliding himself inside my wet core. "I've wanted to do this for so long," he groans.

"I never imagined it could be this good," I say, wrapping my arms around his neck.

"Oh, you're going to get a lot of this."

"Promise?"

"Cross my heart." He smiles, still moving slowly inside me, as though he's savoring every thrust. "I don't know if I can last much longer, Angel." His rhythm grows faster. Harder. "This is all yours," he says in a raspy voice. He continues to push into me until he pulls out, releasing a warm wet stream down the center of my belly. His cries of pleasure are music to my ears.

He lay beside me, my head on his chest. With the light still burning, I admire his bare body. I had no idea when he first kissed me and it felt so right that being in his bed would feel even better.

"Olivia Palmer, what am I going to do with you?" he says, squeezing me with the one arm he has draped around my shoulder.

I smile. "Whatever you want."

He chuckles. "You've made me the happiest man today. I can't imagine any man ever being as happy as I have been today. As happy as I am at this moment." He pulls my face to him and brushes over my lips with his. At first, his kisses are soft and sensual, but then, as if he can't get enough, they become demanding, and he takes a fistful of my hair. Then he lifts me to sit on his swollen shaft. "See what you do to me," he rasps, guiding my hips up and down until I get the rhythm of it, then he moves his hands to my breasts. Pulling me to him with one hand around my waist, he takes turns drawing my swollen peaks into his mouth.

"Damn it, you're stunning," he says breathlessly between mouthfuls of my aroused nipples. "How did I ever get so lucky?"

I'm wondering the same thing. If I'd known being with him was going to be this way, I'd have done it much sooner.

"Oh yes, Angel, ride me," he yells out as I grind onto his rock-hard cock. I cry out in ecstasy as our bodies jolt in unison. He groans once more as we move to a slower pace, then to a stop.

"Damn, woman. I don't think I'm ever leaving this bed again." He wipes the sweat from his brow with the back of his hand. I laugh and lie beside him with my head on his chest, wet with moisture. "Yep, I think we're gonna stay right here forever," he whispers.

"You'll have to get up some time to eat."

He lets out a raspy moan. "I got breakfast, dinner, supper, and dessert right here," he says, giving my damp behind a good slap.

"Ow, you just smacked my derriere." I rub my buttock with a giggle.

"That won't be the last time, believe me."

# 42

## Justus

I wake this morning to find Olivia gone from the bed. It occurs to me that I slept soundly and without nightmares, which brings a smile to my face. I slip on my drawers and make my way downstairs. The scent of coffee wafts from the kitchen. "There you are," I say. She stands at the window in her robe with a cup in hand, long locks falling over her shoulders and down her body. The sun is rising from the eastern plains and the only light inside is the faint illumination from the lantern on the counter.

"I was just thinking someone needs to pinch me. I feel as if this is all a dream," she says.

I come up behind her and wrap my arms around her waist, looking out over the countryside. "It does feel like a dream, doesn't it?" I pull her hair back and lay light kisses on her neck, inhaling the scent of her delicate skin. The exact thing I yearned to do yesterday morning when I saw her at the counter pouring her coffee.

She turns to me. "I love it here." Her hand is soft and warm over my bare chest.

I place my palm over hers. "I love you being here." I mean it. I don't want her to ever leave. Her face is all I want to see every morning when I wake.

"Can I get you a cup of coffee?" Her eyes search my face.

I take her mug and place it on the table. "I'd love a cup of coffee, but first, I'd love something else." I escort her around the table, away from the window, slide off the robe, and unbutton her nightgown.

"Justus, right here? What if someone comes in?" She grabs my hands.

I spin her around and lift the garment up and over her head. "No one's coming. Remember, I gave Mary the morning off." Running my hands up to her full breasts, I gently nibble her ear. She lays her head back on my shoulder and lets out a sigh. I move one hand to her neck while moving the other between her legs. She's wet and warm, as I anticipated. Slowly, I bend her over the table and pull down my underpants.

Standing to one side of her with a hand on her back, I guide her legs open with the other, then slide my palm over her bottom. Damn, she's so delightful and her skin is soft as silk. I grow harder at the sight of her sprawled over the table. Wanting to take her now but also wanting to enjoy every curve of her body, I give her behind a light slap. Then another, harder this time. She lets out a soft yelp. "Do you like that?" I ask, giving her another solid smack before smoothing it out with my hand.

"Yes," she pants, peering over her shoulder at me and

opening her legs wider.

I tap at her flower, splashing the wetness with my fingers. I give it a slap, harder, then faster. Her moans tell me she's enjoying every bit of it. Then I slide a finger in. It's soft, warm, soaked — begging to take me in, to swallow me whole.

I bend toward her and whisper in her ear, "You've got me hard as a boulder. You want it, don't you?"

She nods. "Yes."

"Tell me you want it and I'll give it to you."

"I want it. I need it." Ringlets of hair fall around her face. She's the most magnificent woman I've ever seen, and she's all mine.

I position myself behind her and slide inside, slowly, watching my hard staff move in and out. She feels so good. Tight and warm. I thrust, hard, penetrating her depths. She lets out a throaty whine. Then I thrust faster. My breath is heavy and my heart races. With my hair falling in my eyes now, I can't think straight. I haven't felt this out of my mind since eating peyote just after the war. Moaning my name, she tightens and claws at the table. Satisfied I've brought her to ecstasy, I give it to her harder until I feel myself coming to the brink. I pull out with a shudder and an explosion. She's doing things to my heart that I can't explain. I lay a trail of kisses up her spine and onto her cheek. "You're a dream come true, Angel."

She smiles. "So are you."

My heart expands a little more as she gently bites her bottom lip. How do I tell this woman I'm falling in love with her?

# 43

## Bridget

*(Five days later)*

Standing at the display cabinet of Harold Jenkins's Mercantile, poring over the jewelry, I admire myself while holding up earrings, necklaces, and brooches. No doubt I'll be the most exquisite woman at the church's fall social following the parade tomorrow. How I do wish the old man held a better selection of jewels. No matter, Daddy has the money to buy me the finest of what the store carries.

I eye a beaded comb for my hair. It will go perfectly with the emerald green dress I'll be wearing to the event. The gold beads dangle, shimmering just right. This I must have. Turning the comb this way and that in my hand to catch the light, I barely notice the tinkling of the bell hanging from the front door.

"Good afternoon, sir," says Mister Jenkins. "Is there anything

I can help you with?"

I continue to glance over the accessories, imagining how they would look on me. Making myself known is something I relish. Especially on an occasion where the entire town will attend. I lift my chin as a tingling radiates through my chest. Yes, I *will* turn the head of every bachelor there, including Justus Bennett. He will rue the day he turned me down.

"I'm looking for a girl. Her name's Livvie. Livvie McLain. She stands about this tall and has light reddish-blonde hair."

My eyes remain on the goods in front of me, but a smirk plays on my face. *Well, well, well.*

"I don't know anyone by that name and I'm afraid I don't pay much attention to the ladies' hair," says the storekeeper. The man is so old he probably can't even see well enough to know what anyone's hair color is.

"Much obliged," says the man. The bell on the door chimes with his exit.

I pull on my gloves. "Oh, Mister Jenkins, I can't decide at the moment, and I just remembered I have somewhere I must be. I'll return later." I'm out the door before he can utter a word.

I hadn't gotten a look at the gentleman in the store. But the looming man eyeing his surroundings as if he were deciding where to go next must be him.

I reach up to touch his shoulder. "Excuse me, sir?" I flash him my sweetest smile. He isn't all that handsome, but no matter, this may be just the opportunity I've been hoping for. "I heard you asking about a young woman, Livvie McLain, is it?" I think of the newest resident of Laurel Springs with light reddish-blonde hair and a name that could certainly be shortened to Livvie.

"That's right." His voice is deep.

"I have a sneaking suspicion I may just know her."

"I'm listening."

"Why don't we get out of this awful cold." I tug at the collar of my coat. "You can buy me a coffee." My eyes rove down his frame, then back up to his face before taking hold of his arm and steering him toward the hotel restaurant.

# 44

## Wes

After buying coffee for that little goody-two-shoes gal, who was more than eager to tell me all about Livvie and her cohortin' with some rancher, I found this empty cabin nestled in the woods some miles from the town of Laurel Springs. I'll call it home while hatchin' a plan to take what is rightfully mine—Livvie McLain. I can't believe she thought she'd get away with runnin' from me. Must not have put the fear in her good enough over the years. If she was any other woman, I'd kill her, but something about her makes me grow hard in my drawers. I've wanted the woman from the moment I laid eyes on her.

I recollect the night I came home to her cookin' in the kitchen and Royal tellin' me she was his wife. Doggone little prick. How'd he go and get someone as beautiful and graceful as her? She wasn't even a whore. So many times, I wanted to take her to my bed, but instead, I'd grab her by her hair or send a palm across her face. The only way I could touch her was to lay hurt on her. How many times had I set traps for her to do or say something that would make me angry? More than I can count. I grin to myself.

She's mine. I'll make sure she'll never forget it. I won't kill her, but I'll make damn sure no other man will want her.

I twirl the knife around in my hand, letting the sun glare off the blade. I'll cut her face up real good, that's what I'll do. No other man will even see her cuz she'll be too ashamed to show her face outside. I'll have her right where I want her, bound to me.

---

After scouting out the town, I return to the dark cabin, ready to put my plan into action tomorrow. There's to be a parade, then a social at the church. I'll lay in wait and take her at the right time.

"Mm-hmm, Miss Livvie, by tomorrow night, you're goin' to be all mine." I lick my lips. I've waited three long months to finally have her in my bed. I'll never have to pay for a whore again. I howl with delight. Of course, I still will while out of town. A man can't be expected to go long without a woman.

There's a tap on the window. I grab my rifle that lay on the floor beside me. The tapping stops. Probably just a branch from the tree. The muscles in my shoulders relax as I lay back and cover my eyes with my hat.

My horse whinnies. There had better not be a bear out there gettin' my only way outta here with my woman, damn it. I jump up and run out the door. "Yah, yah!" My rifle is snug against my shoulder, ready to shoot that damn animal. The light of the moon casts over the forest. I don't see any shadow of a bear.

There's a crunch of snow and cold metal presses to my cheek. "Put the rifle down, Wes." The voice is deep and slow.

My nostrils flare and I keep my rifle pinned to my arm. "Who are you? You that son of a bitch that's got my woman?"

The metal digs in further. "Put the rifle down or I'll blow your goddamned head off," says the voice.

I just might kill that little whore now, once I get my hands on her. I lower my gun slowly, but quick as a whip, I spin and fire a shot.

Where is that scoundrel? I search through the moonlight. He's gone. "Come out, you bastard." I turn this way, then that, listening for the slightest crack of a stick or crunch of snow. "You better show yourself." Something falls to my right, and I whirl and fire. When I turn back, *bam*, I get the butt of a gun to the nose and fall to the ground. Dropping my gun, I clutch my face in agony. There's a boot on my ribs and the barrel of a gun digging into my head.

"We've been tracking you for quite some time, Wes." The foot presses harder. "You're under arrest for the murder of Deputy Charlie Carson." The man spits in my face.

# 45

## Livvie

*(The following day)*

The church ladies have pulled off a wonderful fun-filled parade. There are plenty of scarecrows and pumpkins. Mimi, Chet, and Thomas "ooh" and "ahh" at the men walking on stilts. Jenkins's Mercantile has provided sweet taffy and peppermint sticks. There are barrels of apples for the children to bob, and magic shows to amaze all.

Miss Bea is thrilled at the job Justus and I did on the float. Justus had painted a sign promoting the good doctor of Laurel Springs and I created the likes of Doc and Miss Bea administering care to a patient from scarecrows. Miss Bea stands beside the display, waving with pride to the parade-goers below.

The sun has been out all week, melting snow and warming the air. "We couldn't have asked for a better day," says Miss

Bea. "We've been getting so much snow as of late, I feared we might have to cancel." Justus helps her down from the back of the parade wagon.

The best part of the day for me has been sitting beside the handsome cowboy as he guides the team through the streets. I sit tall and smile proudly, waving to the crowd as if I've just won a pageant. I've found my love and I couldn't be prouder.

---

Wonderfully decorated, the church smells of sweet ham and baked goods. A pumpkin display with cornstalks stands in the corner of the room. Moved pews make way for tables piled with meats, vegetables, and all the sweets one could want.

Justus takes my coat and muffler. He's so bold as to kiss my cheek and puts his hand to my lower back.

I smooth out my dress and look around for judgmental eyes. "Would you care for a cup of coffee?" I ask.

"Just the thing to warm me up." He leans in and presses his mouth to my ear. "Until I can have you again."

Heat rises in my cheeks. "I'll come find you with that cup of coffee," I say before stepping away.

As I pour rich cream into a mug, a familiar female voice breaks into my thoughts of the man I've left holding my coat.

"Are you enjoying yourself?"

Bridget.

"We just arrived, but everything looks and smells lovely."

"We?"

"Yes, Justus and me."

"Of course." Bridget's tone drips with contempt. And the ringlets in her hair make her look like a schoolgirl. No doubt she believes herself to be the prettiest woman here this evening. I refrain from rolling my eyes.

Picking up the cups, I turn, but she catches my arm. "You know, I had the most interesting conversation yesterday."

"You don't say." I couldn't care less about Bridget Murphy's conversations.

Once again, I attempt to walk away, but the girl grabs my arm and lets out a chuckle. "Does Justus know you're engaged?"

I pivot fully toward her now. "Whatever would make you think such a thing?"

Bridget puts her hand over her mouth and giggles. "Oh, I must have misunderstood."

"Yes, I shall say you must have."

I turn, but what comes out of her mouth next makes my blood run cold. "Livvie McLain."

My feet halt and my breath catches in my chest.

"Your name, it is Livvie McLain, is it not?" She speaks as if she's completely innocent of trying to bring ruin to me and Justus.

Wes is here.

I set the cups on the table and without a word to anyone, and without my coat and muffler, I run from the church into the crisp darkness.

# 46

## Justus

I lay my and Olivia's coats over a pew.

Silas approaches, holding out his hand. "I'm happy to see you, Justus."

"Well, I'm not about to miss an opportunity to spend time with Olivia, even if it is at a church social." I keep my eyes on her. She's in conversation with Bridget Murphy at the refreshment table. How stunningly beautiful is Liv? She's surely captivated my heart and I couldn't be happier.

The reverend is talking, but I'm only partly listening, as my thoughts and eyes are on my gal. She's the prettiest woman here.

I shift as I see her prepare to come toward me, but then she stops, looking as though she's seen a ghost. Placing the cups on the table, she runs from the building. Bridget laughs, then takes a sip from her drink.

"Excuse me, Silas." I place a hand on the preacher's shoulder. Anger rises in my chest as I stomp to Bridget. "What did you say to her?" I ask the girl.

"Why, I was just telling Livvie McLain about an interesting conversation I had yesterday with her fiancé." She puts her hand on my bicep. I look at her hand and remove it from my arm.

Livvie McLain? Fiancé?

I run out the door. "Olivia. Olivia." There's no one, only horses and wagons tied up around the church. My heart races and the cold stings my lungs as I run, calling out for her. I must find her.

# 47

## Livvie

I dash to Doc and Miss Bea's to get my belongings and leave town. Wes has found me and if he gets to me, he'll kill me. Surely Bridget told him where I'm living. What is he waiting for? *I can go to the Sheriff.* And say what? I haven't seen Wes for myself. If Justus finds out the truth about me, he won't want me. It's best I leave.

I pull out my trunk from under the bed and throw my belongings into it. The next stagecoach won't leave until tomorrow. I don't know what to do until then, but I can't stay here.

My coat. I left it at the church. Piling on shawls, I grab my trunk and run for the stairs.

"Olivia." It's Justus. He stops at the top of the steps, panting.

My body shakes. "Please," I cry. I want to drop my trunk and fall into his arms. "Please. You have to let me go."

He holds his hands out in front of himself, as if telling me he won't touch me. "What's going on, Olivia?" His eyes are pleading.

"Please, Justus." With the back of my hand, I wipe the tears from my face.

"I need you to talk to me." His hands still show me I'm safe. But his stance tells me he won't allow me passage down the stairs, not until I talk to him.

I turn my face away and sniff.

He steps closer. "Is Olivia Palmer your real name?"

I nod and wipe my nose on the sleeve of my blouse, taking a step back.

"Do you have a fiancé?" He drops his arms.

I shake my head.

"I need you to talk to me. I know Andrew sent you here. Does this have anything to do with that?"

"Please, Justus, you don't know me."

"Help me, then. Help me to know you." His face is as pained as my heart. "Please, Olivia, don't do this without talking to me." He rests a hand on his chest. "I'm in love with you, and I've never been in love in my life." He reaches out and takes the trunk from me. "I just ask that you give me a moment to tell me what's going on." He holds his arm out toward the door of my room. Setting the trunk down, he guides me to the bed.

Again, I wipe my nose on my sleeve. Hesitantly, I begin. "No one has ever called me Olivia, except for teachers. I've always been called Livvie. Roy was my husband. Not legally. We just lived together as husband and wife and I went by his name, McLain." I play with the fringe on one of the shawls that's wrapped around me. "He always said he'd marry me, but he never did."

"How long were you together?" Justus's voice is kind.

I shrug. "About eight years, I guess."

"Is he here in Laurel Springs?"

"No. He's dead. His brother Wes killed him. Wes is here. He thinks he has rights to me now that Roy's gone. That's why Andrew and Marybeth sent me here." I glance up at Justus. "No one pulls one over on Wes and gets away with it. He's here to kill me."

"Do you and Roy have children?"

I finger the fringe on my shawl. "No. I can't have children." Surely, he won't want me now.

"So that's why you didn't appear troubled when I didn't pull out while making love the other night," he observes, rubbing his forehead. "What happened? That you can't have children. Were you injured? Was it sickness? How do you know you can't have children?"

Not a soul knows what happened, except for Mini and the girls, and now Rebecca. Roy didn't even know. I take a deep breath and slowly recount my story.

"My mother worked at the laundry in town and didn't come home until late into the evenings. It was my job to make supper after school. One day, her husband, her *third* husband, Vernon, arrived shortly after me." I falter while fidgeting with the fringe on the shawl. I want to go on. I need to. "I was sitting at the table, peeling potatoes, when he came in." I wipe away a tear that slips down my cheek.

"It's okay, I got you," says Justus, wrapping an arm around me. "He had grown bolder in his advances on me but on this day, he didn't hold back. He immediately came and knelt beside me and began rubbing my leg." Justus exhales. I can feel his warm breath in my hair. "And my breasts," I cry. "Then he led me to the room he shared with my mother." Covering my face I confess, "I know I should have run, but fear made my feet follow him." I dare to look at Justus, whose eyes are anguished. "He stole everything special and innocent from me that day. I'm so ashamed."

Justus pulls me closer. "I'm so sorry, Angel." His voice trembles. "He's the one who should be ashamed."

I now feel numb as I continue my story. "Afterward, when he got up to dress, I took my clothes from the floor, meaning to run to my room, but Mother walked in. I don't know why, but she had come home early that day." I cackle without humor, wiping my soaked face. "He told her I'd seduced him. I actually thought she'd believe me and protect me, but she just wailed on me, called me a whore, and put me out."

"Oh, Mother." *I run to her with tears soaking my face and shame invading my body.*

*The woman doesn't embrace me back.* "What is this? How long has this been going on?" *she yells.*

*Vernon quickly pulls his pants from around his ankles.* "S-she t-tempted me, Mabel," *he stutters.* "I tried to tell her it wasn't right."

"You little whore!"

*I feel a sting as hot as fire burns my cheek. I hold my face with a gasp.* "No, Mother."

"*How dare you parade around here tempting this man who has been a father to you. You make me sick.*" *She spits on me.* "*Get out of my house. I don't ever want to see your face again. You're nothing but a whore.*" *She pushes me out of the room and slams the door. I hear Vernon talking to her in a reassuring tone.*

*I take what I can as quickly as I can, even the case that holds my grandparents' letters and grandmother's ring. As I step outside, a tickle itches my thigh. Something is running down my leg. Sobbing, I wipe myself with the inside of my dress before walking down the long sandy road, not knowing where I'm going.*

"Oh, Liv." Justus puts his lips to my temple.

My story's not over. "Mini was the madam of a brothel. She took me in to clean and sew. It was a good, safe place and she and the girls became my family. Weeks later, I was quite sick and Mini said I was with child. When the herbs didn't work to end the pregnancy, she took me to Missus La Belle."

It's still so raw, it's as if it happened yesterday.

*A coolness meets Mini and me as we enter the basement off Twenty-Third Street in the dark of night. The only light that shows is the glow from a pair of oil lamps and a few candles. I imagine even in the daytime it isn't much brighter than this. Missus La Belle sets to work quickly, boiling water and laying out instruments and gauze. The woman is lovely. Much too lovely for this dungeon. She's young and her moves are graceful. Mini trusts the woman with her girls, so I, too, shall trust her. I'm in too much pain to be fearful of what I see around me.*

*The woman speaks tenderly to me as she bustles around.* "*We'll get you feeling better in no time at all, sweetheart.*"

*Mini leads me to a small cot near one corner of the dimly lit room. Missus La Belle cleans between my legs. The rag is scalding hot.* "Mini, give her the wine, please."

*Mini urges me to drink the liquid. I've never tasted wine before. It's bitter and makes me grimace with each swallow.* "Take another," *Mini tells me.* "You must drink this down."

*Before I finish the jar, my head feels light and the muscles in my body are loosened.*

*I hear Missus La Belle's voice again.* "All right, honey, I need you to turn and put your feet on the chairs on either side of me. That's it. Now just relax." *Her tone is calming.* "Now I'm going to do a swipe."

*I never expected the affliction that comes and I scream out into the room. The torture radiates through my body. I don't care at this moment if I die. I just want the suffering to end.*

"Breathe," *says Mini in my ear. But I can't think to breathe, I can only think to scream as I twist the bedsheets in my fists.*

*Missus La Belle speaks softly and kindly to me.* "You're doing great, child. So brave."

*You'd think she was helping me spell my name with the way she speaks her praises over my cries. Her loving tone never wavers as she keeps scraping. Will it never end?*

*My cries echo throughout the room.* "I can't do this anymore!" *My body shakes and my breathing becomes labored.*

*Mini soothes my hair.* "It's all right, sugar, you can do this. It will all be over soon. I just need you to breathe now, you hear."

"Please stop. I can't," *I cry out again with little energy left in me.*

*Justus takes me by the chin.* "I wish I could take it all away, Liv." *He brings my head to his chest.* "God, I wish I could take it away." His chest rises and falls with heavy breaths.

"You still love me after all I've told you?" I ask, fear of his answer gripping me.

He slides to the floor, taking my face in his hands. "I can't imagine my life without you, Olivia Palmer." He brushes my tears away with his thumbs, searching my eyes. "I love you more than all the granules of sugar on all the earth. I will eat sugarless pie for the rest of my life for you."

His words make me chuckle.

"That's my Angel." He leans in and kisses my lips.

# 48

## Justus

Frank's planning a trip to Denver in a couple of days and I'm thinking of riding along, now that I know Olivia is safe from Wes McLain. She was inconsolable at the news of the deputy's death, but she's faring much better now that Wes has been taken back to Missouri to be hanged for his crime of killing a lawman.

I sit in my aunt's kitchen, watching Olivia as she and Rebecca take turns churning butter. I dream of burying my nose in her silky hair and trailing my mouth down her neck to her milky-white breasts.

Her laugh brings me back to reality and I smile. I need to officially make her mine, but the timing must be perfect. Nothing but the best for this amazing woman who has been through so much in her lifetime.

"Rebecca, I have an idea," Olivia says. "Why don't we place an ad in the newspaper asking for the whereabouts of your husband and daughters?"

Rebecca stops churning. "How could that be possible? We don't know where they are. How would we know which paper to put the ad in?" She continues churning. "I don't have money to pay for that."

"I'll pay for it," says Olivia.

"Me too," I offer.

Both women turn to look at me. "What?" I say. "I think it's a great idea. The first good idea I've heard from you since we met." I grin at Liv, pleased with myself for that tease.

Rebecca wags her head and returns to moving the churn dasher. "Don't pay no mind to him, Olivia."

"In all seriousness, ladies, I think it's a wonderful idea. What paper do you think we should put it in?" I look to Olivia.

Her voice is hesitant. "I don't know." She gives me the side-eye.

"Why are you looking at me that way?" I ask.

"Because she doesn't trust you." Hannah comes into the room with Clint behind her. "What did you do this time?" She puts her hands on her hips.

"Olivia thinks we should put an ad in the paper to find Rebecca's family, and I agree."

Hannah throws her hands up the way her mother does. "Olivia, that's a splendid idea. Why hadn't any of us thought of that before?"

"Because apparently, she's the brains in this house." I give Hannah a grin.

She turns to her husband. "Sweetheart, will you find something for my dear cousin to do?"

"All right, all right. I can take a hint. Come on, Clint. Let's go where we're wanted."

Clint chuckles. "You mean outside, playing with the children?"

Days later, before leaving for Denver, I bring Liv money and the addresses of a few newspapers that might be a good place to start. I had inquired with the town printer for suggestions. Olivia insists on paying for half and giving me any remaining monies, then reassures me she'll send out the mail the next day. I'm not the least bit worried.

I kiss her and hold her in my arms for a long moment. "I'll miss you, Angel."

She lays her head against my chest and inhales. "Don't be gone too long. I don't know if I can bear to be without your hugs."

"I'll have you back in my arms before you know it." Right here in my arms is where she belongs.

I caress her lips once more with mine. "Hurry back," she whispers.

There's an apprehension that nags at me as I pull away from the house.

# 49

## Livvie

A knock sounds from the front door.
"Miss Olivia, there's a lady here to see you," says Thomas.

I glimpse from Rebecca to Miss Bea, who shrugs. The loveliest young woman with nut-brown trestles flowing from under her hat stands on the porch.

"Olivia Palmer?" She clears her throat.

"Yes? How can I help you?" There's a sudden emptiness in the pit of my stomach.

The woman's eyes are pleading. "May I come in?"

"Certainly." I open the door wide to make way for her. "Can I take your coat and hat?"

"I don't believe I'll keep you." She scans the room.

I hold my breath. She's here to deliver bad news. I inhale, bracing myself for what's to come.

The woman studies me. "You're beautiful." She drops her

gaze to her gloved hands.

I tilt my head. "I don't believe you've told me your name."

"Adelyn McDaniels." She glances around once more.

"McDaniels? You're Asa's sister?" She looks nothing like Asa, I'll admit.

Tears well in the woman's eyes. "No." She draws in a deep breath, then stands tall and firm, as if trying to appear confident. "I came to ask you to stay away from my husband."

I gasp. Asa's married! How could I have been so blind? I'd been the other woman. Queasiness flows from my stomach to my throat and I cover my mouth.

The woman goes on. "We're to have a child." She runs her hands over her round middle that I hadn't noticed until now. "Due any time. I will pay you any amount if you'll agree to stop…" She shakes her head, as if trying to free terrible thoughts from her mind. "Stop doing whatever it is you do with my husband." Her lips form into a thin line.

I don't know where to begin. "How did you find me?"

She straightens once more. "My husband wrote about you in his diary. I never read it before. I trust…trusted him completely, but mistakenly knocked it off his desk and it opened to a page describing his feeling for you." A tear slides down her face and she quickly wipes it away, as if she doesn't want me to see it.

The thought of Asa writing about me in his diary makes my skin crawl.

"My family has a way of learning information, and I used my connections to find you. I've come a long way to face you, Miss Palmer."

I close my eyes and lay my hand over my stomach to calm my nerves.

Adelyn continues, "You must leave my husband alone. Can't you see he has a family?" The tears are streaming now. "As I said, I can pay you any amount."

*Stay calm, Livvie.* I'm unsure if I should tell this woman her husband tried to force himself on me. That he abused me. Surely, she has a right to know. It's possible he's done the same to her.

"I can assure you, I had no idea he was married, and if I had, I would not have courted or continued to court him. I can also assure you that nothing beyond kissing or hand-holding took place between us." The pendulum in Miss Bea's tall clock ticktocks. "Not that it makes things any better." A tingling sweeps up my neck and over my face.

Miss Bea comes from the sitting room and puts an arm around my waist. "I know this is none of my business, dear, but I must interject here." She faces Adelyn McDaniels. "Missus McDaniels, this must be so difficult for you. I can't imagine being in your shoes at this moment. You seem like such a lovely young lady who deserves so much better than what your husband is providing you."

"Please do not speak of my husband that way. You have no right." Her tone is firm.

Miss Bea continues, "I'm afraid I must. And yes, I do. You need to know the whole truth." Miss Bea folds her hands in front of her. "Are you aware that your husband is wanted by the law?"

Adelyn's eyes widen. "The law? Whatever for?"

Miss Bea rubs my back. "For hurting our Olivia."

"What do you mean?" Her eyes move from Miss Bea to me.

"I think you should have a seat," says Miss Bea.

"I think I will stand." She's defiant.

"He tried to violate our Olivia. He abused her badly in the process. Thank the good Lord she was able to escape. When she did, he fled, and now the law is looking for him."

"This can't be. He wouldn't hurt a soul." The girl wrings her hands.

Miss Bea peers at her. "Wouldn't he?"

Adelyn holds out her arms, as if feeling for something to grab onto. "I think I'm going to be sick."

"Come, dear." Miss Bea takes her by the arm and guides her into the sitting room. "Rebecca, will you get Missus McDaniels a glass of water, please?"

Once the woman appears calm, she speaks again. "I told Asa I was going to visit my sister in Denver. He suspects nothing." She gazes down at her water. "My husband doesn't love me. I've known it from the beginning. We both pretend it's not true, but it is. As much as I've longed for his heart, I always knew it'd never be mine."

"Why did you marry him?" I ask.

"I never wanted to admit it to myself, but the truth is, he married me for my family's money—I married him for love. My father is an influential man in the Colorado banking industry." Her eyes are sad. "I'm sorry he hurt you. I'm so ashamed," she says to me before bowing her head and crying.

Rebecca hands her a handkerchief. "There's nothing for you to be ashamed of."

"That's right," says Miss Bea. "You didn't do anything wrong. Don't blame yourself, dear."

Adelyn pounds a fist into her lap, spilling water on her skirts. "I never should have wed him. My cousin, in not so many words, warned me about marrying him. I knew what she was saying, but I acted as though I didn't. I pretended to believe he loved me. It's all I ever wanted, for him to love me. When I discovered I was expecting, I thought his heart would change, but it's only caused him to grow more distant," she sobs.

I know all too clearly how this poor girl feels, but I'm at a loss as to what to say to her. Then she lifts her head and wipes her face. "I wish to help." Her focus is on me. "I can help the authorities apprehend him."

My mouth falls open. His own wife.

"He deserves to be punished for his crime. Besides, I do not wish him to teach this to our child. I do not wish for my child to grow to be an abuser or a, a…" She closes her eyes. "Something worse."

Rebecca speaks up, "I'll send Thomas for the sheriff if you wish."

Over the next couple of hours, we have a pleasant visit with Adelyn McDaniels. The sheriff comes briefly, so the details of how to seize this evil man can be worked out.

Before walking out the door, Adelyn stops and turns. "I just thought of something. I'm missing a necklace. It's not worth much, but it's priceless to me because it was my mother's. She's gone now. Anyway, I thought one of my staff had stolen it, but now I wonder if it was Asa. He didn't give you a necklace, perchance?"

"I'll be right back." I run up to my room, take the necklace from my bureau, and shuffle back down. "Is this it?"

Adelyn's eyes water as she holds the pendant. "I thought I'd never see this again."

"Oh, Adelyn, I'm happy to return it to the rightful owner." I place a hand on the girl's arm.

"Thank you, Olivia, for your kindness and understanding."

"Thank you, Adelyn, and please write when the little one is born."

Miss Bea wraps the young woman in a hug. "Oh, do come back and visit when you can."

She smiles. "I'll be sure to do that, now that I know I have friends here."

Miss Bea closes the door behind the young woman and claps her hands together. "Wasn't that something?"

"It sure was," seconds Rebecca. "How are you feeling about all of this, Olivia?"

"I have a mix of emotions, I suppose. I'm thankful Asa will finally be caught, but my heart aches for his wife. She is such a lovely girl and to have a child with that man…" I put my palm to my heart.

Miss Bea places a hand on my arm. "Something tells me she will be quite all right. Between her beauty, sweet disposition, and her family's money, she'll fare just fine, in time." She nods, as if to say *mark my words*.

But will she? This just seems to be a reminder that men cannot be trusted.

# 50
## Livvie

Lying in bed, I can't get Adelyn McDaniels's visit out of my mind. Oh, how I do hope she'll find her own Justus someday. Thinking of that sweet man brings a smile to my face. I'm in love with him, something I couldn't say about Roy or Asa. Did I love Roy? Yes. But I always knew I wasn't *in love* with him.

Justus is different. I can't imagine him laying a hand on me or calling me awful names. Snuggling into my pillow, visions of his tender kisses on my lips play in my mind, and I fall asleep with ease.

---

The next morning, I peer out the window for what seems like the hundredth time. Justus left for Denver over a week ago, and I long for his return.

"Dear me, you're going to wear the floorboards down if you keep pacing." Miss Bea's voice sends a flush to my cheeks.

I'm acting like a child who can't wait for Christmas morning. "Oh, Miss Bea, I worry about Justus. What if there's been a snowstorm in Denver?" I collapse onto the sofa. At least I don't have to concern myself with him frequenting any brothels.

I remember a time when Roy, Wes, and me sat at the dinner table.

*Wes teases Roy about the whore he was with the night before. Roy pushes his food around his plate; obviously he wants Wes to shut up.*

*I slam my napkin on the table. Chair legs screech across the plank floors. Wes howls with delight, and I stomp off to my bedroom and cry myself to sleep.*

*I wake to Roy pulling at my skirts. I tug them back down.*

*"Come on, Livvie. You can't expect a man to be away from his woman and not get any pleasure, can you?" He pulls at my skirts again.*

*This time I let him do his business. This is my lot in life, after all.*

*When he's finished, he gets out of bed. "You better go get the kitchen cleaned up now," he says, buttoning his pants.*

"He's a grown man, dear." Miss Bea's words bring my thoughts back to Justus. "He's also a trained soldier. He knows how to take care of himself."

"Yes, I know. But I do miss him so." With my elbows on my knees, I plop my chin onto my hands. I do miss him. I long to wrap my arms around his body and let him hold me. I feel safe there, in his arms.

"Ahh, and there lies the truth." Miss Bea smiles.

I grin.

"I'm sure he misses you just as much, dear, and he'll be back as soon as he is able. Such is the life of a rancher."

"I wish it weren't a Saturday. I'd go to work to keep my mind off him." I peer out the window once more. The panes are frosty and a blanket of white covers everything. At least I'm inside, where it's warm. God willing, Justus is warm wherever he is.

"Why don't you go pay Lenny a visit?"

"I've never visited outside of work. I'd hate to intrude." Perhaps that isn't such a bad idea, though. What does Lenny do outside of shop hours? Probably more sewing.

"I'm sure it's no intrusion. Take her some of the cookies Rebecca and Thomas made last night. I bet she'll welcome the visit. She's such a sweet young lady, that Lenny Johnson. Yes, she is."

Lenny could be feeling boredom today, too, I suppose. "All right. I do need something to keep my mind off that nephew of yours." I inspect my nails. "And I could use the fresh air."

Miss Bea chuckles and returns to her reading of *Little Women*.

Once outside, I find the air to be warmer than it appears from indoors. Thomas plays with other children in front of the house. Snowballs are flying and a dog leaps around, as if he's in on the game, too.

The sight makes me chuckle. Those children have no idea how good their life is, frolicking in the snow, without a care in the world. Laughing, yelling, running, and jumping is all they must do. If only my childhood could have been that simple. An ache pains my heart at the knowledge I'll never see my own children playing blissfully in the fluffy white snowflakes like this. I'll never know the joy of raising little ones.

Within moments, I knock on Lenny's shop door. Thank God

for Lenny. This visit will take my mind off everything. It'll take my mind off Justus, my barrenness, and my past.

No answer.

I knock again. Perhaps she's not home.

A woman's laughter comes from the alley that runs along the side of the building. It grows louder as it draws nearer. Lenny. Her coat hangs open, revealing a rather skimpy dress, and she's on the arm of a man I've never seen before. He's clean-cut, possibly in his thirties. His coat is long, and I get a flash of a pistol on his hip.

"Olivia." Lenny looks like a child caught with their hand in the cookie jar. The rouge on her face is overly done. She unlocks the door. "What are you doing here on a Saturday?"

"I thought I'd come for a visit." I eye the man who walks past Lenny and into the shop, as though he's familiar with the place.

He smacks her behind. "Come on, darlin'. I ain't payin' you to stand around chatterin'."

Lenny wrings her hands as she peers over her shoulder. "I'll be right there, sugar."

"I'm so sorry, Lenny. I'll see you Monday." I turn, nearly running away.

Lenny's a harlot. How could I, of all people, not have known? What will I say to her on Monday? A pain grips my chest.

So many questions whirl in my mind as I clutch the cloth-wrapped platter of cookies tighter. The damn cookies! Now at a near run, tears sting my eyes. Nothing is ever as it seems. Everyone and everything, it's all lies. Why hasn't Lenny ever told me? I wouldn't have judged her.

I scurry down the snowy street, clutching the plate of cookies.

"Excuse me, miss. Can I offer you a ride?" A man's voice comes from somewhere. I don't care. Can't he see I'm upset? Of course, he can't, he's a man. He'll get no attention from me.

"Olivia. Are you all right? Olivia."

It's Justus.

I pivot. Tears run down my cheeks. I must look a sight, standing here crying while holding the plate of confections.

He steps from the sleigh and takes me in his arms, smooshing the stoneware between us.

"What's wrong, my angel?"

My knees grow weak every time he calls me that. He said the first time he saw me, he could have sworn he was looking at an angelic being.

"Oh, Justus, it's so silly." I sniffle.

"It can't be too silly if you're crying over it." He steps back and lifts my chin, forcing me to look up at him.

How I've missed those brown eyes. I ache to kiss his whiskered face. A smile plays on my lips.

"Oh now, there's my girl." He kisses my nose. "Come on, let's go for a ride."

In the sleigh, I lay my head against his arm. I can breathe again. Justus feels like home. I've always wondered what home felt like, but now I know. It's a feeling you can't really explain, it just is. I sigh. He's too good to be true.

# 51
## Adelyn

I leave Asa's office after reminding him our guest will be arriving any moment. Dietrich's voice carries from the foyer, which tells me they've come early. Thank goodness. I'm anxious to get this over with and get that man out of my house. He has no idea what I've arranged for him today. I close my eyes and fill my chest with air. I'm doing this for myself, but more importantly, I'm doing this for my child.

"I don't know if we should sit on this furniture. It doesn't look as if this room gets touched at all," one detective says to the other, not knowing I'm right behind them. They're both tall men, but one has a rather large mustache that covers his entire mouth.

"It rarely gets used. But please, do have a seat." I motion for them to sit, however, they remain standing until I take my chair.

They appear rather apprehensive in my presence, fidgeting with their suit coats and glancing about. Hoping to put them at ease, I lean forward and whisper, "It will bring me great pleasure to watch this for myself. And…" I pause, looking out of the corner of my eye. "It will bring me closure, I believe."

"You're a strong woman, Missus McDaniels," the man with the mustache voices.

"She is, indeed," says Asa as he enters the room with a smile, until he notices the badges displayed on the men's coats. He glances from them to me, then clears his throat and his smile reappears, albeit quite shaky.

"You look as though you've been caught doing something wrong, Asa." I chuckle.

"I don't know what you mean." He fusses with his tie and glances at me. I produce a smile that's as sweet as I can muster for him.

The mustached man stands. "I'm Detective Roberts and this is Detective Comstock."

Detective Comstock stands beside Roberts with his arms at his sides, his shiny pistol resting on his hip, prepared for any fight Asa may be ready to bring. "We're here to arrest you for the battery and attempted rape of Miss Olivia Palmer."

Asa laughs. "Is this some kind of joke?"

I come to my feet. "It's no joke, Asa. I know what you've been up to. I met with Miss Palmer myself." I pull my mother's pendant up from the collar of my dress.

His mouth goes slack.

I continue, "And if you ever come around me or our child, you *will* live to regret it." My words are stern and I feel as though I'm standing a foot taller.

Detective Roberts grabs Asa by the arm and escorts him out of the house without incident.

Detective Comstock turns to me before I close the door behind them. "Good day, Missus McDaniels."

"Miss Chastain." I continue to stare out the doorway at Asa being ushered onto a wagon. "I'm going back to my family name, and I filed for divorce yesterday." I turn to the man. "Thank you, sir, for taking out the trash."

Closing the door behind the detective, I lean against it, cradling my swollen belly. "Just as soon as you arrive, my little one, we're going to make a change."

## 52

## Livvie

I nervously arrive at Lenny's on Monday morning to find her with her feet propped up by the stove, drinking coffee.

"Morning," she says with a grin. "I thought I'd scared you off."

I pour myself some of the dark liquid. Lenny makes it stronger than any man I know. "Surprised, yes. Scared, no. What you do outside of tending the shop is none of my business."

I feel her eyes on me as I pull up a chair to warm myself from the walk over. "I think I'm falling for one of them, Olivia." Her face is beaming.

"The man you were with on Saturday?"

"No, not him." She rolls her eyes. "His name's Jesse—the one I'm falling for—and he's different from the others. At first it was just business, but now…" I see the magic dancing in her eyes as she searches for the right words.

"Why didn't you ever tell me, Lenny?"

"I don't need to be judged, Olivia."

"Just because I live with the Petersons doesn't mean I believe as they do. I lived at a brothel once."

Lenny sits upright in shock. "You were a prostitute?"

"No, I wasn't a prostitute. The madam, Mini, took me in when my mother put me out. I lived there until I moved in with Roy. Those girls were my family."

"I never would have guessed," says Lenny, wagging her head in disbelief.

"That's because we don't talk about our past," I reminded her. "But tell me about this man." I, too, prop my feet up, preparing myself for the story.

"Well," she says, batting her eyes at me. "He has sandy-blonde curls." She bites her bottom lip. "And green eyes." Her countenance is serious now. "He doesn't make me feel like a whore, Olivia. He makes me feel like I'm worth loving and treasuring." She takes a sip of her coffee and continues. "He's gentle and takes his time. And he always kisses me real tender-like before he leaves."

"Where's he from?" I'm happy for her, but my heart also breaks for her because I know the reality of these girls falling for men they can never have.

"I don't know." She lowers her eyes. "He's not from Laurel Springs, anyhow."

"Is he married?" My heart's sad for the woman who may be at home waiting on a man who's taking up another's bed while away.

"I don't wanna know." Grief's written on her face. "I thought

I was stronger than this. I thought I could keep it to business, but he's got my head spinning." She twirls her finger in the air. "Like when I was a little girl and I'd sit on the tree swing and wind it up, then let go. I don't know what I'm going to do, Olivia. When I'm with the others, I feel like I'm being unfaithful."

"You have to talk to him, Len." I sit on the edge of my seat and lean in toward her. "You must tell him how you feel. You can't continue to let your heart be pulled around. It needs a solid direction."

She stares into her mug and nods her head.

As I walk home from Lenny's to make myself lunch, I think of my employer who's become more like a friend to me. I sure hope she can find her true love, as I have. I wish for every girl to know love to its core. What a beautiful thing it's turned out to be. The muscles in my cheeks pull upward as I walk with a big happy grin on my face.

The music rolls out from the front doors of the saloon and it's obvious the men inside are having a merry time. I shake my head. The thought. Spending your time at a saloon at eleven o'clock in the morning on a weekday. Then I see him. Justus comes out the doors, smiling with the arms of a whore wrapped around his neck.

My stomach drops and lurches as heat and sweat cover my body in an instant. My limbs shake uncontrollably. Thank goodness, I'm near the alleyway where I can take refuge from the sight of him with another woman. It's true. Everything I've feared is true. I wrap my arms around my waist and slide to the ground, too sick and stunned to cry. Imaginary fingers grip my throat, slowly cutting off my ability to breathe. I'd hoped he was different. He isn't. He's the same as all the rest. I swallow back the vomit that threatens to come. Never have I felt so alone and torn in two as I do in this moment.

---

I slam dishes around Miss Bea's kitchen in my attempt at making myself a sandwich. He's completely pulled the wool over my eyes. How could I be so stupid once again? It's best I just be done with men all together. Mother may have been content living with unfaithful men, but I can't. I'd rather be all alone.

"Easy there. You're going to break something." Justus comes over and puts a hand on my arm as if to calm me. His efforts further enrage me.

"I don't need you telling me what or how to do anything." I can't look at the despicable man. I can't risk falling into his arms and forgiving him.

He steps away. "What did I do?"

"You know exactly what you've done." I stop and dare to look at him, and my chest heaves.

"I don't understand."

"You don't understand. Of course, you don't. Men don't understand." I wave a knife around as I rant. "You just go around doing whatever you please, not caring about anyone else, and *you* don't understand." I turn from him and continue to make my sandwich. Since I no longer have an appetite, I don't even want it; I just need something to do. Perhaps chopping wood would have been a better idea.

He crosses his arms. "What have I done that's got you so riled?"

"You really don't know? Or you don't care?" I cackle. "In case no one's ever told you, Justus, you can't have it both ways."

"What the hell, Liv? I don't know where this is coming from."

"So you say." I turn back to him. "I saw you, Justus. I saw you strolling out of the saloon with a wide smile on your face and a whore rubbing her body all over you and her arms draped around your neck." I flail my arms wildly. "It's over." I can't be with someone I can't trust. I just can't. He's pulled out my heart and stomped all over it.

"You've decided this. Without even talking with me. Without asking why I was at the saloon."

"My decision has been made. Is there another way you need me to say it? Looking at you makes my stomach turn." Tears cloud my eyes. I want to scream. I want to beat at his chest until every ounce of hurt is gone.

He bobs his head. "What can I do? How can I help you to trust me? I'm not Asa. I'm not Roy. I'm not Wes. I'm not your goddamn stepfather. Jesus, Liv. I don't deserve this. I haven't done anything to give you reason to distrust me. What you saw wasn't what you think." He paces the kitchen. "I would never lay a hand on you except out of love and I sure as hell wouldn't be unfaithful to you, married or not. Don't hold other men's sins against me."

I feel pained. Is it possible I only saw what I wanted to prove to myself—that I can't trust him? But what if what I saw was real, and he's playing me like a deck of cards? I've made up my mind.

He won't pull me back in just to hurt me again. I need to take the advice I gave to Lenny earlier today. I must stop allowing my heart to be pulled around and give it a solid direction.

"You know what, Olivia, I shouldn't have to explain myself to you. But because I know it didn't look right, I will. I was there looking for a man by the name of Black Bird. I was told that's where I could find him. His woman makes beautiful jewelry and I wanted her to make something special for you." He motions toward me. "And I'm sure you know how those women at the saloon can be, trying to make a dollar. But you're right, you deserve better than me. I'm just a no-good rancher who isn't right in the head because I saw too much in the war. I used to drink too much to forget my troubles. I still have nightmares about it all and wake in the dark as wet as a Ute chief in his sweat lodge."

I stare at the floor, willing the contents of my stomach to stay where they are.

"I hope you find a great man someday, Olivia." His boots clomp out of the kitchen, down the hall, and out the front door.

My head is light and my limbs wobbly as I reach for a chair. Why? Why is this happening? I put my head in my hands and sob. What have I done?

# 53

## Livvie

*(Three weeks later) Sutton's Creek, Colorado Territory*

I stop scrubbing long enough to wipe the sweat from my brow. Despite the frigid December temperature outside, the little cabin is steaming inside. The pay is decent, but the work is hard. My knuckles bleed and my hands ache as I continue to scrub the wash over the board.

"When you're done with that, let's take a break," says Ginny.

When I'd arrived in Sutton's Creek, Ginny overheard me inquiring about a job and offered me a laundress position.

"I'll pay you in room and board. I live just over the ridge there on the outskirts of the mining camp. It's small and not fancy in the least, but it's cozy enough. And I'll give you a tenth of what the men pay me."

Many people had left the small mining camp when they

realized there wasn't enough gold to go around as they had dreamed. Although there are still a good many who aren't ready to give up.

Ginny confessed later she didn't need help, exactly. She was lonely and I appeared as though I could use a friend myself.

I can see beyond her weathered skin there is a lovely girl. Her blonde hair hangs in a long thick braid down her back. She came from New York with her husband when they were just newlyweds.

"Oh, my mother and father weren't keen on us leaving, but once we were married,. there wasn't much they could say or do." Ginny stares off in the distance with a smile on her face. "My Jake, he was adventurous. Even as kids, he got more whippings than any other child I knew." She laughs. "One time he burned his eyebrows and bangs clean off playing with fire. His pa thought going to school looking like a fool was punishment enough, so he didn't tan his hide that time."

Ginny and Jake were part of a wagon train to come out west. She discovered she was pregnant on the journey, but the harsh realities of food being scarce and inclement weather resulted in her losing the baby.

"It fit in the palm of my hand, Livvie. We couldn't tell if it was a boy or a girl, but it had eyes and the start of limbs with little buds for hands and feet." A tear streams down her face. "I put a piece of gingham inside a jewelry box, and we laid our baby on top. Jake buried it as far down as he could under a tree. He made a cross from two sticks and stuck it in the ground. I sang a lullaby, then we had to go because the wagon train was moving on, with or without us."

"Oh, Ginny." I hug her.

Months after Ginny and Jake made it to Colorado, a gold claim dispute left her a widow. Now she's all alone. I know the feeling.

"*Are you sure? I don't want to impose,*" *I say when Ginny offers for me to stay with her.*

"*I don't have anyone here. No friends. No family. I sleep with my gun to keep the drunk prospectors away, and my dog isn't much of a protector.*" *She smiles.* "*I welcome a roommate.*"

The cabin is so small that we must share a bed, but at least we're warm and have food to eat.

"So, tell me your story," probes Ginny. We both sit on the bed with our backs against the rough log wall. Ginny's beagle Buck lays with his head in her lap.

I tell her most everything. I feel drawn to her, as though we've known one another forever. It feels good to have a friend here. She's a kindred spirit.

"It sounds as if Justus loves you very much," says Ginny. "You know, not all men are cheaters and wife beaters. My Jake wasn't. You should give him another chance."

"I don't think he'd take me back if I returned. Not even with puppy dog eyes and my tail between my legs. I behaved shamefully, Ginny, and I miss him so." I shrug. "I just can't seem to make the right choices in life."

"I believe you're thinking with your head, rather than your heart," she says. "You keep thinking about all the bad things your mother said to you, and Roy and Wes, instead of listening to what you know in your heart to be true." She lays her hand on my leg. "You're a survivor. You're strong. I haven't known you but a couple of weeks, but I can already tell you're caring by the way I see you interact with Old Man Marshall and Buck here." She slides her hand over the dog's head. "And you haven't given me any reason to believe I can't trust you."

We both turn our heads to look at one another. "Have faith in yourself and forget about them," she says.

"Thank you for that, Ginny." I manage a closed-lip smile.

"All right, well, we better heat up more water so we can get the rest of this washing done."

As we work, I think about what Ginny said, listening to my heart. My heart does long for Justus and my life back in Laurel Springs. I must find a way to get back.

# 54

## Justus

I bring Beau to a halt at the sight of Rebecca walking out of the mercantile. "Hello, Rebecca," I holler before pulling the horse close to the boarded sidewalk.

"Justus, it's good to see you. I haven't seen you in a few weeks. How are you holding up?" She tilts her head up at me.

I lean on my saddle. "I don't know, Rebecca. I just can't bear to see Olivia. I think it's best I stay away."

"Oh, you haven't heard, then."

"Heard what?"

"She left town."

My stomach drops. I haven't wanted to see her because the thought pains me, but there is always hope that I'll get just a glimpse. I hang my head. "I hadn't heard." I wonder why Mary hadn't told me. Perhaps she doesn't know or thought I knew, and I did make it clear I didn't want to talk about Olivia. It just hurts too much.

"We all miss her," says Rebecca "She's a right sweet girl. I don't know where she was going, but she promised to write when she got settled. I'm not sure she even knew herself where she was headed." Rebecca leans in. "You both are downright hardheaded."

I nod. "She deserves better, Rebecca."

"Does she? I don't know she'll find anyone who loves her the way you do. I don't know she'll find anyone as gentle and kind. I fear she'll just keep repeatin' what she's known her whole life."

"Well, I can't make her trust me."

"You need to learn to trust yourself first." She gives Beau a pat. "I hope it doesn't take another three weeks to see you again, Justus." She smiles and walks away.

Rebecca sounds so much like Silas. Possibly there is something to what they're telling me. But what can I do now? Olivia's probably done gone back to Missouri.

## 55

### Justus

I ride to Doc and Miss Bea's for dinner now that I know Olivia won't be there. At least I won't have to see her, knowing I can't have her. Of course, if she were there, I'd be eating at home tonight. My heart's heavy and sorrowful. It's best to shove that away because I'll never see her again. She wasn't for me. A beautiful woman like her, she's likely already found someone else. Someone she can trust…or someone she can't. What if Rebecca's right and Olivia repeats what she's known her whole life and finds herself another Roy or Asa? My jaw clenches at the image of her with another man. I must push that thought away, too. I can't let it get the best of me. If she is with another man, my wish is that he treats her right.

I've been working on forgiving myself for my own past. When I recall how bad I've been and how so much is my fault, I remind myself I'm not that man anymore. I'm a good man. I work hard, have a successful ranch, I don't drink whiskey often, and I would never lay a harmful hand on a woman. Never have I laid a harmful hand on any woman. And I have no intention on having sex with a woman until I find the right one. I thought Olivia was the one. Since she's no longer here, it's clear she isn't. Of course, I could have fought for her. I should have fought for her. Part of me believed I was unworthy of her love and it was all right for me to walk away, letting her go, if that's what she wanted. I pick my chin up, set on enjoying dinner, despite my aching heart.

Since Olivia arrived here five months ago, I'm not accustomed to going to my aunt and uncle's and not seeing her. I miss her smile, her laugh, those deep blue eyes, and golden locks. They haunt me. Her hair always smelled of rose and sage.

"Everything all right, brother?" Clint hands me a cup of coffee.

I nod. No need to bother anyone else with my broken heart. "Just lost in thought, that's all. How's business going at the stables?"

"Better than ever. Thanks for asking. As the town grows, business gets better, you know what I mean?" He rubs his fingers together, indicating money is coming in.

I'm happy for him.

"Are you two talking business over here?" Hannah messages her bulging belly. "You know that's blasphemy on a Sunday." She raises an eyebrow.

I motion with my mug toward her. "Are you planning to be pregnant forever?"

Clint holds up his cup. "Don't get her started, Justus."

Hannah supports her back with both hands. "This child

is already disobeying me. I told him last week he was being plain rude hiding in there. It's time for him to come out and be sociable."

We all get a good laugh out of that.

"I'll leave you two boys alone so you can go back to talking boring business." She reaches up on her toes and places a kiss on my cheek. I bend to meet her kiss. She gives my arm a squeeze. "Love you, cousin," she says, wobbling away.

"Have you heard from Olivia?" asks Clint.

I shake my head as I watch the ladies set the table. "She made it clear she doesn't want anything to do with me. I don't expect to ever hear from her again."

"According to Hannah, she seems to be doing well. She got a job laundering and she made a friend, whom she's living with."

My breath catches in my chest. I can't help but wonder if this friend is a man. I swallow. I can't think about that.

That night, I lay in bed tossing and turning. Sleep won't find me, no matter how hard I try. Over and over, I push images of Oliva naked with another lover from my mind. Then my thoughts go to her lying beside me, smiling at me, eyes twinkling as I caress her bare body. I can still taste her lips and smell her skin.

I should have tried harder. I should never have let her leave. But how? How could I have stopped her? How could I have made her see? I couldn't. I just need time. All wounds heal in time.

# 56
## Livvie

I lay in bed, staring at the ceiling, with Ginny sound asleep beside me. There's been a change in my life, and I now have a secret. I don't know what to do with it. I can't bear to reveal it to the family…or to Justus. A part of me is happy about it but another part of me is so ashamed. All I can hear in my head are Mother's words. *"You little whore."*

I'm thankful for Ginny and my heart aches at all she's been through. How she's made it on her own for the last three years, I'll never know. I can't imagine living out here all alone.

"Do you ever plan to go back home?" I ask her.

"If I ever do, I'll let you know," she says. "For one, Jake's here, and two, I have too much pride."

"Pride?" I can't see her being the least bit prideful.

"I don't want to go back and have my folks say they knew I should never have left. I'll hear all about it for the rest of my life." She stops her scrubbing and glances around. "I'm doing all right here. I'm a woman *with her own business."*

I survey our pails of dirty water, scrub boards, and heaps of laundry. It isn't glamorous, but yes, it is Ginny's business.

I know I need Ginny. Does Ginny truly need me? Probably not. The girl is strong on the inside. But so am I. We're made of something not everyone has—grit. Grit is what always gets us through.

What will become of my life, I don't know. I'll just have to take it day by day. The same way Ginny has gotten along over the last few years on her own out here in the Wild West, with its death and sickness and gunslingers.

A tear slides down my face and runs into my hair. I wipe it with the sleeve of my nightgown. Not wanting to wake Ginny with my crying, I swallow around the lump in my throat, willing the tears to stay put.

I shouldn't have left. I should have given him a chance. I should have believed him. Perhaps he wasn't unfaithful. But if he was having jewelry made for me, then why was he smiling when the saloon girl hung on him? Was he truly having something made for me or was it a lie to appease me? I can't seem to rein in my many thoughts.

Images of him kissing and touching another woman the way he kissed and touched me run through my mind. Is another woman running her hands over his muscular frame now? If she is, it's all my fault. I can't stomach the image.

No, I can't think of him. I close my eyes tight and turn on my side. Ginny and I will be spinsters, not answering to any man.

I write to Miss Bea, a letter to share with Rebecca and Hannah.

How I miss them, but I must admit, that ache is lessening each day I spend here in the little mining camp. And Ginny has such a good attitude and is so full of life, always giggling. She sees beauty in everything and finds humor in the simplest things. A mama bird feeding her babies, a mouse eating a crumb, Old Man Marshall staggering around with his bottle of whiskey.

Most of the men are protective of Ginny and me, as if we're the little sisters or daughters they've left behind to seek riches. The newcomers are the ones we need to be concerned about. They're the reason Ginny sleeps with her gun propped up beside the bed.

The men out here are hungry for a woman. I know some are good men who are lonely, but some only want to use our bodies for their pleasure. I shudder at the thought.

I haven't written in my letters the details of my laundress job. That it's in a small one-room cabin where Ginny and I also sleep and eat, or that we are two of the few women here. I don't tell of the roof leaking every time the snow melts or of the cracks in the chinking. I don't want to worry them, and I know Ginny has been doing the best she can. She's proud of everything she has because it's hers. None of it belongs to any man, and no man can tell her what to do with it.

---

An unexpected letter comes, a letter from Justus. My hands shake as I open it.

"What does it say?" asks Ginny. She's practically jumping

up and down.

    I read it to myself.

    *Dear Olivia,*

    *I don't know if I should be writing, but here I am. And please don't blame my family for giving me your address. I saw your letter on my aunt's desk and wrote it down.*

    *It makes me happy to learn that you're still in Colorado. I feared you'd gone back to Missouri.*

    *Anyway, I'm sorry I didn't try harder. I'm sorry I walked out of the kitchen that day. I should have taken you into my arms.*

    *Is it too much to ask for you to forgive me and come back?*

    *Justus*

    I hand it to Ginny.

    "Are you going to write him back?" she asks.

    I can't. "No." I'm not ready.

    Another letter comes a week later.

    *Dear Olivia,*

    *I'd hoped you'd write back. I guess I'm an ass for thinking that way. If you've found someone new, please tell me and I'll never write again.*

    *Justus*

    The letters keep coming every week, short and sad. I anticipate them but can't bring myself to respond.

    *Dear Olivia,*

    *I miss you so much, Angel.*

    I close my eyes and clutch the letter to my chest before

reading on.

*I think about you all the damn time – when I wake in the morning, when I eat, when I work. Hell, I can't even sleep, but for the moments I do, I dream about you. My heart feels as if it's been torn in two. What do I have to do to make you see that I love you and I'd never do anything to hurt you?*

*Justus*

"When are you going to tell him?" Ginny asks.

I wipe away a tear. "I can't."

"You can't or you won't? He has a right to know, Livvie."

"Please don't." I bow my head and sob into my hands. Ginny wraps her arms around me, and I sink into her embrace.

Two weeks pass before another letter comes.

*Dear Olivia,*

*I can't live this way anymore, wondering every day if there's a letter in the mail from you or if you'll come riding up the drive.*

*I won't be writing anymore, but I won't stop holding a special place in my heart for you, either. You'll always be my first love, but it's time for me to move on now.*

*Justus*

# 57

## Livvie

---

Miss Bea had sent a letter inviting me for Christmas, but Ginny and I spent it in a camp tent surrounded by men of every creed and color and fine music. It was a great time, and we didn't have to lift a finger, as the men cooked and washed the dishes. I'm not ready to face Justus, or the rest of the family, for that matter.

Another letter comes, inviting me to come for my birthday.

"Why don't you go?" Ginny asks. "It's time, don't you think?"

"I can't."

Ginny scrubs at a pair of socks. "I don't like it."

"No one said you had to." I sit on the floor, swooshing a shirt in a tub of water.

Ginny scrubs harder. "It's going to be another day of food, banjos, and fiddles for you, then."

"I love food, banjos, and fiddles. And I especially love not having to cook or clean." I smile, daring her to give another poor reason I should go back to Laurel Springs. "And most of all, I love you."

She blows a suds bubble at me, which flies through the air and lands softly on the wood floor. "I love you, too," she giggles.

Just as we figured, the men at camp invite us for a birthday dinner. They love any reason to celebrate and I'm sure Ginny had a hand in it. Warmth and the aroma of food fills the tent. We feast on a meal of biscuits, beans, salt pork, squirrel, rabbit, dried raspberry pie, and coffee. I don't believe I've ever ate so well or received so much attention on a birthday. Afterward, the men put on a show outside where the snow is packed down by the trampling of boots and the sun warms our faces. Men from far and wide play music with their instruments as they pass around bottles of whiskey.

"No, thank you," I say with a smile that probably looks more like a grimace. Ginny, however, takes a swig with the rest of them. After several drinks, she is whooping and dancing in circles to the tune of "When Johnny Comes Marching Home."

*When Johnny comes marching home again, Hurrah, hurrah!*
*We'll give him a hearty welcome then, Hurrah, hurrah!*
*The men will cheer, the boys will shout,*
*The ladies, they will all turn out,*
*And we'll all feel gay when Johnny comes marching home.*

Ginny makes her way back to me and pulls me to my feet. Arm in arm, we hold our skirts as we spin and dance about, singing all the while.

*Let love and friendship on that day, Hurrah, hurrah!*

*Their choicest treasures then display, Hurrah, hurrah!*
*And let each one perform some part,*
*To fill with joy the warrior's heart,*
*And we'll all feel gay when Johnny comes marching home.*

Justus was one of those brave men who made it home. He must have been so handsome in his uniform. Guilt thickens my throat. Ginny's right, he deserves to know the secret I've been keeping. How can I tell him? He'll never forgive me. He'll despise me.

"Ginny, I need to go lie down." I smile at the girl, hoping to hide my sadness.

"All right." Ginny pats my arm and kisses my cheek, then goes back to dancing. I chuckle at her free spirit.

---

"You know it's okay to cry yourself to sleep every night, but you don't have to." Ginny beats the eggs as if she hadn't said a thing.

I flip the pancakes. How did she know? She was asleep, wasn't she? I start to speak, but she goes on, still not looking up from the eggs. "Seems to me, you have a man who loves you and treats you well. If it were me, I'd run back to him." She peers up then. "You're lucky."

No one has ever called me lucky before. I'm not lucky, though. Am I? I don't respond. I know Ginny speaks from the broken heart of a woman who lost a child and a husband. A husband who loved her in return.

Perhaps I am being selfish. It's also possible I'm letting my pride get in the way of going back and apologizing. But now I'm torn. Going back and leaving Ginny would also be selfish.

"Don't get me wrong," she says. "I'm not trying to get rid of you. I want you here. This is the happiest and safest I've felt since Jake died, but…" Tears form in her eyes. "As much as I love you, I'd give anything to have Jake back." She hugs her arms around herself. "To feel his strong arms around me." She snickers. "Every time he came through that door he was whistling." Staring me in the eye, she says, "I won't get that back, but you—Justus is alive and well. There's still time for you. And if he won't take you, well, at least you tried. You can come back, and *we* will live happily ever after."

My heart beats painfully against my chest. "Oh, Ginny," I say, pulling the girl into my arms. We cry together until the odor of burnt pancakes and smoke fills the tiny cabin. Tears give way to laughter as poor Buck howls to be allowed outside. Ginny opens the door to let the smoke and the beagle escape, and I set to making a new batch of flapjacks.

Valentine's comes, not with a letter from the man I wish to be my sweetheart, but from Miss Bea.

*Dearest Olivia,*

*Your letters to the newspapers have worked! Rebecca's Samuel has written that he will be arriving on the train Monday the tenth of March. Oh, Olivia, you must come. This would not have been possible without you.*

*Your room is waiting for you and I just cannot bear to take no for an answer.*

*I hope to see you then.*

*Yours truly,*
*Beatrice Annette Peterson*

I chuckle at the way Miss Bea always signs her letters.

"This is your chance," Ginny says.

"I don't know. I don't want to overshadow Rebecca's good fortune with my troubles."

Ginny takes hold of my hand. "If you prolong this, you will only make it harder. This is your opportunity."

I exhale. "Will you come with me?"

"Of course, I will," she says with eyes wide. "We can tell them together, if you like."

"What about Buck?"

"Oh, I'm not worried about him one lick. The men will see to it he's cared for."

"Thank you, Ginny." We hug, then turn to making plans for our trip to Laurel Springs.

# 58

## Justus

I have an uneasy feeling come over me as I dress to attend supper at my aunt and uncle's. My aunt insists on an early celebration for Rebecca, since she's found her husband. It's all thanks to Olivia's brilliant idea to place ads in a few newspapers. I can't help but speculate if she'll be there. Of course not. She has a new life now. I push the thought from my mind as I run my hand over my beard and sit my Stetson on my head.

My heart is unsteady as I ride Beau slowly into town. The weather has been mild as of late with Mother Earth showing signs of spring on the horizon, but dark clouds loom in the distance; perhaps rain is coming.

The desire to turn Beau around is strong but I press on. *She won't be there.* I'm not sure if I'm nervous at the thought of seeing her or not seeing her. A part of me longs to have one last look, and a part of me hopes to never see her again. It would be too much. Too painful.

"How am I ever going to get over that woman, Beau?"

The delicious aromas as I walk into the house take my senses hostage and my stomach rumbles. I didn't realize how hungry I was. Food hasn't been a priority over the last months as I've wallowed in my self-pity.

I peek into the sitting room where Doc and Clint sit reading, and Thomas plays marbles on the floor with Chet and Mimi.

"Oh, hi, Justus," says Thomas when he notices me.

Doc lowers his book and peers up at me over his glasses. "It's good to see you, son."

Thomas jumps up. "Justus, Miss Olivia's here." The boy's eyes are wide and his grin excited.

I look to Clint, who gives me a nod and a sympathetic smile.

My body shakes. I take in a deep breath and walk to the kitchen. It's time to put on a brave face.

"Well, hello, beautiful ladies." I open my arms wide.

"Justus." Miss Bea wraps me in a hug.

A girl I don't recognize spins to Olivia with raised eyebrows and a tight-lipped smile.

Miss Bea holds out her arm to the girl. "Justus, this is Olivia's friend Ginny."

With a slightly exaggerated bow, I offer her my hand. "Ginny, it's nice to meet you. I wish I'd heard all about you."

She glances at Olivia, then shakes my hand. "Justus, it's nice to meet you. As a matter of fact, I have heard all about you." She grins from ear to ear..

I don't know how to respond to that. She's most likely heard about what a wretched man I am; a liar and a cheat.

I tip my head to Olivia. "Liv."

She mimics my motion. "Justus."

I guess I taught her well when I educated her on keeping a stone-cold countenance while playing poker because her face doesn't conceal her thoughts at seeing me, not even the cute little nose wiggle. She wears a large shawl that covers her figure. It isn't flattering but her eyes are as stunning as ever. I long to wrap my arms around her, smell her hair, and kiss her lips. The invisible force between us is so thick I can almost see it as we stand staring at one another.

Someone clears their throat, bringing us both out of the trance we seem to be in. I hug Rebecca and Hannah. "All right, then," I say nervously. "I'll just go back to the front room with the men."

I try to engage in talk with Clint about horses, and I even play a game of marbles with the little ones. But I can't get Olivia out of my head. I should go home. No, that would be rude. I just need to get through the next couple of hours. This is Rebecca's evening.

At dinner, I find myself sitting across from Olivia. My leg jiggles under the table and my heart pounds against my chest, unsure of how to get through this meal. The talking and laughing around me is muffled, as if I'm listening from under water. My eyes don't leave my plate, moving the food around aimlessly. The feeling of hunger I walked in with has gone. I have to say something. No, I can't. I shouldn't. I've said enough in my letters. Surely, she received them. They were pathetic. She ignored them. She's ignoring me now. It's clear she wants nothing to do with me.

"Justus?" My aunt's voice brings me back to the present and all eyes are on me.

"Are you all right, dear?"

I sit my fork down. "Actually, I need to go. I'm sorry." I place my napkin on the table and stand. "I'm really happy for you, Rebecca, and I look forward to meeting your husband," I say, pushing in my chair. "Good night, everyone."

"Justus." Olivia's voice holds me back. "Justus, please stay," she chokes out.

My stomach twists. I swallow around the lump in my throat.

"I'm sorry," she says. "I was wrong. I was awful and I've been selfish. No man has given me what you have—love, gentleness, kindness." She lowers her eyes. "Faithfulness."

I step forward slowly. My heart races, unsure of what is happening.

"Justus, I'm an awful person," she sobs.

Ginny places a hand on Olivia's arm. The room is silent except for her cries. I don't know if I should go to her or stay rooted where I am.

She pulls the shawl from her shoulders and hands it to Ginny, then runs a hand over her protruding belly. *She's pregnant.* There are audible gasps from the table. She's pregnant with another man's child. A pain like a punch to the stomach shakes me to my core and bile rises to the back of my throat.

"I swear I didn't know when I left," she says. "I didn't realize until weeks later." She still sobs and Ginny hands her a handkerchief.

I can't wrap my head around her words. I narrow my eyes, trying to comprehend.

"I was too prideful and scared to tell you." She glances around the table. "To tell any of you. I'm so sorry." She sniffles and plays nervously with the cloth in her hands. "And I know this goes against your religious beliefs for Justus and me to have a child out of wedlock."

"He who is without sin shall cast the first stone," Miss Bea speaks up defiantly.

*Justus and me?* She carries *my* child. She needs me. And I need her.

I walk around the table, move her chair from behind her, and take her into my arms. She lays her head against my chest and weeps into the handkerchief. Her hair is soft against my hand and lips, just the way I remember it. "It's all right. I know now and it's all right. It's not too late."

She pulls away to wipe her eyes and nose. "Your last letter said you were moving on."

I lift her chin and place my lips on her wet cheek. "You think I could replace you that quickly?" I whisper.

Hanna comes over and wraps one arm around her, the one that doesn't hold her infant son. She whispers into Olivia's ear, then returns to her seat.

I remember the gift I had made for Olivia. "I'll be right back." I rush from the room to my saddlebag that rests on Beau. I had placed the small package there and left it. I don't know if she'll accept it, but this is my chance.

# 59

## Livvie

I take my seat, feeling both relieved and scared. Scared of what will come next from the family. But the faces before me hold smiles and laughter, sending a warmth over me. They're not judging me. They haven't banished me, yelled at me, kicked me out, or condemned me to hell. They're excited. Questions are coming at me as fast as I can answer them. When will the baby arrive? Have I seen a doctor? Have I started sewing for the baby?

Hannah lifts her infant from her arm to her shoulder. "Oh, Olivia, they'll be cousins and playmates."

"Yes." I manage a shaky smile, not knowing what will happen now that my secret has been revealed.

Justus bounds into the room and bends down on one knee beside my chair, breathless. He hands me a small gift in brown paper wrapped with twine. I move my chair out some to better face him. The outside cold emanates from his body.

"What is this?" I ask, taking the package in my hands.

"Remember when I told you I loved you more than all the granules of sugar and that I'd eat sugarless pie for the rest of my life for you?" he asks.

My hands shake as I slowly open the paper. "A ring." My breath catches. I look at him, puzzled. It's a ring, clearly made by the hand of a skillful Navajo woman. The gift he said he was having made for me. I run my finger over the turquoise stone. "Wings?" I glance up at him again.

"Because you're my angel."

I slip the ring onto my finger. "It's breathtaking."

He rests a hand on my belly and the other on his heart. "Olivia Palmer, will you do me the honor of being my wife?"

"Oh, Justus." I quickly lay the paper on the table and wrap my arms around his neck. "Yes, I'll marry you," I cry.

Claps and cheers erupt around the table.

Justus stands and lets out a whoop. "We're getting married."

I shift to Hannah, who flashes a bright smile.

"Where's Silas?" asks Justus as he fidgets.

Miss Bea speaks. "I believe he's having dinner at the McCalister's."

"We need him."

I grab his arm. "Now?"

Thomas shoots up. "I'll go get him."

Rebecca pulls the boy back down. "You will do no such thing."

Justus bends down and kisses my cheek. "I'll go get him."

"At this moment?" asks Miss Bea.

"Justus, I don't have a dress to wear, or flowers." I pull at his hand. "We don't have to do this today." The man has lost his mind.

He cups my face. "I don't care. To me, you're beautiful just the way you are, and we're getting married tonight. If I have to ride to Denver to find a preacher, I will. I'm not losing you ever again." He kisses my lips and leaves.

"I have a dress you can wear, Olivia." Hannah turns to Clint. "Sweetheart, will you go home and get that blue cotton dress with the Chinese pagoda print and gold trim? I wore it at Thanksgiving."

Clint smiles at me. "Hannah looked beautiful in that dress, and so will you."

I'm getting married. Tonight. I've struggled with so much self-doubt, but it's all turning out even better than I could have imagined. Perhaps I'll wake and find this all a glorious dream.

# 60

## Livvie

I sit on the edge of the bed in my old room; Hannah's room. Everything is happening so fast, and my most pressing concern is Ginny.

"I'll be all right," she reassures me in her sweet voice. "I've lived in that cabin laundering the miners' clothes for three years just fine."

"I don't want to leave you," I choke out.

"I'll come visit you when I can." She lays a hand on my belly. "I want this for you. This is your chance to have a family and you can't give that up for me." Waving her hand and shaking her head, she says, "I'll be just fine. Promise."

I smile and lean in to hug my friend before she pulls me to my feet. "You're so fortunate Hannah had this dress for you to wear. It fits you perfectly."

I study myself in the mirror, admiring my growing bump as I smooth my hand over it. "Yes, I am fortunate. And this dress is just beautiful."

"Silas is here," says Rebecca from the doorway before coming closer with her arms out. "Don't you look pretty."

"Thank you, Rebecca." I kiss her cheek.

"Who's Silas and why does he need to be here?" asks Ginny.

I chuckle. "Silas is the preacher."

"And you don't call him preacher or reverend or brother?"

"He prefers to be called by his first name," Rebecca offers.

Ginny shrugs. "All right. Let's go have a wedding."

---

When I walk into the sitting room, everyone, including Frank and Mary, whom Justus insisted on going to the ranch to get, ready or not, are gathered. Justus and Silas stand before the fireplace.

Rebecca made me a simple but beautiful bouquet of pine, holly, and berry branches wrapped in gold ribbon to match the gold trim on the dress Hanna has loaned to me.

Justus reaches for my hand as I draw closer.

Silas smiles with delight. "All right. It looks as though we're having a wedding this evening. This will be one to tell the grandchildren about, won't it?"

We chuckle.

"Let's pray." He bows his head. "We are gathered here today before God, family, and friends to witness the union of these two, Justus and Olivia, in holy matrimony. God established the bond and covenant of marriage in creation with Adam and Eve.

It signifies to us the union of Christ and the church. May God bless the joining of these two people as husband and wife, as long as they both shall live. Amen."

"Amen," echoes the room.

"I don't think I have to ask this, but is there any reason someone can show just cause for this couple to not be lawfully wed? If so, speak now or forever hold your peace."

I stare into Justus's eyes. He winks, making my insides feel like warm caramel.

"That's what I thought," Silas jokes. "This day was destined to happen. God put everything and everyone in place to bring us all together at this moment."

"Olivia, I don't know when Justus confessed his love to you, but he confessed it to me about five months ago." He shakes his head. "Not his love for me; his love for you."

Laughter erupts.

We speak our vows, declaring our love and commitment for one another, then Silas scans the room. "Who gives this woman to marry this man?"

My breath catches in my throat. I have no parents here, no family of my own. How can he ask such a question?

Heads turn back and forth, looking at one another. "We do," they all say in chorus.

A weight lifts from my chest. I do have family to call my own. Everyone here is my true family. Blood doesn't make you family. Loyalty, love, and kinship makes you family.

"Let us bow our heads and recite the Lord's Prayer," says Silas.

The room prays in unison as Justus and I squeeze our sweating hands together. To me, this wedding is more magnificent than I could have ever planned or dreamed. Everything about it is perfect.

"It is my joy and honor to present Justus and Olivia Bennett as husband and wife." Silas places a hand on Justus's shoulder. "Sir, you may kiss your bride."

Justus beams. "My bride." He leans in. With both hands, he cradles my face and kisses my lips.

My heart flip-flops with joy. I am Missus Justus Bennett.

Clapping and whistling fills the room.

Miss Bea shouts above the crowd, "Let's celebrate with dessert."

"Can I have pumpkin pie?" asks Thomas.

"You sure can, if you help me." Miss Bea taps his nose.

Ginny leans into me at the table and whispers, "Shouldn't the preacher's wife be here?"

"He doesn't have a wife," I whisper back.

She shrugs her eyebrows. "Oh, I guess that's a good reason, then."

At the table, everyone's attention is on Silas as he tells of Justus storming into the McCalister's. "Justus came in, fumbling over himself, begging me to marry him and Olivia."

"Last I checked, the Good Book said thou shalt not lie," says Justus with a grin.

"You're right, Justus." Silas turns to the others. "He didn't fumble…" He stares down at the bite of pie on his fork. "He *stormed* in and *begged* me to marry him and Olivia."

I laugh at the image, but I'm suddenly gripped by pain. The kind of pain I have during my courses. I squeeze Justus's arm and grab my stomach. The happiness on his face turns to worry when he notices my anguish. "Doc, something's wrong with Olivia." Justus takes me into his arms and Doc moves swiftly to my side.

## 61

### Livvie

Justus wraps an arm around my waist. "It's time to go home, Angel." After a thorough examination, Doc has concluded there's no reason for concern. I have no bleeding and the cramps have subsided. He says these things are perfectly normal and we need not worry.

I pull Ginny in. "I'm so sorry to leave you alone with strangers."

"Are you serious? These folks are like family already, and it'll be kind of nice having a bed all to myself again." She widens her smile and I know she's partly teasing. Although, I wouldn't blame her if she was telling the whole truth. I have been taking up more of the bed as of late and have trouble finding a comfortable position to sleep in.

"I'll be back tomorrow. I want to show you the ranch." I give her another hug before exiting the front door that Justus holds open for me. It's raining and he clutches me close, so I don't slip.

"I wasn't expecting to bring you home tonight when I rode here on Beau. Clint was nice enough to bring us a wagon. Looky here." He points to the team of horses.

I pull the shawl Ginny loaned me over my head to take some cover from the water that falls from the night sky. I hadn't anticipated going home with him tonight, either. But here I am. And married, too.

"There you go, Missus Bennett." He helps me onto the wagon.

"Why, thank you, Mister Bennett."

When we reach the ranch, Justus insists on carrying me into the house, up the stairs, and into our room. *Our room.* I play his words over in my mind as I ready myself for the night.

He sits on the edge of the bed and pulls me to him, resting his head on my belly. "Can you feel him?" he asks.

"I feel flutters. As if there's a little bird frolicking around in there." I hold his head to my bump and run my fingers through his messy hair.

"You said you couldn't get pregnant." He pulls my nightgown up and kisses around my belly button.

"The midwife in Sutton's Creek said it's not always the woman. Sometimes the man just can't get a woman pregnant. And all those years, I thought it was my fault."

He reaches up and touches my cheek. "Come, lay with me."

In the glow of the lamplight, he caresses my stomach. "I gained a wife and a child all in one day. I'm certain I don't deserve such blessings."

I watch him, so tender and loving with my rounded middle.

I run my fingers through his hair once again. How I've missed him. "I've been asking myself the same thing. I thought there was no fortune left for me."

He moves himself between my legs. "We have all the fortune we need right here, you, me, and our little one."

He kisses from my belly button down. Opening my legs wide, he teases the inside of my thigh with his tongue.

My breath clenches in my chest. This is truly happening. I'm not dreaming. I'm Justus's wife, in his bed, our bed, making love. A tear rolls down my cheek. I've never been so happy in all my life.

My back arches at the sensation he's causing as he caresses the folds between my legs. He slides a finger in, then two, moving in and out as he continues, hungry, devouring every last drop of my juices.

*Don't stop. Don't stop.* I grip the blankets around me. "Justus. Oh God, Justus." I scream into the room as my body convulses.

He comes up with a grin, eyes sparkling. He wipes his mouth with the back of his hand, as if he had just thoroughly enjoyed a meal. "I can't tell you how many times I've imagined doing that to you again." He shakes my nightgown. "This needs to come off." More than happy to oblige, I slip it over my head.

He feels my breasts, gently squeezing them. "They're so swollen."

"They're preparing for baby."

"Well, they're mine, for now." He takes a nipple in his mouth, sucking gently at first, then harder. He reaches down between my legs, sliding himself in. Slowly, he begins to move.

"Let me turn over," I say.

He sits back on his heels as I maneuver my behind in the air and my head toward the pillow.

"Oh now, this is a real nice view." He rubs at my backside and down my thighs. He moves in again, filling me with his girth and length. I close my eyes at the wonderful sensation. His movements are slow. I know he's savoring every bit of me and that brings a smile to my face. He reaches around, massaging my breasts and kissing my back and shoulders. "I've missed you so much, in so many different ways," he says, continuing to move in and out gently. He's making *love* to me. I can feel every ounce that he has for me in this moment. "I can't ever lose you again," he says.

"You won't." I lay my hand over his hand that holds my breast, and our fingers entwine.

"I love you, Angel."

"I love you, too, Justus."

He pulls himself upright, grabbing my hips and moving into me faster, faster, pounding harder. I can't get enough. I move with him, wanting him deeper, deeper still. Our bodies slam together. Sweat beads on my brow. My breaths come in heavy waves. "I need you, Justus. Don't stop. I need you," I cry out.

The sounds of our wet bodies slapping together echo through the room.

"Did you miss this?" he asks, breathless.

"Yes," I pant.

"Oh, Liv," he cries out as his body jerks before coming to a stop and pulsing inside me.

We fall into a heap on the bed, regaining our breath, soaked with sweat. He pulls me into his arms, and I lay my head on his chest. He inhales the scent of my hair. "My bride."

I smile at his words.

"I am the luckiest, happiest man on the planet. I thought the night I brought you to this bed was the best night of my life, but tonight I am infinitely joyful because tonight, you're my wife. Life cannot get any better than this right here."

"I agree." I wrap my arm around his waist and squeeze. Lightening illuminates the room and thunder crashes as branches scratch against the window.

"This storm reminds me of that first day in Denver," says Justus. "You grabbed me when you fell."

I smile at the memory. "And you swept me up and helped me to safety." The room lights up with another flash of lightening. "I never thought love would come to me, but here you are." I snuggle even closer into the safety of his arms.

"I never thought love would come to me," he says. "And then you arrived in a rainstorm and turned my life upside down." He squeezes me. "Because I'm not a bible man, I don't agree with everything Silas said tonight, but I do agree we are destined to be together."

"Yes, we are." I kiss his chest and take in the scent of his skin, fresh and clean. I'm safe and loved. If only I could crawl inside him and live there.

The storm is lulling me to sleep when Justus's voice causes my eyes to flutter open. "What did Hannah whisper in your ear this evening? After you announced your pregnancy."

I smile at the remembrance. "Welcome to the family."

He laughs. "God love her."

# 62

## Livvie

"Oh Livvie, your family has been just wonderful," Ginny says with much animation.

*Your family.* I roll those words around in my mind. I've always thought of them as my family, but now they truly are my family. I melt a little with that knowledge.

"Oh—" Miss Bea puts her hand to her heart "—it has been our pleasure having you here, dear," she says to Ginny.

Ginny gives her brightest smile. "Thank you, Miss Bea."

Miss Bea turns to me. "We were up way past our bedtime last night. We had popcorn and played hide the thimble at Thomas's insistence. Silas even stayed and joined in the fun."

I'm stunned at the idea of Silas playing hide the thimble. "He didn't."

Rebecca, who sits sewing, chuckles. "Yes he did, and when I tucked Thomas in last night, he said Ginny was the best hide the thimble player and asked if we could keep her."

"Oh, he's so fun," says Ginny. "I'd put him in my bag and take him home with me if I could," she teases.

"Oh heavens, where are my manners." Miss Bea gets up. "Olivia dear, let me get you a cup of tea." She is out of the room before I can protest.

"So, tell me," asks Miss Bea when she returns, passing the steaming cup to me. "How does it feel to be married to that boy?"

I smile and gaze into the oak-colored liquid. That tall, rugged, handsome cowboy is all mine. I can hardly believe it. "It feels amazing." I flutter my eyelashes, feeling dreamy. "And our little wedding last night, here in this room, will forever be one of my favorite memories."

"Well, dear, I know it all happened so fast, but did you discuss taking a honeymoon?"

"Yes, we talked about it over breakfast this morning. I just can't imagine being anywhere but the ranch, so we decided instead of us leaving, we'd send Frank and Mary for a getaway. Justus said they haven't left the ranch in years, aside from Frank going on cattle drives and whatnot. And Mary deserves to have someone else cook and care for her for a week or two."

"I'd say that's a lovely plan." Miss Bea leans forward. "I just want you to know, dear, that we are thrilled about this baby." Her eyes threaten to spill over with tears. "Little ones are such blessings."

"Oh, thank you for saying so."

Ginny speaks up, "I told them how worried you've been and how we almost didn't come."

Miss Bea nods. "I'm certainly glad you did come, after all."

"Me too," seconds Rebecca. "Otherwise, I wouldn't have been able to make this." She holds up what appears to be the start of a baby gown.

My heart softens and I run a hand over my bump. "This baby will not want for anything, will he?"

"No, he or she will not," says Rebecca, who returns to her sewing.

I then remember the reason I came back to Laurel Springs to begin with. "Rebecca, I haven't heard the story of how you found your husband."

Rebecca beams. "Would you want to read his letter? I carry it with me." She pulls it from her apron. "I'm so nervous to see him, but so elated. He doesn't know we have a son. Imagine. Of course, I could have shared that news in a letter but decided I'd surprise him instead."

I read the letter aloud.

*My Dearest Rebecca,*

*This is the day the Lord hath made! My employer, Missus Caroline Jones read your ad in the newspaper on her recent trip to Springfield. When she brought it home to me, we knew it was you. We just knew it.*

*I have thought about you day and night since that fateful morning so many years ago. I've heard rumors about who purchased our Ellen and Lydia, but that's all I have is rumors.*

*If you write me back, I'll be on the first train I can get.*

*Your dearest Samuel*

I shake with excitement and my tears spill over. I sit the tea and letter on the table beside me. "Oh Rebecca." I go to her and put my arms around her.

"Of course, I wrote him that very moment," she says, "and he wrote back that he'd arrive on the train in Denver on Monday, the tenth of March. Two more days, can you believe it? It just doesn't feel real."

I know exactly what she means.

"I can't thank you and Justus enough for this. If it weren't for the two of you, I wouldn't have gotten that letter, ever."

"We love you, Rebecca."

Rebecca's eyes soften. "I love you, too."

"Oh, Olivia," says Miss Bea as she claps her needlework into her lap. "I have completely failed to tell you that Adelyn McDaniels has moved to Laurel Springs. She's Adelyn Chastain now, as she's taken her maiden name. She has the sweetest baby girl, Clara Mae, she calls her. She looks just like Asa with black hair and blue eyes, but we won't hold that against her, now will we? Oh, she has those dimples, too. Just the loveliest little thing. You must arrange a visit with Adelyn, she'd be so pleased."

That gives me an idea. "Perhaps we should invite her to Samuel's welcome party on Monday."

Miss Bea clutches her bosom with her sewing. "Oh, what a splendid idea. I'll pay her a visit this afternoon."

So much has changed over the months since I left Missouri. I can't help but wonder what the future has in store for me here now.

# 63

## Livvie

Ginny sits in the backseat of the sleigh as Justus guides the team into the small camp. Last night's rainstorm turned to several inches of snow overnight. The ride has felt much different than it had on the stagecoach going to Laurel Springs. This time I'm beside my husband, without a care in the world.

"I wonder how Buck's faired without me. I sure miss him," says Ginny.

I chuckle. "He's probably lying at the door waiting for you." I tell Justus, "That dog does not leave her side."

"Dogs can be faithful protectors if treated right," says Justus. "We should get one before the baby arrives."

"I love that idea." I know there's a dog on the ranch, but he's a ranch dog, not a companion dog.

"Well, it's settled then, we'll find us a good mutt first thing. Every boy should have a dog as a child."

"Did you have a dog?" I ask.

"Sure did. Red, an Irish Setter mix. He died while I was gone fighting Johnny Reb."

A scream from Ginny grabs our attention. Justus manages to bring the sleigh to a halt before she tries to jump from it.

The men of the camp stand holding buckets before a smoldering heap that used to be Ginny's cabin.

She breaks loose and runs to the wreckage. "No, no, no!" she shouts. Her hands fly to her head in despair.

I run to her side. We've both lost everything we own except what we'd taken to Laurel Springs with us. My stomach turns as I swallow back the vomit that threatens to come up.

Justus asks the men, "How did this happen?"

One man wipes his blackened face. "We don't know. We were panning down river and smelled smoke. When we came running, it was ablaze." He steps closer to Ginny. "We were too late Ginny. We're so sorry."

She falls into my arms. Great waves of sobs erupt from her petite frame. It takes all my strength to hold her. We fall to the ground and cry together. Justus wraps his arms around us both, holding our heads to his chest.

As if having a sudden realization, Ginny draws back, eyes wide and arms out. "Where's Buck?" She turns toward the men. "Where's Buck?" she yells.

"I haven't seen him," one man responds.

"Oh no!" She runs to the burned-out cabin, looking inside. "I need Buck," she cries as she presses her hands to her face, desperately searching the rubble.

As I stand with Justus's arm around me, I feel something tug at my skirt. It's the dog, begging for attention.

"Ginny! Ginny, he's here." I bend down and pull him into my arms, laughing with relief.

Ginny runs to us and grabs the animal. A laughing cry comes from her as she squeezes him and lets him lick her face. "Oh Buck, I thought I'd gone and lost you, too. Why'd you scare me like that?"

After a moment, she sits on a stump and stares at where her home used to be, petting the sleeping beagle in her lap. I sit on a stump beside her. "I don't know what I'm gonna do, Livvie. I've lost everything. And you…" She looks to me with a tear-streaked face. "You've lost everything, too. I'm so sorry. I feel as though somehow, it's my fault. I should have stayed behind."

Although my heart does ache for my only worldly possessions, including my grandparents' letters and Grandmother's ring, I know I haven't lost everything. I gained more than I could ask or hope for—a family. It's a small fortune, but I feel as rich in wealth as the Queen of England.

I wrap an arm around the woman and pull her close. "I've got you, my friend, and for that, I'm so thankful. What if you'd stayed and had been in there?"

"Oh, I would've gotten out," she says confidently, as if it were that simple.

"But what if you hadn't?"

Justus squats down by the two of us. "Rumor has it that some men who didn't take too kindly to you ladies turning down their advances did this. I'm thankful you weren't here. Who knows what they would have done to you."

A shudder runs through my body. We are lucky to be alive. I ponder this as I stare at the burned-out pile before us.

"The sheriff will be coming," says Justus. "But my guess is those men are long gone now. Ginny, I think you should come back to Laurel Springs with us."

"Oh, I can't do that. You two need your time together as husband and wife, and I don't have anywhere to go. I think it's probably time I just go on back to New York."

Justus chuckles. "Trust me, my aunt would be over the moon if you stay with them. I'm not saying you can't go home. I'm just saying you should come back with us until you figure it out."

"I agree, Ginny." I lay a hand on her arm.

Ginny nods.

Justus helps me to my feet.

"I have one thing I need to do before we go," says Ginny solemnly. "I have to tell Jake goodbye."

Tears sting my eyes. I tip my head to my friend.

With Buck by her side, Ginny walks slowly to the spot with rocks piled where she sits every day to "talk with Jake," as she says.

Justus and I watch her as she kneels beside the pile of stone and lays her head on them. Her body shakes. I step forward to go to her, but he catches my arm. "She needs to be alone with him right now."

He's right.

He takes my hand. "Let's go see if there's anything salvageable in here," he says, pointing to the charred remains of the cabin.

After saving what we can, Justus goes to fetch food for us.

I sit on the stump I'd sat on a hundred times. The view is different today. How quickly life can change. "Grit," I whisper to myself. Grit keeps me going.

Ginny's shuffling feet in the snow catches my attention.

"It's okay, Livvie. Jake said I can go. He said he'll be with me wherever I am." There's a light in her eyes I hadn't seen before, and I know she believes what she says.

I stand and pull my friend into my arms. "Yes, it's only his body that rests here."

"That's what he said." Her voice is calm and sweet, a lullaby to my ears.

Then, I pull away while still holding her shoulders. "I have some good news."

Ginny studies me.

"We found the tins we were saving our coins in. It's all there, can you believe it?"

"This is good news." She stares at the cabin. "I still have so much to be thankful for, I suppose. Sometimes rays of sunlight still shine through the clouds when it's raining, and I guess you could say our lives and the money are the rays of sunlight. Buck, too, of course."

The way Justus was my ray of sunlight when I arrived in Colorado during a thunderstorm. Yes, I understand completely.

# 64

## Livvie

Justus gives his hands a single clap. "Are you ready to come see the barn?" We've been preparing for a party in celebration of Rebecca's husband's arrival today.

"You're done already?" I ask suspiciously. "I better, so I can make sure it was done right." I grab my coat and follow him out the door.

"I think you'll be pleased," he says.

With my hand in his, we head out to the barn.

Hay bales are stacked so folks can sit comfortably, and space is cleared for a nice dance floor. "Oh Justus, you all did a wonderful job." I nod my head as I glance about. "I'm very impressed."

He takes me by surprise as he pulls me in and kisses me. A peck, then a nibble of my lip, slipping his warm tongue into my mouth. Grabbing my backside, he presses my body to his. One hand slides up, cradling the nape of my neck as he kisses me deeper. It's as though he's ready to make love to me right here in the barn. I grow warm and my knees soften. I pull my mouth from his. "You better stop this, Justus Bennett, or else you'll have to take me right here on these bales of hay."

He kisses me again. "Oh, that's definitely going to happen," he says through heavy breaths. His mouth moves to my cheek and down my neck, then up to my ear. "Not today, but it *will* happen."

I smile and weaken a little more at the image.

Voices come from outside the barn door and Justus steps back, reaches down, and readjusts himself from the outside of his pants.

"I see I've still got it," I say, cradling my little bump.

"You don't even know." He gazes at me hungrily, causing a tingle to run right through me.

Thomas comes bounding into the barn and jumps on the nearest stack of hay. Ginny strolls in behind him with Buck at her heels. She thought Buck would be happier on the ranch than in town, and Justus and I agreed.

"I get to meet my pa today." Thomas jumps excitedly from stack to stack.

"You're a lucky boy," says Justus.

"We came to help you all get ready for this barn dance," says Ginny. She stops. A sly smile plays on her lips. "Were we interrupting something here? We can go," she says, hiking her thumb over her shoulder.

"No," I say, patting at my hair. "Justus was just showing me how proud he is of the work he's done."

Ginny saunters over with her hands behind her back and her head bobbing. "Compared to how it looked on Saturday, this is great work."

I take Ginny by the arm. "Let's go see what decorations we can find. I want this to be perfect for Rebecca."

"Wait for me," says Thomas, jumping down from the haystacks.

Justus stops him. "Actually, Thomas, I could use your help." The boy's face lights up. "All right."

---

Everyone waits in quiet anticipation for Silas to bring Rebecca's husband Samuel to the barn doors. My stomach flutters as I watch Rebecca, who wrings her hands and smooths out her skirt. After all these years of thinking she'd never see him again, he's coming. And he'll be so surprised to learn about Thomas. A child no one can take from them.

When the two men appear in the doorway, Silas steps to the side. I think Rebecca is going to fall on the floor at the sight of the man who stands before her. She chokes on her sobs and bends in two. He comes to her quickly and grabs her, wrapping his arms around her waist. She hangs on his neck and wails.

I dab at my own silent tears, watching the couple. Peeking around, I see I'm not alone.

Justus stands with his hand on Thomas's shoulder. When Rebecca regains her composure, she steps back from her husband and waves Thomas over. Justus gives the boy a pat and Thomas walks slowly to his ma.

"Thomas, meet your pa," she says with a smile.

The man holds one arm out, as if to balance himself, and the other goes to his chest. He glances from Thomas to Rebecca. "I…you…he's our son?" He looks to Thomas again.

"Yes, soon after we were separated, I learned I was carrying him. I've had a part of you with me all these years, Samuel."

The man falls to one knee and opens his arms to Thomas.

The boy embraces his pa. Samuel's tears are no longer silent. He cries out with joy. Pulling Thomas away from him, his hands cup the boy's face. "Let me look at you, son." Then he brings him back into his arms as though he never wants to let go.

Samuel stands, wipes his face with a handkerchief he's pulled from his pocket, then surveys the faces of the strangers. "I s'pose I'll get to learning who the rest of you are as the night goes on." He opens his arms wide. "Shall we celebrate?"

"Here, here," says Frank as he pulls his fiddle from the box and begins to play.

I pour over the variety of pies. "Which one does this baby want?"

"Oh, stop blaming the baby and just eat, already," says Ginny.

I shush her with a wave of my hand.

"I think he wants mincemeat." I give Ginny a look as I serve myself a slice of pie.

"Awful," she says. "Worst pie ever."

"I agree," says Silas, who snuck up behind us.

I turn to see Ginny straighten and look away. I grin to myself as I take a bite of pie and watch the pair in conversation. Ginny fidgets as if a man has never talked to her before.

"I hear you're going to be making Laurel Springs your home now," Silas says to her.

"Yes, Miss Bea and Doc have offered me a room in their home."

"I'm happy to learn you'll be staying. It'll be nice seeing you around."

Ginny bites her lip and glances at the floor.

A new song begins from Frank's fiddle and Silas holds out his hand to her. "May I have this dance?"

"I'm afraid I'm not very good," she replies, looking to me. I already know the girl loves to dance. I've seen her waltz and stomp to the beat of the fiddle and banjo many times. I smile at her and slowly move my head from side to side.

"That's all right. Just follow my lead," he says, his hand still extended and a firm smile planted on his face.

Ginny sways, as though she's thinking about it. "You won't laugh if I fall on my face?"

"Not too hard." He chuckles.

Ginny looks back to me again and I quickly use my fork to prod the girl on.

"Well, all right," she says as she takes his hand.

My heart is full as I sit on a stack of hay and watch the couples on the dance floor turning and curtsying. I remember the day Rebecca told her wrenching story. There is so much gratitude in my heart that she has found her love once more. Now, if only they could find their daughters, their family would be complete.

I laugh aloud at Justus, who has the job of caller on the dance floor. I can see he is taking his job seriously as he bellows out the instructions. "Bow to your partner and your corner, too. Allemande left. Right hand turn." He moves his arms and taps his foot with great vigor.

How did I get so lucky to find and marry this man? And I'm blessed with carrying his child within my womb. I eat my pie and tap my foot to the music.

"Olivia."

"Lenny." I set my plate and fork down and stand to give her a hug.

"Look at you," says Lenny, stepping back to eye my little bump. "And I hear you and Justus are married now."

I nod and grin.

"Wow, a lot has happened since I saw you last. Sure have missed you."

I pull her to the hay where I had been sitting. "Oh Lenny, I've missed you, too. Tell me, did you ever talk to Jesse about your feelings?"

She bows her head. "I did, but nothing's changed. He said we shouldn't ruin a good thing."

I press my fist to my lips. "Oh Lenny, I'm so sorry."

She waves her hand. "Never mind. I suppose I'll just be happy that I still have him, even if it's only part of him."

No one should ever accept just part of a person. My heart aches for my friend.

"Well," she says, clasping her hands in her lap. "I'm glad you're home. Come by the shop and see me, won't you?"

"Of course, I will."

"I had better go congratulate Miss Rebecca and meet this handsome man of hers." She leans into me for a hug before strolling across the floor.

I sway to the music, watching Caleb and Adelyn lock eyes as he spins her around to the rhythm of the fiddle. Could there be a flicker of something between them? Only time will tell.

# 65
## Livvie

Rebecca and Samuel sit beside me on the hay. "Thank you for doing all of this for us," Rebecca says, leaning into me.

"It's the least we could do. You have been such a beautiful light in our lives, Rebecca. Anyhow, you deserve this and more," I say.

Rebecca embraces me. "Thank you."

Samuel, who sits on the edge of the haystack, peers around his wife. "Rebecca tells me you and your husband are the ones who put the ad in the paper and paid for it. I want to thank you for that. We'd have never found each other if it hadn't been for you two. You tell me what I owe you and I'll pay up."

"Just seeing your family together is repayment enough. We're so happy for you." My heart is nearly bursting, seeing them together.

He nods his head and tears fill his eyes. Lenny is right, he is a rather handsome man, clean-shaven with a strong jawline and a cleft chin.

"I hope you're enjoying yourself tonight," I continue.

"Yes ma'am, we sure are," he says with a smile that shows a set of pearly whites. "And I still can't believe I have a son I knew nothin' about. What a joy that boy is."

"Yes, he is." I lay my hand on Rebecca's. "Your wife has done a fine job raising him."

"I can see that." He gazes at Rebecca with every bit of love. "But I'd never doubt it for one moment." He lays a smooch on her cheek.

I watch them with a smile on my face and love squeezing my heart. "Samuel, I hope to see more of you two very soon." I take my plate and fork from the haystack beside me and stand. "For now, I think I shall call it a night. Please excuse me."

Rebecca hugs me, Samuel shakes my hand, and they promise they'll see me tomorrow.

Mary is busily washing dishes in a tub of steaming water. "Thank you for helping, Mary."

She gives me a wave of the hand. "Now, you know this is what I love to do. Besides, I'd rather be here than out on that dance floor." She tips her head in the direction of everyone still spinning their partners around the open space, which makes me laugh.

"It appears your Caleb is enjoying himself." We both watch Caleb and Adelyn still dancing with upturned faces and eyes only for one another.

"She's a sweet girl, that Adelyn," says Mary. "But I'm not sure Caleb is ready to be a father to that little girl of hers."

An arm swoops around my waist. "How's my bride?" Justus asks in my ear.

"I was just about to find you and ask that you walk me to the house. I don't want a bear or mountain lion getting me."

"I can do better than that. I can tuck you in bed," he whispers.

I smile as his words flutter through me. "Excuse us, Mary. I'm going on up to bed."

---

Justus lay on his side, resting his head in his hand, as he traces his fingers around my bare nipples.

"I love the way you tuck me in," I say, tilting my head to look up at him.

He moans. "I love the way you let me tuck you in." Our lips meet.

Feeling a lot of fluttering inside, I pull the sheet down away from my belly. "I think we woke the baby."

"You can feel it?" he asks.

"I can." I bite my bottom lip.

"You pregnant is the most beautiful thing I've ever seen." He moves himself down so he can caress my midsection. "What should we name him?"

I think about this a moment. "Justus Ethan Bennett the second."

"No. He needs his own name." Justus looks thoughtful as he massages my belly. He leans in closer, as though he is going to place another kiss on my skin. "What's your name, son?"

My heart overflows at the sight of him loving on my bump. "I think we'll know once we meet him," I offer.

He nods. "I think you're right." He cradles my belly with his arm and relaxes his body.

I run my fingers through his hair and over his back. He's the man of my dreams and I never knew it. I wish it hadn't taken us so much time and heartbreak before finding each other and coming together for good. But we wouldn't be who we are today, would we? Perhaps I can find it in me to be thankful for what I lived through over the years, if it meant bringing me to this man in this moment with the soul who lives inside my body. "Justus?"

He gives me a sleepy groan.

"I'm grateful we found each other."

He lifts his head and pushes himself up to face me. "I didn't even know you were who I was looking for all these years. But here you are, filling my heart, my mind, and my life. I'm never letting you go, Angel." He leans in, claiming my lips passionately. I can feel the depth of his love in that one kiss. He swallows my entire being in his embrace.

"I can't get enough of you, Justus. I need you closer, inside of me again."

"I'm right here," he says, as if the words awakened him. He makes his way down my neck to my full breasts. He takes my leg, guiding me to lay on my side, and I savor every inch of him as happy tears roll down onto my pillow.

# 66

## Livvie

"Justus, Justus, can I show Pa ole Beau?" Thomas jumps up and down excitedly.

"We'll get there, little fellow," Justus says, laughing.

Rebecca and I watch the men from the porch as they make their way out to the barn. My heart is full, thinking of Justus as a father to our son. "Let's go inside where it's warmer," I say to Rebecca.

Mary hands Rebecca and me each a cup of tea before taking hers and sitting on the sofa. "I'll understand if you do, Rebecca, but I sure hope you're not leaving us. I know Samuel just got here yesterday, but have you discussed a plan at all?"

Rebecca bows her head. I can see the words are coming hard for her. "Samuel has no job here. He's already employed in Chicago, so he believes it only makes sense for us to go back there." She wipes a tear with the back of her hand. "It's bittersweet."

Mary holds out a handkerchief to her. "We'll miss you, but it's the right thing to do. Samuel's right."

"He wants to put more ads in the papers to find our Ellen and Lydia."

"Oh, that's wonderful, Rebecca," I say. I sure hope they find their girls.

"I'm just so thankful I found Samuel." She dabs at her eyes. "I could pinch myself. I still can't believe it."

This is Rebecca's ray of sunlight through the rain clouds. She found her husband and he gained a son. I put my hand to my heart, thinking of Rebecca's plight. Happiness and heartache, all at the same time. Oh, life can be so complicated.

"Thomas and I will be leaving with him on the next train back at the end of the week. I wanted to make sure you got these now." She reaches in her bag and pulls out two sweet little baby gowns and an infant-sized quilt.

"Oh, Rebecca." I sit my cup and saucer down. "How on earth did you get them finished so quickly?"

Rebecca chuckles. "I needed something to keep myself busy while waiting for Samuel."

I start to get up, but Rebecca puts out a hand. "You just stay where you are. I'll bring them to you."

"Rebecca. I'm pregnant, not an invalid."

"You just stay put."

"These are lovely." I examine each item with care. Tears threaten to spill as I swallow back a lump in my throat. "I will think of you every time he wears them, and every time I wrap him in this blanket." Tears cloud my vision. "Now look, you have me crying." I wave my hands at my face until Mary brings me a handkerchief. She must keep a half dozen stowed away in her pockets.

Mary's level head sets us straight. "It's going to be all right. We'll miss Thomas and Rebecca, and they'll miss us, but we'll all get so busy in our new lives without each other that it will start to feel normal. Before we know it, we'll all be just fine. *And we'll write letters.*" She emphasizes the last sentence with a firm bob of her head and a hook of her arm. "Now, who'd enjoy a slice of chocolate cake? I baked it fresh this morning."

"We'd love cake," I say with a sniffle.

The men's laughter echoes through the house as they come in from the kitchen. I love the sound of Justus's laugh; hearing it now gives me a sense of comfort.

"Why do you ladies look so sad?" he asks.

I wave my hand at him. "It's just pregnancy and babies. You know us women can be sentimental."

With his hands in the pockets of his britches, he rocks back on his boots. "I have some news that I think will turn your frowns around."

"All right." I glance at the women, then back to Justus.

"Samuel, you want to tell them?" he asks.

Samuel turns to Rebecca. "Would you want to stay in Laurel Springs?"

She sits up straighter, as if composing herself. "I wish to be wherever you are. You and Thomas are my home."

I hold my breath, waiting to hear what comes next, although I have a feeling I already know.

"Justus has offered me a job."

Rebecca's hands go to her mouth.

"And," Justus adds, looking at Samuel.

"And." Samuel's face is alight. "One of his head ranch hands moved west, so there's a house for us to live in."

Rebecca flies from the couch to Justus. She grabs his face in both hands. Standing on her toes, she kisses both sides of his cheeks.

He takes her by the arms. "Easy Rebecca, our spouses are watching."

She swats his chest and moves to Samuel. Wrapping her arms around his neck, she sobs into his chest. Pulling her head away to look up at him, she asks, "Are you sure you're all right with this?"

He smiles down at her. "I'm more than all right."

She stands back and puts her hands to her cheeks, her brow furrowed. "Justus, thank you."

Justus tips his head. "Thank you, Rebecca. I can already see Samuel is a hard worker and knows the ins and outs of a farm." He turns to me and holds out his arm toward Samuel. "And he's a blacksmith," he says with raised eyebrows.

"That's wonderful news."

Rebecca takes my hand. "I'll be close to you again. Justus, when does he start?"

"As soon as he is able."

"I'll have to take the train back to Chicago to pack my belongings and give Missus Jones the news. She's been good to me, but I think she knew this was a possibility."

Justus puts a hand on the man's shoulder. "It sounds as if she wants what makes you happy."

"I believe she does." He nods in agreement.

"Where's Thomas?" Rebecca glances about the room.

"Oh, he's scouting out where to build himself a fort." Justus chuckles.

Rebecca laughs and waves her hand. "Oh, that boy."

Samuel lifts a finger into the air. "I do have one request." His eyes dart between Rebecca and Justus. "Don't let him build it until I get back to help him."

Justus offers the man his hand. "You got it, sir."

"Thank you, Justus, for everything."

---

"It will be so nice to have them here on the ranch, won't it?" I ask as Justus and I stand in the yard and wave them off.

"Yes, it will. I look forward to it."

He slips his arm around my waist. "You know what else I look forward to?"

"What's that?"

"Seeing you naked." He bends down and presses his mouth to my cheek.

"You're just like a rabbit, Justus Bennett," I laugh.

"Tell me you can't get enough, either."

I bite my lip. He's right. I long for him almost every moment of the day. If this excitement never wears off, I'll be an extremely happy woman. "I can't get enough."

"Mm-hmm. I think it's time for your nap, Missus Bennett." He swats my bottom.

I peek around to see if anyone noticed. "Justus."

Once inside, Justus calls for Mary as we make our way up the stairs. "My wife needs a nap and I think I'm going to join her."

"You two go right on ahead."

Justus speaks again. "Don't worry about lunch. I'll make us sandwiches when we get up."

"All right. I'll see myself on home, then."

On the landing of the stairs, Justus takes hold of my behind and leans into my ear. "I can't wait to sink my teeth into this." I practically run up the steps.

# 67

## Livvie

"What holiday traditions did you grow up with that you want to continue for our family?" asks Justus, while holding me in his arms.

I shrug. "We didn't do anything special. My mother didn't see the sense in celebrating holidays. She would get me one gift for Christmas, but we never had a big dinner or a tree."

He sits up. "You never had a tree as a child?"

"I've never had a tree, ever."

"You've never had a tree? Not as an adult? Not at Ginny's?"

"No."

"Why not? How could a person never have a tree? They're magical," he asks with a grimace of confusion.

"I guess I was used to not having one, and Roy didn't care less. Ginny's cabin was too small. We did hang some pine boughs, though, and ribbons she had previously used."

"I have to change this," he says. "And I'm not about to wait for next Christmas to do it, either. How do you feel about getting out of the house?"

"Now? To go where?"

He gives me a big smile. "Hunting."

"Hunting?" This man has gone mad.

"That's right. Hunting for a Christmas tree."

I arch a brow. "It's March."

He jumps out of bed. "That's all right. Come on, get dressed. We're having Christmas."

I chuckle. "All right. Let's hunt for a Christmas tree. Some fresh air will do me good."

"That settles it, then. Make sure you bundle up. I don't want my girl catching a cold."

*This man is a dream come true,* I think as we wander out toward the wooded area to search for the perfect tree.

"Do you have any special traditions from when you were a child?" I ask.

He smiles, as though lost in a time long ago that is sweet as a peppermint stick. "Oh, yes. I made cookies with my ma."

"You bake?" I'm surprised to learn this bit of information.

"Sure do." Justus pulls a sled for the tree as we trudge through the deep snow.

"Was there anything else you and your ma did?"

"We'd string popcorn for the tree, and there was always a peppermint candy and a penny in my stocking."

"Your ma sounds real special."

"She sure was. She would have loved you, Angel."

My breath catches. I never tire of hearing him call me Angel.

There's something special about it. Something sacred. A name just for me—from him and no one else.

"I'm sure I'd have loved her, too." I squeeze his hand.

"Yes, you would have."

I spot the tree. "Right there." I point.

"That there's a blue spruce."

"I love it."

"Then that's the one you're going to have." He kisses my nose and proceeds to cut down the tree.

Back at the house, he sits it up in the living room in the same corner he says his ma always put it.

"Wonderful," I exclaim. "Now I think we need to honor your ma with her Christmas traditions. What do you say we get some corn popping and make cookies?"

"Gingersnaps?" Justus peers at me with those big brown eyes, the way a little boy would look at his mama.

I giggle. "Of course."

Before I know it, we're stringing popcorn, eating gingersnaps, and drinking coffee.

"What's all the ruckus in here?" Mary asks as she enters the kitchen to start supper.

Justus and I laugh as we throw popcorn at one another and try catching it with our mouths. "Makin' memories, Mary. Makin' memories," says Justus.

"I love that. I love that a lot. What I don't love is the mess you two have made."

I start to clean up. "We'll take care of this, Mary."

Once the popcorn is on the tree, we stand back to admire it.

"Perfect," we say in unison, then chuckle.

It truly is perfect. This is the best Christmas ever. If only I could get to town to buy something for Justus. That's when I have an idea, and I'm sure with Mary's help, my plan will come together beautifully.

Two days later, the house is abuzz with Christmas dinner preparations. Ham, vegetables, and pies. Justus has managed to get the whole family and our friends on board with his Christmas in March idea.

After dinner, we move into the sitting room to have coffee and sing Christmas carols by the tree. Justus stops short. "What do we have here?" He notices his stocking hanging over the fireplace.

"Go ahead. Look in it," I say with delight.

Justus pulls out a peppermint stick and a penny. He wipes his eyes with the back of his hand.

"Frank helped me with that one." I give Frank a wink of thanks for bringing a peppermint stick back from town for me.

"Thank you, Angel." Justus pulls me to him and kisses the top of my head. "Thank you," he repeats.

After everyone is gone, we sit on the sofa, cozied up by the fire and the tree. "I didn't get you anything," says Justus. "I guess I forgot about that part."

"I got you and our baby; that's all I need." I kiss his whiskered cheek.

"Well…" He shifts himself off the sofa and onto one knee on the floor. "I hope this will make up for it." He holds out my grandmother's ring, better than new.

I gasp. "Oh, Justus. I thought it was gone." My eyes cloud over, and I wipe them to see clearly.

"I found it in a tin case and took it to the jeweler, who cleaned and repaired it. I thought about telling you when I found it, but I didn't want you to see it in that condition. So I decided to surprise you."

I move it this way and that, inspecting it as I had done when I first discovered it long ago. Tears roll down my face. This man is too good to be true.

He continues, "I hope you'll wear it."

"But I have a beautiful wedding ring that you had made especially for me." I will not trade my ring for anything, not even for my grandmother's.

"You can wear it on your right hand." He takes it from me and slips it on my finger.

"I suppose you're right." The last time it was on my hand, it slipped from side to side, but this time it fits just right.

He brushes his lips against my fingers. "I bet she'd be right happy to have you wear it, rather than keep it in a box tucked away."

"Oh, Justus. You have given me the best day."

"You gave me the best day when you married me." He leans in and presses a tender kiss on my mouth.

# 68

## Livvie

July is stifling and dry. I'm not sure how much more I can take of this heat while I'm so big and round. Justus insists I let him and Mary do everything, since I'm clearly about to have the baby any day. I sit on the sofa with my swollen feet propped on a stool while he rubs them, and I lay a cool rag around my neck for comfort from the sweltering temperature. "I feel as big as a heifer," I say, rubbing my bulging belly.

"If it makes you feel better, you still get me hard."

I would swat him if I could reach him. "Justus," I whisper. I'd be mortified if Mary heard him talking that way.

"She can't hear me. She's banging around in the kitchen, as usual."

"I hope this baby arrives soon. I don't know how much more I can take of this extra weight in this heat." I blot my neck and face with the cold cloth. "Will you help me up?"

He stands. "What do you need? I can get it for you."

"I just want to get up. I'm not feeling so comfortable, even with the piles of pillows behind me. I think I'll go in the kitchen and see what Mary's up to and if I can help her."

"I don't want you standing."

"I'll sit at the table. I promise." I give him my sweetest smile.

As soon as he helps me to my feet, there is a loud pop and a gush of water from between my legs. We gape at each other. "I think it's time," I say.

"I'm getting you up to bed." Justus hollers for Mary to come quick.

She hastens to the stairs, where we're slowly making our way up. "What is it?" she asks excitedly.

"The baby's coming. And the rug by the sofa may be drenched," says Justus.

"Oh dear! Are you having pains?"

"No, I feel fine. Just large and hot."

"I'm going to get Doc," says Justus as he helps me into bed.

"But I feel fine."

"I'm not taking any chances."

He fluffs my pillows. "Can I get you cold water and a cloth, or water to drink?"

"All of it, please. And if you could get a breeze to come in through that window, that'd be wonderful, too," I say sarcastically.

He kisses me. "I'll be back before you know it."

I smile at how sweet this man is. "Thank you."

He peeks his head around the door at me. "We're having a baby."

"I'm having a baby. You're going to get me cold water and Doc."

A few minutes later, Mary arrives with her arms full and announces, "Justus left. Here's a basin of cold water and a rag, and a pitcher of cold drinking water and a cup."

"Thank you, Mary."

"You poor thing. You'd think we were living in an oven. Can I get you anything else?"

I laugh at how they're worrying over me. "I don't need anything else, thank you. Except, perhaps, a good book, since my husband has confined me to this bed."

"Oh, he frets over you." She smiles. "And he's excited. I remember when Frank Junior was born. You'd a thought I was dying with the way Frank fussed over me."

I chuckle, knowing exactly what she means. Then the familiar cramping begins, only this time, I'm sure it means the baby is coming soon.

# 69

## Justus

After learning Doc is out of town, I return to the ranch to find Rebecca hanging laundry on her clothesline. "What brings you over here, Justus?"

Still sitting on Beau, I remove my hat, wiping my forehead with my sleeve under the relentless sun. Sweat soaks my hair and shirt. "Olivia's having the baby and Doc's out of town. Can you help?"

"I know a thing or two about delivering babies. Let me grab some supplies."

"Thank you, Rebecca."

Inside, Liv's cries come in waves down the stairs and strike me in the gut. Rebecca shoots me a look of concern. She was fine when I left.

"Justus, I need you to start some water to boil."

I nod, but the floor has my boots glued to it.

"Justus. Water," orders Rebecca in a calm but firm voice.

I blink. I have to move. My wife needs me.

A short time later, Mary comes down and takes the boiling pot from the stove.

"What do I do?" I ask, shoving my fingers through my hair.

"Pray," says Mary as she swoops past me and up the stairs. That doesn't feel like a good sign.

The cries that meet my ears as I sit and I pace, sit and pace, bring back memories of the war. Flashes of soldiers falling, sounds of gunfire, and cannons booming go off in my head.

*Explosions surround my men and me. The sun is setting and it's getting harder to see. Dirt flies around us as the cannons from both sides wreak havoc. I see Clint from my periphery. "Get down! Get down!" I shout at my friend, knowing my screams are in vain.*

*Seconds later, Clint's feet shoot up from under him.*

*"Nooooo!" I crawl to him, not knowing what I'll see. I've seen enough mangled men on the battlefield, but this is one I can't bear to look at. I need to get to him, no matter what I might find.*

*"Justus," Clint chokes out.*

*He's still alive. Thank God. His face, arms, torso, legs…leg. My stomach moves into my chest. "We gotta get you outta here." I yell to another soldier, a boy, nearby, "Billy, help me."*

*The boy helps me hoist Clint over my shoulder, then I run. I try not to look at Clint's butchered leg. Just get him out of here. Just get him out of here. A surge moves through me like a lightning bolt and I run faster than I've ever ran.*

I cover my ears, willing the memory to stop. Minutes run into hours. I don't know how much more I can take. I don't know how much more Liv can take.

"Shouldn't you be seeing to Olivia?" I ask Mary angrily when she comes down to prepare supper.

"Birthing babies takes time. We all need to keep our strength up to help her. Besides," she says, "I don't see *you* making a meal for us."

I can't think of food at a time like this.

"You must eat," she says. "We don't have time to tend to you if you pass out." She sits a cold pork sandwich and a peach in front of me. "I'm taking Olivia some broth and relieving Rebecca."

I nod and force myself to take a bite. Then I sit with my head in my hands. This has to be over soon.

Rebecca's voice is tired. "Olivia is sipping her broth. You better at least take another bite."

"How's she doing?"

Her cries tell me the situation isn't getting better.

"She's coming along."

"I want to see her."

Rebecca shakes her head as she pats her mouth with the napkin. "No, you don't. You should go for a walk, get out of the house. I know this ain't easy for you. It's never easy to hear someone you love in so much pain." She stares off, as if going to a faraway place. "It feels as if someone's tearing your heart out."

I nod. Yes, I'd give anything to take my wife's pain from her.

"She'd feel the same, you know, if it were you up there," says Rebecca, as if reading my mind.

"I imagine you're right." I peer down at my food and decide I had better eat more than one bite.

About an hour later, I jump from the sofa at Olivia's words.

"I can't. I can't do it," she cries.

I run to the foot of the stairs and stop to listen.

"I can't. I just can't. Please."

I dart to the top of the stairs and stop again. I can hear Rebecca. "I need you to push, honey. Push real good."

Olivia heaves.

"That's real good. Now I need you to do it again."

"I can't do this anymore."

My heart breaks into pieces at her words. She's surrendering. I exhale, realizing I'd been holding my breath.

"You have to. That little boy needs your help."

I brace myself against the wall.

Liv lets out another loud heave, then a scream that pricks every nerve in my body. The only sound now is of my heart beating in my ears. My knees are jelly. I clutch my stomach and slide to the floor.

A cry. Not from my wife, but the strong loud cry of an infant.

Tears stream down my face. "Thank you. Thank you," I cry out.

The banister creaks against the weight of my head as I await the command that it's all right to see my wife and son. Moments later, a gentle touch on my shoulder causes me to jump.

Mary's eyes are rimmed in red. "You can go see them now," she says, giving me an exhausted smile. She and Rebecca slip past me down the stairs, and I slowly make my way to the bedroom.

Propped up in bed is Olivia. Bare breasted, she holds the baby to her. Her hair is damp and disheveled, but she is even more beautiful than I've ever seen her look before. If I were an artist, this would be the picture I'd paint. She gives me a weak smile as she watches me make my way around the bed and lay beside her.

"You did it." I place a kiss on her silky shoulder.

The baby's cheek is soft under my rough finger. I don't know what to say. This is a sacred moment.

"What do you think?" she asks.

"I think he's sucking on my teat," I say, admiring the little one.

"She."

I draw back. "What?"

"*She's* sucking on your teat. We have a daughter, Justus."

I hadn't considered having a daughter. I study her little hand resting on Olivia's breast. "A daughter." My heart fills with pride at seeing my two girls lying there in that bed.

"Isabella Rose Bennett."

Oh, Mama, I wish you were here. "My ma's name." I can't take my eyes off my daughter as she enjoys her first meal.

"Is that all right?" Olivia dips her head to meet my eyes.

"It's more than all right." I take her face in my hands and kiss her passionately. Heat grows in my body. "I don't think I've ever wanted you more than I do at this moment, my sweet angel."

# 70

## Livvie

Justus has fallen asleep with his head on my shoulder and Isabella has fallen asleep over my chest. I let my body relax into this moment.

Everything Mother told me about being unfortunate and unlucky was all a lie. The woman placed her beliefs from her own hapless circumstances onto me, as though they were facts. I pity the woman, in a way. Perhaps if she had different beliefs, she would have met with providence.

I press my lips to Justus's head. How I love this cowboy. Isabella's cheek is smooshed, and her little mouth forms an "O." I am rich beyond measure. No amount of wealth could take the place of the treasures I have right here in this bed with me.

A year ago, I boarded a train for the unknowns of Colorado, fearful and believing everything bad was my lot in life. Today, I'm basking in love's arrival.

## Author's Note

Thank you so much for taking the time to read Justus and Livvie's story. If you enjoyed it than someone else will too. Please, I kindly ask that you take a moment to leave a review on Goodreads, BookBub, and/or wherever you purchased this book from. If you post about the story on social media, please be sure to tag me. You can find me on Instagram and TikTok at @amandajspeights and on Facebook at AmandaSpeightsAuthor. Also, be sure to sign up for my newsletter at www.AmandaSpeights.com so you don't miss a thing about book 2, *Love's Call*, of my Laurel Springs series.

## Acknowledgments

Ted, my sweet loving patient husband. Thank you for believing in me, encouraging me, and supporting me (in more ways than one) through this book's evolution. I so appreciate how your steadiness always balances me out. You're my rock and the Jim to my Pam. ♥

John, you bought me a typewriter many moons ago so I could write my first novel. As we know, the only thing I managed to do was teach myself to type. But here I am at last, and something tells me you're smiling from the other side of eternity. You always knew I could do it and I thank you for that.

Melissa, my little sister. Thank you for putting up with my requests for feedback, frustrations, and at times oversharing of information. The faith you had in me to see this through was one of the many things that kept me going.

Amanda, the best daughter-in-law with the greatest name ever. (wink) Although you may never see this since you don't really want to know what goes on in your mother-in-law's head "in that way" I still want to thank you for letting me share cover and interior design ideas with you. You know I'm super indecisive so thank you for your input.

Mrs. Arter, my fourth-grade teacher. Whether you ever see this or not I still want to acknowledge you. Your class was my safe place, and you gave me a love for reading that turned into a love for writing. I wouldn't be where I am today without your loving instruction so long ago. Thank you for being a light in my life when I needed it most.

To my editor, Chris Wheary, at www.CMWheary.com thank you for helping me find the diamond in the rough with this story. Your education and encouragement mean more to me than words can express. I look forward to working with you on book 2!

Shout out to my cover designer, Roseanna White, at www.RoseannaWhiteDesigns.com for turning my vision into something more magnificent than I could have imagined.

Thank you to Steve, Research Volunteer at the Colorado Railroad Museum in Golden, CO for helping me with Livvie's train ride from Missouri to Denver. Steve was so gracious and extremely thorough.

I must also recognize the ladies of the Women's Fiction Writers Association (WFWA). Your support, education, resources, writing retreat, writing dates, and new friends have been a wealth beyond measure and something to treasure. I feel so blessed to be a part of such group and I am so grateful to this organization and all the ladies who encompass it.

Finally, thank you my amazing reader. I can't express enough the gratitude and joy I feel that you chose to pick up this book. My heart is full! This story has truly been a labor of love and I hope you enjoyed spending time in it as much as I enjoyed writing it. I look forward to bringing you book 2, *Love's Call*, of my Laurel Springs series!

## About the Author

Always accused of daydreaming and teased for having her nose in a book, Amanda decided to combine those best qualities and write steamy 1800s American West romance.

Although a West Michigan native, she now calls the foot of America's Mountain home, where she and her husband are raising their young daughter. Amanda has a grown son—apparently, she enjoyed raising him so much she decided to repeat the process.

When she's not writing, you'll most likely find her homeschooling her daughter, or reading historical fiction about badass women or a spicy romance.

Be sure to sign up for her newsletter at www.AmandaSpeights.com, so you don't miss any updates on book two of her Laurel Springs series. She promises not to spam you with unnecessary information. You can also follow her on Instagram at @amandajspeights.

*Author photo: © Melissa DeMers Photography*

This Page is Intentionally Left Blank

This Page is Intentionally Left Blank

Printed in Great Britain
by Amazon

62552318R00190